To Julie,
(awesome fiction nerd)
Thanks for the read!
James Nall

MUNGWORT

A NOVEL

JAMES NOLL

ALSO BY JAMES NOLL

Tales of the Weird
A Knife in the Back
You Will Be Safe Here
Burn All The Bodies
Mad Tales (Compendium)
Don't Turn Around (Illustrated Compendium)
Thirteen Tales (Short Story Compilation)
The Wounded, The Sick, & The Dead (Short Stories & Novellas)

The Bonesaw Trilogy
The Rabbit, The Jaguar, & The Snake
Blood & Gold

The Topher Trilogy (Novels):
Raleigh's Prep
Tracker's Travail
Topher's Ton
The Topher Trilogy (Omnibus)

The Hive (Serialized Novel):
Seasons 1-4

Audio Books
A Knife in the Back
Thirteen Tales
The Hive: Seasons 1-4
The Wounded, The Sick, & The Dead
The Rabbit, The Jaguar, & The Snake

MUNGWORT

JAMES NOLL

SILVERHAMMER
STUDIOS

Fiction * Audio Books * Film
www.silverhammer.studio

This is a work of fiction. Names, characters, places, and incidents either are products of the author's imagination or are used fictitiously and are not to be construed as real. Any resemblance to actual events, locales, organizations, or persons, living or dead, is entirely coincidental. I tell you true

MUNGWORT Copyright © 2021 by James Noll

All rights reserved. Printed in the United States of America. No part of this book may be used or reproduced in any manner without written permission except in the case of brief quotations embodied in critical articles and reviews. SILVERHAMMER books may be purchased for educational, business, or sales promotional use. For information, visit www.silverhammer.studio

Cover design by Robin Vuchnich
Book Design by James Noll

First Edition

Digital Edition October 2021 ISBN: 9781733744348

Print ISBN: 9781733744355

Hardcover ISBN: 9781733744362

DEDICATION

For Iggy, the best geriatric cat in the world, and Bingly and Darcy, who are similarly best cats in the world, as well as Luna, the best kitty in the world, George (best kitty in the world), and their new counterpart, Grace Kelly, who is, of course, like the others, the best kitty in the world.

A LAUDATORY PREFACE

This book would not have been possible were it not for the efforts of one Chip Warren. This is how excellent of a person Chip is: not only did he spend hours and hours with me on the phone, hashing out the plot, helping me with the structure, and generally guiding this project from beginning to end, he also wrote a good amount of the script from which this novel is adapted (a little backward in process, I know, but that's how we did it). In addition, even though I used some of his descriptions in this novel, and even though I took some of his dialog, when I told Chip that I wanted to credit his name on the cover too, he demurred.

"Why muddy the waters?" he said. "It started with your story and will end with it. You can give me full credit in a laudatory preface, introduction, or both."

So here you go, Chip, you humble bastard: your first and only laudation.

CONTENTS

The Hard Kind	1
Ben Doth Murder Sleep	15
What In The Happy Horseshit Is This?	27
Sumac On Steroids	39
Pick Your Poison	53
Mungwort	69
Fresh Meat	85
Creeper	101
This Does Not Meet OSHA Workplace Safety Standards	117
Aren't You Just A Little Velma Dinkley?	131
Phytoviral Spillover	139
Ed is Dead	157
Pendejo	171
The Dwarf, The Witch, & The Troll	191
Mérida	203

THE HARD KIND

Virginia weather was a bitch. Anybody who ever spent more than a few weeks in the Old Dominion knew it. The wild switchbacks from sun to rain to sleet, or tornado to derecho to lowland flooding, or even (in the coastal regions) from snow to tsunami to tropical depression, could induce a kind of barometric whiplash that wreaked havoc upon body and mind, not to mention gutters, siding, and in-ground pools.

Except for summer.

Especially in July.

Unlike the arid southwestern deserts, Virginia summers included a healthy dollop of humidity—perhaps not as tropical as Belize or Guatemala or Costa Rica but certainly more intense, for on any given day, from noon to noon, May through June, and July and August too (and sometimes September to boot) the cloud cover burned off by seven in the morning, and the temperature soared to over one hundred degrees, and the humidity hovered around 95%, the misery aggravated, at least in Northern Virginia, by the swamp upon which the nation's capital had been built.

And woe to any landscapers, VDOT workers, or farmhands who found themselves digging trenches or laying down asphalt or mowing or picking or pounding or shucking or doing pretty much anything outside when a heat wave struck. Code red air conditions indeed. No amount of hydration could properly replenish a human body in such conditions because such conditions were out of the range of human tolerability.

All hail the great Virginia heatwave! Where footpads burned, asphalt baked, and power-grids browned.

One night at the beginning of just such a heat wave, a semi pulled into the parking lot of the Rt. 1 Diner a few miles south Fredericksburg, Va. Nobody cared about the driver. Nobody cared about his truck. And nobody cared about the girl who, once the semi hissed to a stop, popped out of the cab.

"Thanks, Bobby!" she said.

"You got it, Cece. Be careful out there, kid."

Cece patted a knife sheathed on her hip.

"You know it," she said, and she slammed the door shut.

Bobby waved out the driver's side window and put his truck into gear. Cece watched him rumble away, but then, seeing something she didn't like, she ran up alongside the cab and pounded on the driver's side door.

"Whoa! Whoa! Whoa!"

The semi came to another whining stop, and Bobby rolled his window down.

"Dude," Cece said. "You've got brake fluid leaking out the back."

Bobby leaned out for a useless look.

"Shit, really? I just got that fixed."

"Well…" Cece squinted down Rt. 1. "I think I know a place. If it's still around."

"They're not gonna fuck me, are they?"

"Nah. Old friend of my dad owns it."

Bobby shook his head.

"Yeah. I got a haul ass up to Philly."

"It's right up the way. Thornburg Truck Repair. Ask for Deandre. If he's still there, he'll hook you up."

"He available 24-7?"

"Last I remember."

"Alright. Thanks, Cece."

"Take care!"

Cece watched the truck growl out of the lot, shaking her head as it took the ramp to I-95 instead of continuing down Rt. 1. She checked her phone, tapped at the screen.

"Route 1 Diner. Nine o'clock sharp," she murmured.

She looked up at the diner. The blinking neon sign on the roof welcomed her with a friendly yellow HELLO. As she watched, the "O" blinked out. She snorted.

"Got that right."

A blast of cold air hit Cece in the face when she opened the door and stepped inside. She folded her arms over her chest, suppressing an involuntary shiver.

The diner looked like any number of greasy spoons in the world, but only if they'd been decorated in 1974 and never renovated. Dirty linoleum floors, harvest yellow tabletops, avocado green counter stools. The place was nearly empty, too. A trio of giggling teenagers occupied a corner booth in the back, a figure in a sleeveless hoody hunched over the counter, and a man in flannel blew on a mug of coffee near the bathrooms in the corner. But that was it.

"Have you seen my son?"

It was an old woman sitting in a booth to the right. Her eyes were rimmed red, her skin seemed to sag off her face, and her bird's nest hair was so thin that Cece could see her scalp.

"What?"

"My son. Bennet. Have you seen him?"

Cece turned away. Why had she done that? Rule number one: don't talk to the loonies. The old woman stared at her for much longer than she had any right to, but when it became clear that no reply was forthcoming, she returned her gaze to the window and continued her lonely monologue.

"... think they can just push me. Take my *knife*, take my *wife*, take my *life*..."

Taped to the hostess stand was a torn piece of notebook paper with the words *Ring Bell To Be Sat* scrawled across it in red crayon. Cece flipped it up, revealing a tarnished call bell. She slapped it, and a pot in the kitchen crashed to the floor, followed by a man yelling in Spanish.

"I don't care if you just washed it, Luis!" a woman yelled back. "Maybe if you wasn't so lazy, you'd've hung it up out the way!"

A set of double doors swung open behind the counter, and the owner of the voice, a pile of red hair with a pen clenched in her teeth, poked her head out.

"Seat yourself, hon! I'll be out in a jiff!"

The yelling from the kitchen continued as Cece made her way up to the front counter. She aimed for the stool as far away as possible from the guy in the sleeveless hoodie, slung her backpack on the floor, and plopped down. A menu with a splotch of red sauce on it was wedged in a metal holder between a dented napkin holder and a pair of ancient sugar dispensers. She picked it up by one corner and pretended to read. The girls in the back giggled. A knife clinked on a plate. The waitress's voice preceded her as she bumped open the swinging doors with her butt.

"Your shift don't end until eight, Luis, so you're workin' until eight." She hefted a rack of glasses in front of her and eyeballed Cece's menu. "That's an old one, hon."

With athletic grace, she set the rack of glasses down on the drink cooler, swiped up a menu from a stack next to the register, and slapped it on the counter. Her name tag read "Lydia."

"Coffee?"

"Yeah."

"Leaded or unleaded?"

"Leaded."

"My kinda girl."

Lydia grabbed an ancient coffee pot off the burner sitting on the counter without even looking.

"Mind yourself, hon," she said as she poured. "This one runs hot. Creamer?"

She was already reaching for the bowl of pods when Cece said, "got any skim milk?"

Lydia stopped and blew a lock of hair out of her face.

"Yeah. In the walk-in."

She said it as if someone just asked her to unclog a toilet. When Cece didn't amend her order, she snapped her gum and retreated to the kitchen, bumping the doors open with her hip.

"Luis! You ain't got time to be sittin' around!"

The dining room fell silent. Even the giggly girls stopped giggling. Cece craned her neck around to see what they were doing, but the booth where they'd been sitting was empty. Her eyes fell on the guy at the end of the counter. He hunched over a piece of blueberry pie, his arm curled around the plate like a practiced felon. His hood obscured all but the tip of a malformed nose and the glassy surface of a burned chin. Feeling her gaze, he stopped eating and looked up. Cece turned away and studied her reflection in the mirror behind the counter. *Okay. Deep breath. Count to ten. Glance to the right.* Now he'd turned to face her, a hint of a smile on his deformed lips.

Here we go.

To distract herself from what was about to happen, she pulled a worn postcard from the back pocket of her jeans. On the front, a vintage illustration of the Chatham Bridge drawn in the style of the 1950s. Bel Airs and Hudson Hornets drove across it, going in and out of the city. A couple of skiffs floated below. VISIT HISTORIC

FREDERICKSBURG spanned the top, written in bubble letters. Cece ran a finger over the picture. Smiling, then unsmiling, she flipped it over and read the farewell:

Love, Dad.

"Been road-dogging it?"

She snapped to attention. Scarface was leering at her. He'd pulled his hoody off, and Cece realized she'd nicknamed him appropriately. Puckered slugs laced the left side of his face, the corner of his dead left eye drooped and pulled down, and the beard he'd grown to cover it all was loose and patchy.

"No offense, buddy, but I'd like to be left alone."

"Oh, come on now, little girl. I'm just trying to be friendly."

"Laying it on a little thick, aren't you?"

"For a fine-looking filly such as yourself? No way."

"Not interested."

Cece folded the postcard and jammed it in her back pocket.

"What you got there?" Scarface asked.

"Postcard from my boyfriend. He's into Muay Thai, and he's almost here."

Scarface slid the fork into his mouth and slowly pulled it out, making hard eye contact the whole time.

"Muay Thai, huh? You must like the rough stuff."

"Give it a rest, creep."

Cece cracked her knuckles. Scarface was not to be dissuaded.

"This pie is delicious. Let me buy you a piece."

"Fuck off."

"Whoa! No need for that kind of language."

With a bump and a bang, Lydia backed out through the double doors amidst a flurry of Spanish.

"Cry me a river, Luis."

"Hey darlin'," Scarface said. "Get this young lady a piece of your finest blueberry pie, would ya?"

Lydia ignored him and put a couple of creamer pods on the counter in front of Cece.

"We only got these little ones."

"You hear me?" Scarface leaned over the edge of the counter and pretended to read her name tag. "Lydia?"

Lydia lowered her eyes at him.

"You got enough to pay for that first one?"

"What the fuck business of it is yours?"

"Because if you dine and dash on me, I swear to God, I will run you down."

"Just get her the pie, sweetheart."

"I already said no," Cece said.

Lydia's eyes slid from Scarface to Cece.

"You okay, hon?"

"I'm fine."

"You sure?"

"I said I'm fine."

Lydia snapped her gum.

"Alright, then. You get what you get."

She wiped her hands on her apron and strolled down to the end of the counter, snatching up a spray bottle and a rag along the way. The smell of bleach tinged the air soon after as she moved from table to table. Scarface tucked his chin, half-watching her as she cleaned. When she was far enough away, he leaned an elbow on the counter and scratched his patchy beard.

"Boyfriend's late. Maybe he's at karate class, sweatin' it up with the boys."

"Muay Thai."

"Whatever. He don't seem like that great of a boyfriend, do he? Lettin' a pretty thing like you travel around all by her lonesome?"

Cece pulled her shirt up just a bit, exposing the bowie knife sheathed on her belt. Six-inch blade. Hand-carved antler handle. Bone inlay of a blazing sun on the grip. The initials "C.S." had been burned into the leather on the sheath.

"Who says I'm lonesome?"

She lowered her shirt without a word and blew on her coffee. Scarface gave her a crooked grin. He ran a finger down the scar that stretched from the corner of his eye into the thatch of his beard.

"Ain't nothing you can do to me that ain't been done before."

Cece scanned the dining room. No sign of Lydia. The old woman muttered at the window. The man in the back looked up from under his cowboy hat, and Cece now saw that it wasn't a man at all but a woman, a stout woman at that, with broad shoulders and thick hands. She caught Cece's eye and nodded. Cece looked quickly away.

"You know who you remind me of?" Scarface said. "My sister. She had a little sass to her, too. It was funny until it wasn't. Had to adjust her attitude now and then if you know what I mean."

He hopped over a few stools and leaned in.

"That it? You sassy?"

Cece turned to look him right in the eye, a smile creeping up as she tilted forward. She reached up, curled her fingers through his greasy hair, and whispered something in his ear. Scarface's smug leer turned into a scowl.

"I'd like to see you try."

"Well," Cece said. "You like it rough, right?"

Her fingers tightened into a fist, and she slammed his face down onto the counter. Scarface popped up, nose gushing.

"Fuck!" he yelled. He brought his hand up and looked at the blood. "You broke my nose, you bitch!"

With a growl, he lunged for her. Cece leaped off her stool, snatched the coffee pot from the burner, and flung the contents in his face. Scarface stopped short, his hands shaking in midair.

Then the shrieking started.

Cece shot a look over her shoulder as she fast-walked through the parking lot. The door to the diner was still closed. She picked up her pace, hopped onto the shoulder of Rt. 1, and aimed for an island of trees up ahead on her left. The traffic on 95 whooshed nearby. A siren sang in the distance. Cece rapped a rhythmic mantra under her breath as she walked, the words matching each step.

"Fuck, fuck, fuck, fuck."

A car honked as it sped past, and she jumped.

"Nice ass, honey!" someone yelled.

"Get fucked!" Cece yelled back.

She threw another look over her shoulder. The lot remained empty; the door remained closed

"Come on, dude," she muttered.

Someone burst out of the entrance. Short, stocky, cowboy hat. The woman who'd been sitting in back. Cece slowed her pace. The woman scanned the area. Caught sight of Cece.

"Hey! Stop!"

With a smile, Cece trotted forward. She heard a door slam, the roar of an engine. It took a little longer than she expected, but soon a truck growled up the road. Everything about it was black: black exterior, black rims, black roll-bar. Cece stepped onto the narrow shoulder to let it pass, holding her hand up to block the lights, but the truck rolled up alongside, hogging both lanes. The passenger side window rolled down with an electronic whirr, blessing the night with Axel Rose's screeching caterwaul.

You're one in a million, babe/Yeah, that's what you are/You're one in a million/You're a shooting star.

The radio cut off.

"You need a ride, kiddo?"

"No."

"You sure? That guy back there—"

"I'm fine, thanks."

Cece picked up her pace. The truck matched it.

"Can I help you with something?" Cece asked.

"You're a ballsy little girl, aren't you?"

"Interesting choice of words coming from you."

"What's that supposed to—oh, I get it."

"I don't swing that way, okay?"

"I ain't trying to pick you up. I'm trying to help. My name's Karen. Karen Boemer."

"Good for you."

The empty road stretched out in front of Cece. Four lanes, woods on either side. If she needed to, she could just duck to the side, double back, and disappear into the brush.

"Listen," Karen said. "You did a number on that guy, and guys like him don't take too kindly to stuff like that. It's only a matter of time before he runs you down."

"He's probably balled up on the floor, crying."

The door to the diner slammed open, and Scarface lurched out. He scanned the night, spotted Cece.

"I'm gonna fucking kill you, you bitch!" he screamed.

"Don't look like it."

"Fuck," Cece muttered.

Scarface jumped into an old Mazda B-series and started it up. The tires smoked as he peeled out of the lot.

"The way I see it," Karen said. "You can wind up in my truck, or you can wind up in his."

Five minutes later, they were barreling down what Cece could only describe as one of the backest of back-country roads she'd ever been on. While there were technically two lanes, it was only in the sense that if pressed, two cars could squeeze past each other with about a foot to spare, maybe less. Not that it mattered to Karen. She hogged the double yellow with every inch of her truck. Trees whipped by in a blur. Cece white-knuckled the panic handle.

"I think you lost him."

"Can't be too careful. Guy like that knows these roads better'n me."

They hit a turn too hard, tires squealing, and the truck lurched onto the shoulder, churning up dirt and gravel. Branches ticked off the side-view. Karen let out a gleeful whoop and jerked the wheel, and the truck popped back onto the blacktop.

"American made, baby! American made!"

"Please slow down."

They squealed around another turn.

"I SAID SLOW DOWN!"

"Okay, okay," Karen said. She eased off the gas. Sixty. Fifty-five. Fifty. "Didn't think a girl like you'd be so uptight."

Cece loosened her grip and let out a breath.

"You don't know a thing about me."

"Didn't mean to offend you."

"You didn't offend me. You scared the shit out of me."

"I apologize."

"Let's just get into town."

"You got people there, huh?"

"Boyfriend."

"This the one who's into Muay Thai?"

"You were eavesdropping?"

"It's a small diner. Voices carry."

Cece suppressed a grin.

"Thanks for getting me out of there, but I just want to see him, okay?"

"Message received."

They rode in silence. The trees, tall and dark, canopied the way, blocking the light of the moon. They came to an intersection, and Karen turned onto an even narrower road. Then another intersection and another turn. They passed under a bridge, swung around a switchback, and straightened out onto a long, flat stretch of road. They encountered no other cars, passed no houses. Just woods, woods, and more woods.

"Are you sure we're heading into town?" Cece asked.

"Sure as the north star."

Cece checked her side-view. Darkness and blacktop.

"Good, because—"

"Mind if I listen to some music?"

Karen flipped the radio on without waiting for a reply. The blare of what sounded like a passing train came over the speakers, followed by thumping bass and the unmistakable growl of Eddie Van Halen's Frankenstrat.

"I saw these guys in '78. Virginia Beach," Karen said. "Won tickets on WNOR. Can you believe that? Rouge's Gallery. I was right. Up. Against. The stage!"

"Mm."

"Listen, this is gonna sound kinda weird. But are you looking for a job?"

"A job?"

"I saw you hitch a ride in with that semi. I'm guessing you got about, what, ten bucks on you if you got a nickel."

She hit another curve without braking.

"I'm fine. Maybe you could take it a little easy on the—"

"Honey, I can drive these roads blind in the rain."

A couple of drops spattered on the windshield.

"Look at that!" Karen cried. "You wanna hear my proposition or what?"

"I told you I don't do that."

"Not that kind of proposition. Think of it more as an opportunity."

"You want me to sell cosmetics for you or something? Build a team of my own?"

"What? No, I ain't AMWAY."

Cece put one hand on the sheath of her knife. She eyed her backpack on the mat by her feet. The road twisted and turned and bottomed out. A break emerged up ahead, and they sped out of the forest and out into the open. Boundless fields lined each side. The clouds disappeared, and a full moon beamed down from above. Karen laughed.

"You know what they say: if you don't like Virginia weather, just wait a few minutes!"

"I'm not looking for work, Karen."

"Just hear me out. I think this is a job a girl like you would love."

"A girl like me?"

"Yeah. I don't know if anybody's told you this, but you're a bonafide badass. The way you handled that creep back there? Shoowee!"

"I didn't mean to take it that far."

"He got exactly what he deserved. Like I said, we could use people like you."

"Okay. I'll bite. What kind of job is it?"

"The hard kind. You'll be working the land, serving Mother Nature. But it's one hundred percent organic, off-the-grid Bohemian living. We even have yurts!"

"Yurts?"

"Yurts!"

"So farming then? You need pickers?"

"Kind of."

Cece winced.

"What's the matter?" Karen asked. "You afraid of a little grind?"

"It's not that. I just finished a two-month maintenance pull in Lubbock. I was hoping to pick up something where I could spend the rest of the summer in the air conditioning."

"Lubbock! Golly day, you'll fit right in with us! Got a lot of hard-asses out there just like you. There's this one girl, Harlow, she actually worked on an oil rig."

"Harlow? Sounds like a rich girl's name."

"Oh, trust me. Harlow ain't rich."

Karen glanced over. Cece was still holding on to the panic strap and looking out the window.

"Free room and board. Pay's good, too."

"Heard that before."

"$40.00 an hour."

Struck, Cece shot her a look.

"Bullshit, $40.00 an hour. For farm work? You're shitting me."

"I shit you not."

"What are you doing out there? Growing weed?"

Karen gave her a double-take, then she started laughing.

"Weed! That's funny. Weed."

"'Cause I'm not getting caught up in that shit, Karen. There's no wage worth going to jail for."

"No, we ain't growing weed. It's close but—"

"Close?"

"We ain't doing nothing illegal. I promise."

"Then what are we talking about? Digging cesspools? Mending fences?"

"Clearing and carving, mainly."

"Clearing and carving what?"

"Nothing you can't handle."

Cece watched the landscape roll by. The air conditioning blasted out of the vent.

"So what do you think?" Karen asked.

Cece thought about how to respond for a moment. Then she said, "you know how many farms I've worked on?"

"Two or three?"

"Ten. You know how many of them pay $40.00 an hour? Zero."

"It's pretty specialized work. I ain't gonna lie. It's a bit dangerous. Think of it as hazard pay."

"Hazard pay," Cece scoffed.

"*Der'mo.* I guess you're going to be an asshole about it."

Karen popped open the middle console and rummaged around with one hand, keeping the other on the wheel.

"I'm not being an asshole," Cece said. "I'm being realistic."

"Where is that thing?"

"I don't know what kind of scam you're running, but you can count me out."

"Uh-huh."

"So why don't you pull over and let me out. I'll hoof it into town."

"Just got a new one last week."

A four-way stop appeared up ahead. Karen pressed down on the accelerator. Cece renewed her death grip on the handle.

"Karen, seriously. Slow down."

"There it is!"

Karen pulled a full-face respirator from the console and strapped it to her head. Cece didn't know whether to laugh or scream.

"What the fuck are you doing?"

Karen's muffled voice came out from behind the mask.

"Always hate doing it this way. Dust gunks up my cab."

Cece lurched for the door handle. Karen hit the auto-lock.

"It's easier if you just let it happen, darlin'."

She mashed a button on the panel. A blast of yellow powder shot out of the vents, hitting Cece in the face. Cece's vision doubled. She felt herself slide down on the seat. Her legs went limp. She rolled to her side and slapped at the steering wheel, but Karen knocked her hand away.

"Double trouble, huh?" she said.

She mashed the button again.

BEN DOTH MURDER SLEEP

Cece's dreams were vivid and vicious, populated by a series of torturous images.

Rotten teeth biting into a heart-shaped apple.

A bark-covered tumor pulsing on the trunk of a tree.

A body swinging from a gleaming meat hook.

She was in the diner again, her hand gripping her knife. Scarface leaned toward her, that creepy smile on his face.

"You remind me of my sister."

His face glitched. Cathode static.

The scars disappeared, the creepy smile replaced with a genial gentleman's confidence.

"She likes coffee in her sugar too."

A vacuum ripped her out of the diner and into Karen's truck. She white-knuckled the panic grip as they careered around the dark back roads.

Karen, her eyes glittering behind the filter mask:

"I guess you're going to be an asshole about it."

Her face glitched. Cathode static.

Karen's mask vanished, her gimlet eyes gone merry:

"You're a bonafide badass, Cece."

Sonic distortion.

Cece spun in a vortex. Stars flashed in strange patterns. Whispers in an alien tongue. The static morphed into the calming rush of a mid-summer breeze. Branches appeared overhead, blurry at first, then sharp. The leaves defined to the veins. Darkness to light. A sun-filled sky. Puffy white clouds.

She was walking behind her father, heading for his shed. His brown work boots, his worn work jeans. The knife on his belt was the same as hers: Hand-carved antler handle. Bone inlay of a blazing sun on the grip. The initials E.E. burned into the sheath. He turned, his laugh-lines wrinkling.

"C'mon now."

Cece sat up with a gasp.

She lay on her back on a lush, green lawn. Not a cloud in the sky. Birds chirped. Cicadas swelled. The sweet smell of sassafras filled the air. She rubbed her eyes and her fingers came away covered in pollen.

"What the hell?"

She shook her head, showering the surrounding space with a yellow cloud. An image flashed into her head. Karen, wearing a face mask.

Double trouble, huh?

It worked. Not quite the way she thought it would, but it worked.

She took in her surroundings. To her left, a stately white farmhouse. To her right, a wide-open field. In the distance, a chain-link fence cowering beneath a wall of trees. The top third seemed to buckle under an onslaught of vines and brush. She twisted around the other way, blinking. A half-circle of white tents stood around an open field like a village. Tibetan prayer flags decorated the entries, clothes dried on lines strung between each one, and a fire pit blackened the dirt in the middle.

"Sleep no more! Ben doth murder sleep!"

A young man in a floppy hat crested a knoll holding a plate of food in his hands. He was, if not portly, rotund, but his legs were thick and strong, and the muscles in his arms and chest filled out the loose tunic draped over his shoulders. He stopped in front of her and held out his arms as if he was standing in front of a grand audience.

"Innocent sleep. Sleep that soothes away all our worries."

Cece shook her head.

"Not a fan of the bard, huh?" the boy asked.

"Bard?"

"Yeah. You know, Shakespeare."

"No."

He held out his hand.

"I'm Ben."

Cece ignored it. She stood up and looked around again. Woods, fence, house, yurts. Ben dropped his hand and wiped it on his pant leg.

"Tough night?"

"I don't know. I… don't really know what happened. I was in a diner?"

"Oh, my god. Were you sleepwalking?"

"I don't think so. I don't think I even slept."

"Well, that sucks. Harlow hates lazy workers."

"Harlow?"

Harlow sounds like a rich girl's name.

Ben nodded at the circle of tents.

"Your yurt-mate? And your supervisor. Kinda. She's pretty badass, though. Sometimes just an ass."

"I don't really—"

"Sorry," Ben said. "Sorry-sorry. I've had, like, six cups of coffee. Maybe. Uh…" He extended the plate. "Break your fast, avoid the lash!"

Cece recoiled.

"What?"

"Oh! It's harmless. It's just something we say here. I tried to change it to 'don't be a fool, get you some fuel'." He paused. Shook his head. "Didn't take."

Cece took the plate, picked up a piece of sausage, and nibbled the edge. Her eyes widened, and she shoved the rest of the link in her mouth, followed by a handful of strawberries, then a piece of toast. Ben watched her, amused.

"Good, right? I'm Ben, by the way."

"You said that."

"Oh. Right. And you're Cicely?"

"Cece."

"Oh, like the song!"

"Please don't."

But it was too late. Ben had already started to sing.

"Cecelia! I'm down on my knees. I'm begging you please to come home. Ho-ho-home!"

Cece, cheeks chipmunked with strawberries, stared back, her face flat and expressionless.

"Right," Ben said. "Guess you've heard that before."

It took very little time for Cece's body to respond to the Virginia summer sun. Her face flushed from the heat, her limbs felt heavy, and her shirt was soaked with sweat before they walked even fifty yards from where she'd woken up. She wolfed down the last sausage on the plate. Ben laughed.

"Man, you really were hungry, huh?"

He removed a bottle of water from the folds of his tunic and handed it to her. She unscrewed the top and upended it, guzzling half in a few gulps.

"Easy there," Ben said. "We still have a full day in front of us."

"Full day of what?"

A curious smile formed on Ben's face.

"A full day of that."

He pointed to a crowd of workers milling around the weed-choked fence in the distance. Two massive trees had fallen through, creating a fifty-yard gap on either side. The top of one of them, the biggest, lay stripped of its limbs, the thick trunk ringed with the stumps of branches. As she watched, a team of workers with chainsaws attacked it.

"This is the job," Cece said. She looked at Ben, waving at a cloud of gnats that seemed to form out of nowhere, a look of understanding dawning on her face. "This is the job, right?"

"Uh, yeah."

"What, exactly, is it?"

"Clearing and cutting, mainly. The brush grows too close to the fence, so we gotta cut it all back."

"And the trees?"

"Yeah, the trees, too."

"No, I mean, do they all fall on the fence like that?"

As if to answer, the sound of cracking wood echoed in the morning, the reports firing like gunshots. Chainsaws cut, farmhands yelled and scattered, and out of the woods crashed an oak tree, easily two hundred feet tall. It landed with a thud that shook the earth, taking out a fifty-foot portion of the fence.

"Yeah," Ben said. "Yeah, I guess they do."

"Does that happen all the time?"

"Nah. That's the first time I… well, I mean, yeah. It does."

An ATV tore over the hill in front of them, heading for the main house. The driver, a short girl wearing a cowboy hat, steered the vehicle like a pro, the muscles in her arms shaking as she sped over the turf. Her hair ran down her back in a long, black braid.

In the passenger seat sat her polar opposite: a tall boy with shoulder-length blond hair flowing behind him like he was in a shampoo commercial. His shoulders were broad and thick, and his biceps bulged out of a sleeveless flannel. He pointed at Ben and Cece, and the driver adjusted her path, aiming straight for the pair. She came to a skidding halt right in front of them and switched the engine off.

"Where the fuck have you been?" the boy demanded.

"Hey, Jake," Ben said. "Nice to, uh…" He turned to Cece. "This is Cece. Cece, this is Jake and Aiko."

Aiko smiled.

"Nice to meet you."

Jake hawked a lunger. He was so tall that his knees were jammed up against the dashboard. He looked like a nose guard trying to squeeze into a kindergartner's desk.

"Dude, Harlow's pissed."

"She told me to take care of the new girl."

"Bullshit," Aiko said. "You just didn't want to puke off the back of the truck again."

"I get carsick."

In tandem, Jake and Aiko said, "we know."

"You know, I might have something for that," Jake added.

"No thanks, man."

Jake was already rummaging around in the pocket of his cargo shorts.

"No, seriously. Here."

He handed Ben a little brown vial.

"Take a little hit of that before you have to drive anywhere and you'll be ship-shape."

"What is it?"

"Ginger oil."

"For better health and wellness," Aiko said. It sounded like she was repeating a line of ad copy.

Ben studied the vial.

"Thanks, I guess."

The Great Oak Field Kitchen had been aptly named. Sixty feet tall, with a trunk at least fifteen feet in circumference, the tree's spread shaded the field kitchen all day long, even at noon. Its vine-covered branches were so thick and strong that the workers often climbed up and sat on them ten to twelve at a time, joking and eating during mealtimes.

Cece sighed in relief when they reached the shade. She plucked at her shirt.

"I'm glad I went sleeveless."

"Yeah, about that," Ben said. "You shouldn't have gone sleeveless."

"Jake went sleeveless."

Ben held up his vial of ginger oil.

"Jake thinks ginger oil cures Kinetosis." He scanned Cece's face for a second. "Plus, it's going to be at least a hundred today. Hundred and ten with the humidity."

He shook his loose sleeves.

"Something like this'll work. Keeps the cloth off your skin, lets the sweat do its job. And you'll need a hat." He looked down at her feet. "And you need to tuck your pants into your socks."

"Dude, I picked fruit in San Antonio. I know how to dress for this shit."

"Alright. You get what you get. Let's load up on water before we go out."

Cece regretted her bravado the moment she stepped back out into the sun. Had it gotten even hotter in the few moments they were in the shade? She bore the heat like a yolk, slumping her shoulders as if shrinking away from it would help. A bee zipped by her ear. The grass made the skin on her legs itch.

The closer they got to the fence, the more she realized just how much work the job required. Vines and brush choked the links, washing over them in thick waves. Some sections buckled with the weight. Others had collapsed completely. It looked like the forest was trying to consume it. Workers hacked and whacked at the overgrowth, toted it to huge piles, and covered it in clear plastic tarps. Others assaulted the trees in the woods, scaling the trunks on lines and grapples, cutting off branches with chainsaws. Still more attacked the new tree that had fallen through the fence. They hauled branches to wood chippers and log splitters. The air was alive with the cacophony of power tools.

It was as clear and bright as any mid-summer Virginia day, and if it wasn't for the heat and humidity, it could have been mistaken for pleasant. Cece thought that she'd be able to weather the weather. She'd grown up in Fredericksburg. Spent over two-thirds of her life there. But as she marched through the fields, she wondered how much of her life she'd truly spent outside and how much of it she'd spent holed up in the basement enjoying the air conditioning, or swimming in the river, or ensconced in dark movie theaters gulping down ice-choked soft drinks.

She unscrewed another bottle of water, took a few gulps, and poured some over her head.

"How do you guys work in this?"

"You'll get used to it."

She was feeling a little better by the time they reached the crew. Maybe it was the water, maybe it was the food, but a familiar strength had returned to her limbs.

She spotted Jake working a massive chainsaw on one of the fallen branches. Sawdust coated his chest, arms, and legs, and a pile had gathered under him that almost reached his ankles, but he didn't look like he was making much progress. The girl working next to him (also covered in sawdust) stopped hauling a branch out of the way and swatted Jake on the leg. Jake cut the chainsaw at the same moment that Ben yelled, "that's Harlow!"

Harlow looked up at the sound of her name, saw Ben, and stomped over. She snatched up a pair of machetes sticking out of the ground, handles up.

"Where the fuck've you been?"

"You told me to get the new girl."

"I told you to make sure she woke up on time, not take her on a date."

Cece held out her hand as Harlow approached.

"I'm Cece."

Harlow ignored her.

"Fuck's sake, Ben," she said. "We got a massive invasion going on and you're playing grab-ass."

"Gimme a break."

"You skirt work again, I'm docking your pay."

Harlow shoved the machetes at both of them.

"Clear the brush and vines over on the western section. Start at the first good post past the break and work your way in."

Both Ben and Cece looked to the left of the breach. The closest clear post was at least a hundred yards away. Another tree had fallen through there, too, and workers were scrambling all around it, cutting off branches and clearing debris. Harlow turned her attention to Cece.

"Where's your hat?"

"It's in my bag."

"No sleeves?"

Ben said, "I told her, but…"

"If you're going to work out here, you need a hat, gloves, and sleeves."

"I know."

"Your boots are fine, but you need to tuck your jeans into your socks."

Harlow bent over and pulled Cece's cuffs up, revealing ankle socks.

"No-shows? Jesus."

Jake started the chainsaw up again.

"Jake, wait!"

She stomped away.

"Who's on the trunk at our section?" Ben yelled after her.

"Rufus."

"Seriously?"

"Make sure he doesn't hurt himself again!"

The operation at their portion of the fence didn't seem all that much different from anywhere else along the line. Workers hacked away at the vines and brush on either side, while a couple of boys with chainsaws mounted a fallen tree. The side of the trunk that faced up was bare, leaving huge stumps sticking out at all angles. The branches on the side that faced the ground were still intact, creating a kind of springboard between the earth and tree.

The tree was so big that it had torn up a swath of forest fifty feet in circumference when it fell. Roots dangled in the air like wooden tentacles, but where the tree met the ground, there were still great stalks the size of tank turrets anchoring the trunk to the earth. Cece thought that if she sat on the stump and started counting the rings, it might take her at least ten minutes to finish.

A gangly boy started jumping up and down on his end of the trunk, cackling as the tree bounced under him. He was so skinny that his body seemed to swim in his loose-fitting clothes. A rebel branch slashed at a young man trying to cut a branch jutting off the side, and the young man cut his engine and ripped his safety goggles off his head.

"Cut the shit, asshole!"

"Come and make me!"

"You jump on that thing again, I'll shove this up your ass."

"Your mom said what?"

"Rufus, I presume?" Cece asked.

Ben nodded, clearly pained.

"Yeah."

The other chainsaw boys cut their engines, and they watched with cocked heads and slumped shoulders as Rufus leaped ever more hysterically on the trunk.

"I'll be right back," Ben said. He marched over toward the fallen tree, yelling, "hey, Rufus! Knock it off, man!"

Cece turned toward the fence. Something in the brush caught her attention, and she knelt to inspect it. It was a bird. A dead bird. She tried to knock it out with the tip of her machete, but vines encased it like a mummy. She stabbed her blade into the ground with a grunt and pulled her knife out of the sheath on her belt.

Leaning closer, she saw the vines had strangled the poor thing. One had cinched around its neck so tightly that the bird's head hung at a ninety-degree angle from its body. Ants crawled over its feathers, in and out of its eye sockets, its open beak. Cece swiped at the vine but only cut a sliver of the meat. She tried again. Nothing. She flipped the blade to the serrated side and sawed at it. The brush shook, the fence rattled, but the vine refused to give.

This is the toughest vine ever.

The sun must have dipped behind a cloud because she felt the heat lift off her back. Good. The sounds of the chainsaws grew dim, the air around her close, and she focused on the job, determined not to let a stupid piece of vegetation win. A few more cuts and that should do it. One. Two. Three. Four. Damn. Damn thing won't give.

"Cece? Is that you?"

It was Ben, but his voice sounded far away. Cece stopped sawing, and that's when she realized brush had covered her completely. The leaves and vines and little branches seemed to have swallowed her up. Must have crawled in without realizing it.

"Fuck me," she said.

She hacked away at a knot of leaves to her left and, with a ripping and cracking noise, crawled out from underneath it all. The sun hit her full in the face, and she held her hand up to block it.

"You're a mess," Ben said. He grabbed her wrist and pulled her to her feet. "What were you doing in there?"

Cece looked back at the mound of brush.

"There was a bird."

"A bird?"

"A dead bird. I was trying to clear it before I started hacking away, but…"

"You don't have to worry about dead birds," Ben said. He pulled her machete out of the ground and handed it to her. "All you have to do is make sure you lean into it when you cut—"

Irritated, Cece wound up, took an expert step forward, and brought the blade down hard and fast, hacking the mound away in a single whack. Ben pulled the corners of his mouth down.

"Okay, you got it. I'll just, uh… I'll just go over there."

Cece got to work, hacking away at the brush that consumed the fence. The sun beat down on the exposed skin of her arms and neck, and the sweat flowed off her face and soaked her clothes. Soon the muscles in her arms and back were burning with the effort, and the grip had rubbed her palms raw. Within an hour, blisters formed on the heels of both hands.

She had just taken a break to wipe the sweat off her brow and get some water when someone started yelling over the buzzing saws. She looked over and saw Aiko's four-wheeler parked by the tree trunk. Jake and Rufus were in each other's faces, jawing and pointing at the tree. Harlow and Aiko were attaching a metal chain to the four-wheeler's hitch. Harlow looked up and saw Cece, said something to Aiko (who nodded), and stomped over toward the fence.

"Fuck me," Cece muttered.

Shaking her head, she sent a half-hearted blow at the next patch of brush. The blade got wedged in a thick knot, and no matter how hard she yanked and pulled, it wouldn't come loose. She reached into the thicket, thinking she might be able to snap some of the vines with her fingers, and pulled it out with a hiss.

"Fuck!" she snapped.

A thorn had cut a valley through the back of her hand and lodged in the meat between her thumb and forefinger. She plucked it free, and blood welled up and poured out. She stuck her hand in her mouth and sucked.

"I thought I told you to get some gloves."

Harlow. Cece spat blood and wiped her hand off on her jeans.

"It's fine. I'm fine."

"You don't look fine."

"I've had worse. It's just a thorn."

"You need to be more careful. You end up in the infirmary, I'm down a worker."

"They're just weeds."

"Just weeds?"

Harlow stepped past her and pulled a thatch off the ground.

"This is poison oak." She grabbed another thatch. "This is poison ivy." She grabbed a third. "This is poison sumac." She jabbed a finger at the woods. "There are wood nettles, leadwort, and hogweed out there. You want your hands to swell up like basketballs?"

"Okay, well, they're not in the fence, are they?"

Harlow snorted and waved at the ocean of green that had taken over the metal links.

"What do you think?"

"Shit."

"Shit is right. Aiko's got some rubbing alcohol in the bag on her four-wheeler."

She pulled off her gloves and slapped them on Cece's chest.

"Those don't come off until the day is done."

"Not even to eat?"

Harlow gave her a withering glare and brushed by, heading back to the trunk. Cece swore that if they had been in middle school, she would have rammed her shoulder.

"Thanks for the gloves," Cece said.

"They're coming out of your paycheck."

Cece rolled her eyes.

"And cuff your fucking pants!" Harlow added.

Eight hours.

Eight hours of hacking and pulling, cutting and stacking. By the end of the day, they had cleared the fence, but the tree looked almost the same as it had that morning. Harlow had them spray a mixture of bleach and vinegar on the brush and cover it with an enormous tarp.

By the time they made it back to camp, the sun was low on the horizon. Other crews were straggling in from the fields, too. Playful shouts and laughter filled the air. The cooks were setting up the field kitchen under the big oak, but even though Cece's stomach grumbled, she aimed for her yurt instead.

"Hey, aren't you going to dinner?" Ben called after her.

"I'm exhausted, man," Cece said. "Just need some rack time."

"Here, wait!"

He ran over to a table and grabbed a bunch of fruit and a loaf of bread. He was grinning as he ran back to her.

"Ben, you didn't have to do that," Cece said.

"I know." Ben unloaded his cache into her arms. "Food is fuel. You'll thank me tomorrow."

They both turned and headed off, Ben back to the old oak, Cece back to her yurt. She stopped almost as soon as she started.

"Ben!" Ben stopped and turned, shading his eyes with his hand. "Which one is mine?"

The yurt was spare and clean. Three cots on a packed dirt floor, an open space with a table and chairs. The string lights hanging from the roof glowed low and warm, and an exhaust fan twirled at the apex, filling the space with cool, if not cold, air.

Cece's backpack leaned against a cot to the right. She dumped the food next to it, unbuckled her belt, put her knife on the ground under her cot.

Her cell phone was sitting on top of everything in her bag. A notification advertising "Regeneren by SingleCorp" popped up, and she swiped it away. She checked the battery. 95%. Awesome. She checked the reception. Two bars. One bar. No bars. Awesome. With a sigh and a groan, she stashed it in her backpack and lay down. Her breathing steadied and deepened in less than a minute.

WHAT IN THE HAPPY HORSESHIT IS THIS?

First call came before dawn the next day. Cece scarfed her breakfast down under the limbs of the Great Oak and then it was back out to the fence. She ambled alongside Ben through the fields, rubbing her neck and shoulders.

"First week's rough on your back," Ben said.

"It's rough on everything."

"I see you're wearing your hat and sleeves."

Cece patted her back pocket.

"Brought my gloves, too."

"Harlow's really going to take them out of your paycheck."

"I don't doubt it. So, what are we going to do after we clear the last few sections?"

"Don't worry, they'll find something for us."

"I don't doubt that, either."

Cece didn't have to worry about their next job. As they approached the fence, she thought she was seeing things, that the gray dawn light only made it look like brush carpeted the links again. But as they drew closer and the other workers started groaning and cursing, she realized it wasn't an illusion at all. The entire length she thought they'd already cleared was awash in green, somehow thicker than before.

"Dude, what the fuck is this?"

"It happens sometimes."

"Yeah, but how?"

"I think it's the fertilizer they use."

"Use on what? All they have are unplowed fields."

"The hoop-house flowers."

"What is that? Some kind of code for something?"

"Nope. It's what they grow here."

Ben glanced at Cece.

"Didn't anybody tell you that?"

"No."

A dozen newly sharpened machetes waited for them near the fence. Next to them, a single chainsaw. Ben adjusted his hat, tugged on his gloves, and pulled his sleeves down.

"No use in complaining."

It was almost lunch when the incessant buzzing of the chainsaw suddenly died. The silence was so complete as to be shocking. Ben came around from the other side of the fence and joined Cece, who was finishing up one last patch of brush.

"What happened?"

Cece raised her chin at the fallen tree where Rufus was hunched over the trunk, scratching his head and looking at the saw at his feet.

"His tool went limp."

Ben chuckled.

"Nothing worse than performance issues."

Jake popped up on the trunk and slapped Rufus's shoulder with the back of his hand.

"What the fuck did you do now?"

"I didn't do anything. It just died."

"Did you check the oil?"

"Yeah, I checked the oil."

"Did you check the gas?"

"I'm not an idiot, Jake. Back up."

Rufus got into position and pulled on the ripcord. The saw sputtered, chugged, and died.

"Pull harder," Jake said.

"I know how to start a chainsaw."

"Doesn't look like it. Let me try."

"No. I got this."

Rufus started yanking spastically on the cord, all to little effect. Cece watched, half intrigued, half amused. He was not a burly person. His arms were more bone than muscle, his chest had a divot in it, and his ribs stuck out like a xylophone. Cece felt that if the urge struck, she could walk over, pick him up over her head, and snap him in half. With every pull of the cord, she expected something on him to break. Everybody seemed to think the same thing because they all stopped what they were doing to watch: Jake standing on the trunk behind him, Aiko leaning on her ATV, Ben leaning on the hilt of his machete.

On the hundredth pull, Rufus paused. He was breathing like he'd just run a marathon.

"God DAMMIT!"

Jake reached for the saw again.

"Here, let me—"

"No!"

Rufus grabbed the ripcord and pulled one last time. The chainsaw miraculously roared to life. He picked it up over his head.

"YESSS!"

Jake backed away, hands raised.

"CAREFUL, ASSHOLE!"

"FUCK OFF, JAKEY BOY!"

"OKAY. YOU GOT IT STARTED. LET ME GET THE BOTTOM CUT DONE FIRST."

"MY START, MY SAW."

"DUDE. WE HAVE TO START UNDERNEATH FIRST OR IT'LL PINCH."

He took a step forward, but Rufus swung the saw away with one hand and put the other on Jake's chest. Jake looked at it. Looked at Rufus.

"MY START! MY SAW!" Rufus yelled.

Goggles affixed, earplugs in place, Rufus started in on the underside of the trunk, angling in. He pressed up, grimacing against the sawdust that flew up into his face and coated his chest. When he finished one side, he angled the saw up to start in on the other. Cece leaned into Ben's ear.

"He's totally going to pinch the bar."

Ben nodded.

Rufus attacked the trunk again. While he really was scrawny to the point of emaciation, he impressed Cece with the way he handled the job. His arms might have been shaking and his torso clenched so tight that each muscle on his abdomen stood out under his sweat-soaked shirt, but he was getting it done. If only he had the sense to stop.

The trunk cracked and shifted, but he pressed on. Another inch, another crack. Jake hopped down and started waving his arms over his head.

"RUFUS CUT THE ENGINE!"

Rufus pressed upward, teeth gritted.

"RUFUS!"

With one final, hefty crack, the trunk pinched. The saw went dead and Rufus let go, leaving it hanging by the bar.

"Dude, what the fuck!"

"I told you, man," Jake said.

"I just needed one more inch."

Jake put his hands on his knees to inspect the damage.

"It's fucked, man. Do you always have to act like a spaz?"

"Only on your mom."

Rufus grabbed the chainsaw by the handle and yanked, but it didn't give.

"I wouldn't do that," Cece called.

"Maybe just jiggle it a little?" Ben suggested.

"I wouldn't do that either."

Rufus put a foot on the trunk and pulled with both hands. Nothing. He put both feet up and hung from the handle, straining in vain. The saw wiggled.

"That's a two hundred dollar bar, Rufus," Jake said. "You break that, it's—"

Rufus yanked once, twice, and on the third time, the bar cracked, the chain snapped, and he flew back and landed on his ass with a shocked "whuff!"

"FUCK!"

"Goddammit, Rufus."

Aiko hopped on her four-wheeler.

"I'll go get one from the west field."

"I wouldn't do that," Jake said. "Warner and Mueller are over there. You really want to let them in on this?"

Aiko opened her mouth to argue, then closed it.

Rufus jumped up onto the trunk.

"We can get this done without a saw. Watch."

He jumped straight up into the air, thrusting his legs down as hard as he could when he landed. The trunk creaked and popped, and the branches underneath bounced like shock absorbers.

"The cut's pretty deep." He jumped again. A louder crack this time. "If we wrap a chain around this end and fix it to the four-wheeler…" Jump, thump, crack! "And a bunch of us get up here and jump together…" Jump, thump, crack!

"I'm not doing that," Cece said.

"Yeah, me neither," Ben added.

Rufus shot Jake a look.

"Jake?"

"No way, man."

"Aiko?"

"I gotta run the four-wheeler."

"Pussies," Rufus spat. "Fine, I'll do it myself. What'd'ya say, guys?"

The broken bar stuck out of the trunk like an accusation. Jake picked up the chainsaw motor and inspected the casing. Finally, sighing, he said, "can't hurt to try."

The chain had a hook on each end. Jake extended it from the hitch, wrapped it around the trunk, and hooked it into the link closest to the hitch. Aiko started the ATV and drove forward a few feet, pulling the chain taut.

"On my signal!" Rufus said.

He positioned himself on the bottom side of the cut, the side closest to the root ball.

"Ready? Set... GUN IT!"

Aiko unleashed the throttle. The tires spun, pelting everybody nearby with dirt and grass. The trunk shifted, cracked, shifted again.

"GO GO GO!" Rufus yelled.

He started jumping up and down on the trunk. It reminded Cece of an old music video from a band her father loved. Joy Division? No. New Order. The tree creaked and cracked.

The four-wheeler gained some traction, spun in place, gained some more. The wood groaned like a dying leviathan, and Rufus, incited by the noise, jumped higher, slamming down again and again.

"Almost there!"

Another crack, louder this time, and the two halves shifted. The top rolled an inch, teetering on the edge of breaking off.

"Holy shit!" Ben yelled to Cece. "It's gonna work!"

The bottom of the tree, the part still attached to the root base, bobbed along with Rufus as he jumped, shaking and swaying. Cece swung wide to look at the hole where the tree used to stand. Two thick roots bent out of the ground and into the trunk, fastening the ball to the earth. Her eyes widened.

"Stop!" she yelled, running toward Aiko. "Cut the engine!"

But it was too late.

Aiko gunned the four-wheeler one last time.

The trunk cracked and rolled forward.

Cece spun and sprinted for the still leaping Rufus. She stepped on a log and launched herself into the air, hitting him broadside and sending them both flying. They dropped to the other side and landed with a thud. With one final, massive report, the section of the trunk chained to the four-wheeler pulled away.

But the other section, the section still attached to the root base, shot up like a catapult and whumped back into its hole. Sticks and errant branches whistled through the air, sailing over the tops of the trees and flying deep into the forest. Aiko turned the engine off, leaving them all in stunned silence. Then, out of the emptiness, Rufus screamed.

"My aaaaaaarm! My fucking aaaaaaarm!"

A mini-truck pulled up, a calico beater with new tires and a rusty grill. It came to a stop with a whine, the gears thunked into park, and the driver threw the door open.

"Fuck," Ben muttered. "Warner."

Warner was a tall, thick man with an impressive belly straining the buttons on his work shirt. He stepped around the front of the truck and hooked his thumbs into his belt, surveying the scene like he'd just stumbled into a geriatric orgy.

"What in the happy horseshit is going on here?"

Jake stepped forward, already explaining.

"Mr. Warner, we were just trying to—"

"Shut up, Jake. Rufus! Quit rolling around like an idiot and get back to work."

Rufus continued to writhe and moan.

"Goddammit, Rufus! You either get up or—"

"His shoulder's out!" Cece yelled. "Give him a second."

Warner cussed under his breath.

"Mueller?"

A second man, much skinnier, with a rugged face etched with sun and dirt and years of hard work, eased out of the passenger side. He hung over the door with a lazy leer.

"Yeah, boss?"

"What do you mean 'yeah, boss'? We got a man down."

"On it."

Mueller shut the door and picked his way through the debris, the sap-covered branches, the blackened twigs, his movements lithe and serpentine. He shook his head when he got to where Rufus was lying on the ground, a crooked smile creeping up one side of his face.

"What do we have here?"

"He dislocated his shoulder," Cece explained.

"I can see that, darlin'. Get him up. Don't let that arm drop."

Cece got to her feet and stooped over Rufus.

"Hold your arm against your chest," she said. "I'm going to scoop you up, okay? On three. One—"

"No," Rufus said.

"Two."

"Wait."

Cece lifted him a beat early, and Rufus was too shocked to scream, letting out a tepid "ehhhh" instead, and then he was standing, holding his left arm as if it didn't belong to his body. Mueller suppressed a laugh.

"Alright, boy. Come on."

"My hat," Rufus said, and without a second thought, he reached for it. With his good arm. The bum limb dropped and dangled from its socket like a dead branch, and Rufus leaned over even farther, arm swinging, and puked all over his shoes.

Cece and Mueller took a simultaneous step back.

"Told you to hold on to that," Mueller said.

After they stowed Rufus safely away in the cab, Warner addressed the crew.

"What a pathetic bunch of assholes are we. Whose stupid fuckin' idea was this?"

"That's not really fair," Ben said. "Jake—"

"Quiet, bacon grease."

Ben's mouth snapped shut. Warner strolled around the site, eyeballing each of them. Most found something of interest to stare at on the ground.

"Anybody want to explain just what the fuck happened here?" His eyes settled on Jake. "How about you, Queen Bee?"

"The chainsaw got pinched, and the bar broke, so—"

"The bar broke? Goddammit"

He whipped around. Found Cece.

"Who the fuck are you?"

Ben stepped forward.

"She's new. Just came in last—"

"How many times I gotta tell you to shut up?" He glared at Cece. "What's your name?"

"Cece."

"Let me ask you something, Cece. Are you a certified arborist?"

"No, I just—"

"Have you even completed the required hour's class on power-tool safety?"

Cece pressed her lips together.

"No."

"Then what the fuck are you doing over here? Why aren't you hacking ass on the brush line with the rest of the grunts?"

"The trunk was about to fly, so I—"

"So you what? Decided to fuck with my job site?"

"Rufus did that perfectly fine all by himself." She indicated Jake. "Him, too."

"Dude," Ben said. "If she hadn't knocked Rufus off that trunk, it would have sent him flying like a missile. We'd be cleaning his brains off of a tree somewhere."

Warner's left eye twitched. He spun and addressed Jake.

"That true?"

Reluctantly, Jake said, "yeah."

Warner nodded. He apprised Cece anew, grudging respect flashing across his face.

"Well, this ain't preschool, dipshits. We're down a fucking man and we're down a fucking chain saw. You have any idea how much one of those bars cost?"

As one, they all said, "two hundred dollars."

Warner's face turned red. His bloodshot eyes settled on Cece, then Jake, then Ben.

"Come on, Warner," Aiko said. "It could've been worse."

"She was only trying to help," Jake added.

Warner's scowl deepened. He spat on the ground.

"This fence has to be repaired, this tree taken down, and all this brush tarped-up. Fast. So you sack up, cut the crap, and make it right before sundown."

"Sundown?" Jake whined. "This is at least a two-day job."

"Then it looks like you'll be late for dinner, don't it?"

Amidst the groans of the workers, Warner stomped back to the truck and swung inside. Mueller hopped in the bed. The tires carved ruts in the soft earth as they peeled away.

The sun had just set when Cece and the rest of the crew straggled in. The bulbs hanging between each tent illuminated the village with a warm glow, and the other workers milled around, talking, playing cards, or just enjoying the evening. Low fires burned despite the heat, including one in the center of the village, as the smoke helped keep the bugs at bay. Jake peeled away, giving Aiko a quick kiss, and Aiko dipped into her yurt. Cece, however, plopped herself down in a chair in front of the central fire across from a couple having a low conversation. Ben joined her. The symphony of the woods, the crickets, the katydids, swelled and fell all around them. Cece removed a crumpled pack of cigarettes from her breast pocket and shook one up.

"That was an enormous pile of bullshit."

"Actually, for Warner, that was pretty nice."

"The guy's a sadist."

"I mean, you did almost kill Rufus."

"Kill him? I saved his life!"

Cece picked a flaming branch out of the fire and used it to light her cigarette.

"I haven't smoked this much in years," she said.

She blew out a cloud and watched it mingle with the smoke from the fire.

"Fucking jiggle it?"

They both laughed, and Ben, feeling the mood lighten, lay on his back.

"It's not my fault we have to jerry-rig everything around here."

"Pretty much par for the course with these jobs, isn't it?"

"Doesn't make it right."

"This your first time working something like this?"

"Kind of."

"There isn't any 'kind of'. Either you have or you haven't."

"Then it's my first one."

"Why?"

Ben shrugged.

"I needed a job."

"But why this crap? You could be washing dishes or bartending or something."

"I'm an Anthro major at W&M. I thought, I don't know, I could spend my summer doing something closer to what I want to do when I graduate." He picked up a rock and threw it into the fire. "Stupid choice, I know."

"Nah. I get it."

"You've obviously done this before."

"Plenty times ten."

"None *exactly* like this, though."

Cece took another drag and flicked the butt into the fire.

"The work's pretty much the same even if the details are different."

"It's okay here. Warner's a hardass, like I said, but he's alright most of the time."

"I've seen plenty of guys like him. They yell and they yell. That other one's a piece of work though."

The couple on the other side stood up and moved away, casting wary glances over their shoulders.

"Mueller?" Ben said. "He's alright. Doesn't talk much. Just a little weird. Aiko hates him. So does Harlow. And Jake." He waited for a beat. "And me, too, I guess."

"He's a creep."

Cece leaned back and looked up at the stars. The night sky was black velvet with bright pinpricks of light.

"The stars are so pretty out here."

Cece turned in a little while later. Harlow was still up, sitting cross-legged on her cot, reading a paperback.

"Hey," Cece said.

Harlow didn't even look up from her book. Cece clucked her tongue and whispered, "fine." She went over to her rack, lay back, and closed her eyes. After a moment, she rolled over and rummaged around in her bag. She dug out her cell phone and tapped at the screen. Still no bars.

"Shit."

"Good luck with that," Harlow said. "No cell service around here for miles."

Cece checked the battery. 90%. She turned it off and stowed it away. Harlow shifted on her cot, and the sheet she'd pulled up over her legs fell to the side, revealing a tattoo of a female tomato sitting coquettishly in a hammock.

"Nice ink," Cece said.

Harlow pulled the sheet over her leg. Cece tried again.

"I think we got off to a bad start."

Harlow turned her book over.

"What you did out there today was super-dangerous."

"You heard about that?"

"Everything everybody does gets back to me."

"Then you know I saved Rufus's life."

"You both could have died."

"I don't want to get on your bad side," Cece said. "Maybe there's some way for us to just get along?"

"This isn't a Disney movie, sweetie. We're not going to end up best friends. You want to get along with me? Keep your mouth shut and do your job."

Aiko, who'd been sleeping with her back to them, took her pillow and squeezed it over her head.

"Oh my god-uh," she moaned. "Will you two shut up?"

"Sorry, A," Harlow said.

She reached behind her and pulled a filter mask from under her pillow. Something about it struck Cece as familiar. An image flashed into her head. Karen in the pickup truck looking at her from behind the same kind of mask.

"Double trouble, huh?"

And then... and then... what happened? She couldn't recall. It was right there on the tip of her tongue, but...

Harlow caught Cece staring.

"Can I help you?"

"What? No. I was just looking at your mask."

"And?"

"Nothing. I thought maybe you have bad allergies or something."

Harlow strapped the mask over her face.

"Do me a favor," she said. "Mind your own business."

Then she leaned over and flicked off the string lights.

The night sounds filled the void between them.

Later.

Cece sat up in her bunk, gasping. She couldn't tell if it was night or morning. All she knew was that she heard a thud and felt the ground shake. She looked around the yurt; all was gray and silent. Harlow lay on her back, her heavy snores muffled behind the mask. Then someone spoke on the other side of the canvas just loud enough for her to hear.

"... sick of this shit. Not enough money in the world for me to stay."

"Come on," a second voice pleaded. "Don't leave. Look at what happened to Deion."

"Deion was an idiot."

"The guy was a Rhodes Scholar."

"He was a mama's boy doing a summer of hard labor so he could go back and virtue signal to all of his douchebag friends."

"Just come back to the yurt."

"No. Way."

"Please."

"I said no way! I'm losing it here, man. They work us so hard. I can't... there's something wrong here. Don't you feel it?"

"It's just the hard work."

"No, I mean… I can't remember stuff."

"Like what?"

"Like, do you remember how you got here?"

"Sure. I answered an add on Craigslist."

"No, I mean *got* here got here. Like, where were you right before you showed up here?"

Silence.

"See! That's what I'm talking about."

"I'm just tired is all…"

Footsteps crunched on the grass as the pair moved away, their voices fading into the night.

Cece listened to the rise and fall of the bugs in the woods, waiting for them to return. When they didn't, she took a deep breath and lay back down and stared at the vent cover. Someone had tied a yellow ribbon to one of the slats, and it shook as the cool air blew.

SUMAC ON STEROIDS

Cece's most vivid dreams always came right before she woke. This one was no exception.

She was standing at the entrance to an old souvenir shop just off of Route 1. The trees on the other side of the road were dark smudges in the night. All was still. A warm breeze blew in from the south. Sweat trickled down her neck.

Someone was sharpening a blade somewhere in the back of the store.

She swept forward, speeding through the shop on stiff legs. Grotesqueries lined the shelves. A stuffed hyena head on a stick. Tentacled faces in jars of green liquid. Pink intestines pressing against clear plastic bags. She zipped past, hooked around a corner, heading for the grating sound. An old man appeared in the back. He was leaning over a grinder, sharpening a bone-handle knife. Sparks showered the air as he bore down on the blade.

The scene changed, and she materialized in the middle of a park. Acres of green grass. Thick woods all around. Her father stood off a ways, beckoning to her. Behind him, his old tool shed, gray and worn and listing, the door swinging open like a mouth.

The scene changed again, and she was in the copse on the fence line. A vine wrapped around her neck and squeezed. Her limbs went numb, her head congested, her eyesight darkened—

Cece sat up in her cot, gasping. Harlow stood in the entrance, tying her hair in a ponytail.

"Bad dream?"

Cece touched her neck with her fingertips. Nothing. She was fine. When she spoke, her voice was rough, hoarse, as if she'd been shouting.

"A vine."

"What?"

"A vine was wrapped around my neck. I couldn't breathe. It felt so real."

Harlow snorted.

"Okay, well, you already missed second call. Better hurry before they start cleaning up. Break your fast, avoid the lash."

At five-thirty in the morning, the field kitchen buzzed with activity. The farmhands gathered for their morning grub, keeping the kitchen staff busy shoveling eggs and bacon, refilling the fruit bins, and making sure the water coolers were always full. Ben lorded over a full table, recounting the story of how Rufus nearly died. Jake and Aiko sat on one side of him, and Rufus sat on the other.

"The tree trunk is bouncing at least three feet in the air, and this idiot is jumping up and down like a monkey, screaming 'Gun the engine!'" Ben slapped Rufus's shoulder, laughing, and Rufus's face went pale. "If this kid'd stayed there one more second? Holy moly."

He mimicked a body flailing through the air, whistling a journey from its apex to its final splat on the tabletop. Amidst the laughter, Cece slid onto the bench across from him, her tray filled with sausage patties and orange slices. Ben pointed at her.

"But Captain America here comes flying through the air like a, uh, like Captain America, and knocks him away a microsecond before the trunk shot up into the air. I mean, come on! Where'd you play college ball, Lawrence Taylor from the New York Giants?"

"Don't mix your metaphors, Benjamin," Cece replied.

The table erupted again, even Rufus.

"Where are you from, Cece?" Aiko asked.

Cece forked some sausage into her mouth and chewed.

"Here, actually."

"Good old Frednecksburg? No way."

"Yep. Grew up in Spotsyltuckey actually. Left after I graduated high school. Haven't been back here in a long, long time. You?"

"Florida. Please, no 'Florida man' jokes. I know them all. Trust me."

"Pennsylvania boy, here," Jake said.

Aiko punched him playfully on the shoulder.

"Jake, no."

"What?"

"Delaware. You grew up in Delaware."

Jake laughed, stopping when he saw she was serious.

"Oh, shit. Right. Wilmington." He looked at Aiko. "Right?"

"I swear to god, Jake. You'd forget who I was if I didn't remind you every day."

She planted a kiss on his lips.

"Gross, guys," Ben said. He threw some bread crumbs at them, and the table laughed again.

The familiar sound of Warner's truck captured their attention, and they all turned to see it burring down from the fields, a trailer rattling behind. The laughter died.

"That's our cue," Aiko said. She nudged Jake. "Come on, baby."

"I'm not done with my bacon."

"Leave it."

Jake popped one last bite into his mouth before he let her drag him away. By the time the calico pickup rumbled to a stop under the oak tree, those who remained had fallen silent and still, sharing knowing glances or staring at the food on their plates. Ben pretended to find something of vast interest in the space over Cece's shoulder. Warner leaned out of his window and pounded on the door.

"Let's go! Let's go! Work ain't gonna work itself!"

"What a dick," Cece muttered.

Ben and a few of the others chuckled. Warner saw it and jolted out of the cab, marching toward the table like a drill instructor.

"I'm sorry, sweetheart. Did you say something funny?"

Cece swallowed her smile.

"No, sir. Just eating breakfast."

"Uh-huh. Because I could've swore I heard you say something right before all your little friends here laughed."

Ben said, "She didn't say—"

"Did I ask you, Lardass?"

"Man, knock it off with the fat jokes, okay?" Cece said.

"Cece, it's fine," Ben said.

"No, it's not fine. He shouldn't talk to you that way."

Warner leaned back and crossed his arms over his ample belly.

"Well, well, well," he said. "You hear that, ET?"

Mueller, leering out of the window of the truck, shifted a toothpick from one side of his mouth to the other.

"What's that, boss?"

"We got ourselves a little social justice warrior."

"Uh-oh. I'll get the dogs and hoses."

"Gimme a break," Cece said.

Warner unfolded his arms and leaned on the table, resting his gnarled knuckles on the graying wood. This close, Cece could smell his aftershave, the faint sour tang of coffee. She refused to meet his glare, choosing instead to stare straight ahead. Ben's eyes flitted back and forth between them, a look of unadulterated fear on his face.

"You listen to me, little girl," Warner muttered. "If I want to call Lardass over here a lardass, I'll call him a lardass. Got it?"

Cece shifted her eyes to the right. The breakfast sounds, the chatter, the flatware, the glasses, had stilled. Cece felt their eyes on her. She clenched her jaw.

"Hey, man," Ben broke in. "Take it easy."

Warner zeroed in on him.

"What's that, Lardass?"

"All she said was 'break your fast, avoid the lash,' okay?"

"What the fuck's that supposed to mean?"

"I-it's just something we say, you know. Because you guys are always harping on us to eat."

"Oh, I see."

Warner grinned. He returned his attention to Cece.

"Well, pardon my manners, boo boo. I thought you'd already filled your tank. Go ahead then. Finish up. You're gonna need it." He stood erect. "That goes for all of you. Finish up here and get your asses out to the north fence. You ain't gonna like what we got in store for you today. Not one bit!"

He strolled back to the truck, chortling to himself.

Cece pushed her plate away.

"What was that all about?" Ben asked.

"How should I know?"

"For a second there, I thought he was going to punch you in the face."

"Ya think?"

"On second thought," Warner called over his shoulder. "Pork Roll, Sugar Lips! Ya'll're coming with us."

Mueller hopped in the bed before they left, giving Ben, scrunched up in the corner against the cab, the side-eye.

"You're sitting back here?" Ben asked.

"Thought I'd get to know the new girl a little better."

Cece, her arms spread over the tailgate, rolled her eyes. Ben threw a look at the cab.

"Can I sit—"

"Nope."

"But it's empty."

"You got a medical condition or something?"

"I get carsick."

Mueller scoffed. He stretched out on the bed between them, his long legs resting on the wheel hub.

"You can stay right where you are, Pork Roll."

Warner steered the truck across the fields, avoiding as many rabbit holes as he could, keeping his speed below twenty-five. The trailer, in the manner of all trailers, rattled behind, the noise from its parts competing with the two clattering wheelbarrows bungeed to the side and the two clinking shovels resting on the bed. Cece let her head roll back and closed her eyes, enjoying the feel of the wind on her face. Then the truck hit a ditch and the bed jolted up and her eyes popped open. Mueller was staring at her.

"What is your job here, exactly?" Cece asked. "Resident creep?"

A slow smile spread across Mueller's face.

"I like the way your cheeks dimple when you talk. Makes you look young."

"Oh, my god," Ben moaned.

He pulled his knees up to his chest and gulped air.

Mueller slapped his leg.

"What's wrong, Piggly Wiggly? Too much syrup this morning?"

"Leave him alone," Cece said.

"Okay. Alright."

Mueller gazed at her. Let his eyes wander down... then up.

"Seems like we got ourselves off to a bad start, you and me."

"We didn't get off to any start at all."

"Whoo! You're spicy, ain't you? I like that. All the women in my family were spicy. My mama. My sister. My aunts. Mama and Bea, that's my sister, Beatrice, they didn't get along. Didn't get along one speck. Bea had herself a sassy way about her. Smart mouth, just like yours. Wasn't really her fault, given the circumstances of her upbringing, but my, oh, my did she and mama get into it!" He smiled at the memory, then let his eyes fall on Cece again, a different kind of smile appearing on his face. "Mama used to strap her right across her bare bottom."

Ben burped, clapped a hand over his mouth, and leaned over the side of the truck.

"Thar she blows!" Mueller chortled.

He squatted forward to bang on the cab, and when he did, his shirt pulled up, riding over a familiar-looking sheath.

Cece's eyes widened. There it was. Out in the open. Hand-carved antler handle. Bone inlay of a blazing sun on the grip. Her hand instinctively trailed down to her own blade. It was still there.

"Pull over!" Mueller yelled.
Warner whipped open the window panel.
"What?"
"Captain Intrepid here just barfed all of your port side."
"Goddammit!"
Warner hit the brakes and skidded to a stop, sending Cece and Mueller lurching forward.
"I told you," Ben said, wiping his mouth with the back of his hand.
Warner hopped out to inspect the damage.
"All over my tires," he grumbled. "You're gonna wash that off yourself."
"Hey, boss," Mueller said. "Better put him up next to you before he wastes the rest of his fuel for the morning."
Warner nodded in agreement.
"You heard him, Deep Dish. Get on up here."

Warner's truck rolled to a stop just inside the property line at the west field. An ancient maple had crushed the fence, taking out multiple sections. The grass was pockmarked with patches of blackened turf, like cigarette burns on a green carpet, no doubt the result of the thick, pustule-like balls of fungus that blistered the trunk. Where the fence still stood, great, waving carpets of vine, thicket, and bramble engulfed the links. Other sections farther down the line listed and bowed under the weight of the weeds. Links bent out like shotgun wounds, the shoots and thorns spilling through the holes. Cece nodded at the black patches.
"Did you guys try to burn it?"
"You're funny," Mueller replied.
He hopped out of the bed as Ben exited the cab.
"… and that's why Picard was so fucked up about killing the Borg queen because in some ways she was his queen, but he also knew she was evil."
Warner got out and stomped around to the trailer.
"So this is our punishment?" Cece asked. "We have to clear all this by ourselves?"
"Oh, no," Warner said, lowering the trailer gate. "We got something much more fun in mind for you two idiots. ET? My head hurts from listening to… whatever it was Stay Puft was talking about. You mind?"

"My pleasure." He faced Ben and Cece. "Them black patches on the ground? That's mungwort residue. Truly disgusting shit. Obviously, we need to fix this part of the fence, but we can't have everybody stomping around in it, tracking it all over the property. So before the main crew comes out, here's what you're going to do."

Warner tossed the shovels out of the trailer.

"Shovel that shit up."

Then he rolled the wheelbarrows out onto the grass.

"Pile it up."

Followed by the gas cans.

"And set it on fire."

Mueller was a creep, but he wasn't a liar. The mungwort residue was indeed truly disgusting shit. At first, Cece thought it would be, well, not easy, but equivalent to digging up a garden. This was most certainly not the case. The fried charcoal surface belied the thick, boggy goo underneath. It dripped off their shovels, steaming even in the heat. Ben, his shirt pulled up over his nose, scooped a tar-like shovelful into his wheelbarrow with a splat.

"What do you think it smells more like: feet or ass?"

"Both," Cece said. She'd tied a bandana around her face.

"Feass."

"Asfeat."

"Assface."

They laughed despite the toil.

After twenty minutes, Cece's shirt hung turgid with sweat, and black filth dotted her arms. After forty, so much crud coated her skin that she didn't know where the mungwort residue ended and she began.

And she couldn't get Mueller's knife out of her head.

"That's some knife you got there," she said.

"Aw, shucks. You like it?"

"Where's a guy like you get a knife like that?"

"Why do you care?"

Cece shrugged.

"Antler handle? Bone inlay? Knife like that tends to have a story."

"Sure does."

Mueller's sleepy eyes remained glued to hers.

"I got something on my face?" Cece asked.

"Nah. I just like looking at you."

"Dude. Just... stop."

She turned her attention back to the fields. Three workers in rubber overalls slumped by. Red splotches marred their faces like acid burns, their arms, too, and their hair looked patchy and bald in places. They stared dead-eyed as the truck passed.

"I need a break," Ben said.

Cece looked up, startled out of the memory.

"Yeah," she said. "Me, too."

They sat down next to each other and surveyed their work. The pile they'd made was impressive, but of the fifty-so-odd mungwort residue patches they needed to clear, they'd only excavated five.

"Fuuck me," Cece said.

"Five an hour isn't bad, right?"

"Not if you want to work for ten hours straight."

Ben emptied his water bottle.

"I'm starving. How close are we to lunch?"

Cece was about to respond when her phone vibrated in her back pocket. She stood up and clapped the dirt off her hands.

"I need to go to the bathroom."

She picked up her shovel.

"Back in a flash."

"The world is your toilet!" Ben called after her.

"Gross, Ben."

The fields were a flat plane for at least a half-mile in every direction. Nothing but wind and grass. So the only place she could get a bit of privacy was on the other side of the fence, in the wild woods filled, according to Harlow, with every kind of poisonous plant on the planet.

She picked her way through the dead branches and mungwort-blackened vines, using her shovel to push the worst of it aside. After a few dozen yards, the underbrush cleared, and she found herself in a kind of leaf and branch-covered dome. The air was stale and stuffy, but it was better than being out in the sun. She dug her phone out of her pocket and looked at the screen. One bar. Fuck. She held it up over her head. Still one bar. And the battery was down to 30%. Double fuck.

Then a text notification from SCARFACE popped up, and she swiped the glass.

U there?

She thumbed a quick response. Hit send.

Yeah.

Three dots appeared on the screen, blinking, blinking. Then they stopped.

"No no no."

She held the phone up, searching for a signal. Nothing. She stepped farther into the thicket.

"Come on, come on."

The dots reappeared. Her phone rang.

"Yes!" she cried, and she swiped the screen open. "Dude! Where the fuck have you been?"

"Can you hear me?"

"Yeah, I can hear you."

"Cece?"

"I'm here! Where the fuck have you been?"

"In the hospital, no thanks to you and that coffee."

"Shit, man. Sorry, but I had to improvise."

"First-degree burns, Cece."

"Good thing your face is already fucked up."

"Not funny."

"Listen, the connection's weak, so we gotta hurry."

Something tickled her ankle, and she pulled her leg back with a gasp. Snake? She looked down. Nothing but a thorny vine. Must have accidentally brushed against it. Back to the phone.

"So listen—"

A burst of static came from the other end.

"Q? You there?"

"Yeah. Listen, you need to watch out for—"

His voice degraded into a digital beep before returning with "… in the basement."

"What's in the basement?"

"No, DON'T go in the basement."

"Basement? What basement?"

"In the—"

"OW!"

Cece looked down again. This time a vine had snaked up her pant leg and wrapped around her knee. What the fuck? She cut it in half with the shovel blade and carefully removed the piece that had sneaked up her jeans. The tips of the thorns were red with her blood, and when she rolled her pants up, she saw three black puncture wounds. She tossed the vine away, disgusted, and rolled her cuff back down, pressing it against her shin to staunch the blood. She looked back at her phone. The signal had disappeared.

"Damn," she whispered, and she put the phone back in her pocket.

She took a step away, heading for the breach, but almost tripped. A third vine had wrapped around her ankle. She cut it in two and, hopping on one foot to rip it off, stumbled into a tree covered in bramble and thicket. The arm holding the shovel plunged into a nest of prickers.

"Fuck!"

She wrenched it down and out, pulling the vines with her, the thorns leaving bloody ruts in her skin. She inspected her wounds. They were deep, but not terminal. The surrounding trees creaked. A warm breeze shook the leaves, bringing with it the heady scent of goldenrod and sweetfern. Was that a footstep? The snap of a twig? She cocked her head, straining to listen. Nothing.

Okay, she thought. *Fuck this.*

She ripped the vines off her arm with a grunt and brought the blade of the shovel down, slicing another in two. As if on cue, the brush rattled to life. Branches shot out of the woods like crooked fingers, vines whipped down from above. Something lashed her cheek. With a scream, Cece wound up and swung the shovel like a bat, swatting down an angry bough shooting straight for her face.

Out in the field, Ben dozed on a clean section of grass, fluttering on the edge of a full-on nap. Cece screamed, and his eyes flashed open. He sat up, wondering if he heard what he thought he heard. Cece screamed again, grunted, and yelled, "GODDAMMIT!"

Grimacing, Ben lay back and closed his eyes.

"Gross."

A vine crept up Cece's pant leg. A third tore at her wrist again. More wound together like rope, wrapped around her shovel, and ripped it free. Another encircled her throat and squeezed. Cece's eyes bulged. Now they bound her ankles. Now they encircled her stomach. Now they wrapped around her forehead. Only her left arm was free. She had maybe a few seconds before they restrained her entirely, and then… and then what?

No time to worry about that.

She grabbed her knife with her free hand, whipped it out of the sheath, and sawed at the vines around her throat. The point of the knife cut into her jaw. Blood ran down her face. One vine popped like a broken guitar string, followed by two more, and then her neck was free. She took a strong, ragged in-suck of breath.

"Alright, bitches," she muttered.

With a feral roar, she hacked at the vines on her arm, her ankles, left, right, rip, rip. She lurched back the way she'd come, but a wall of brambles blocked her escape, encircling her on all sides. She sheathed her knife, snatched the shovel off the ground, and hacked into it. The wall shook, a few branches cracked, but it didn't give. She swung the shovel again. A few more branches snapped, but the wall held.

"Motherfucker!" she screamed, and she threw herself into the attack. "Ben!"

Ben sat up when he heard his name, frowning at the woods. Had he really heard that?

"BEN!"

Ben struggled to his feet, saying, "alright, alright."

Leaning on his shovel, knees popping, he started for woods, grumbling, a tiny limp in his step.

"BEN! HELP!"

At that, he broke into a run. He sprinted through the breach, turned right, and hit a wall of vine and branches that hadn't been there before. Ten feet high and solid as stone, they created an impenetrable dome. As he watched, Cece yelled, and the wall shook as if struck by something on the other side.

"Cece?"

"Ben! Get me out of here!"

"There's a wall. Of vines."

"I know!"

"What do you want me to do?"

"GET ME OUT OF HERE!"

"How?"

The wall shook again, and a hole formed. Cece's eyes appeared.

"You got your shovel?"

"Yeah."

"Use it!"

Her eyes disappeared, replaced by the blade of the shovel. When she ripped it back, the wall shuddered like a thing alive. Ben joined her, and they hacked away at the opening, sticks and leaves flying. It widened bit by bit.

"Almost there," Ben said.

Cece, panting, sweat pouring down her face, grit her teeth, heaved the shovel over her head and, shoulders flexing, biceps bulging, brought it down with a scream, aiming for a knot of tangled vines and branches. The blade cut through the air and sliced deep into the wall. And stuck.

"Fuck!"

She pulled back, grunting, but the blade wouldn't move.

The wall shuddered again, and then right before their eyes, the branches and vines wound their way around each other, reforming the breach into a solid barrier. Cece yelled something, but her voice was faint.

"Cece?"

Another reply, fainter this time, like she was moving farther away. Crashing and slashing, a few labored grunts. The wall pulsed, and a wave rippled across it. Ben took a step back.

"Cece, can you hear me?"

The wall pulsed again. A dimple appeared. Dead leaves and broken sticks flew out of the center. Cece's shovel came next, whirling like a helicopter blade. It whipped overhead and crashed into the branches behind him. The wall puckered one last time, and in a rush of thorns, briar, and bramble, Cece shot out of the center. Ben barely had time to let out a scream before she hit him full in the chest, knocking him flat. She landed face down behind him, skidding in the dirt for a few feet before coming to a stop against a stump. They lay there for a moment, stunned and exhausted.

Then Ben said, "I mean… that must have been some piss."

For the second time that week, Cece limped, injured and dirty, into her empty yurt. Harlow's cot looked military ready, the blanket taut and smooth, two pillows neatly propped against the head. Aiko's looked like a body had been stashed under the sheets. Her pillows were heaped, lumpy and disturbing, and a variety of toiletries, clothes, and essential oil vials dotted the ridges and slopes. A fine mist of yellow pollen coated everything, the cots, the dirt floor, the bedding, even the canvas walls. Cece stumbled over to her bag, rummaged around, and pulled out a half-empty fifth of vodka. She spun the top off, took a shot, grimaced, and poured some over the red, raw wound that was her ankle.

"Ah, fuck that hurts."

"Oh, my god."

Aiko stood in the entrance, freshly showered, one towel covering her body, one done up like a turban on her head. Harlow squeezed past, took one look at Cece, and snorted.

"You look like shit."

"Thanks."

"Told you to cuff your pants."

"You didn't tell me the fucking woods were possessed."

"Whatever."

"What happened to you?" Aiko asked.

"She didn't gear up, that's what happened to her."

"No," Cece said. "The vines attacked me."

Harlow sat primly on the edge of her cot.

"Yeah. Right."

"Ben and I were clearing that mungwort shit out of the west field. I went to take a piss, and they attacked. Like snakes. Like they wanted to kill me."

Aiko watched her with wide eyes.

"Are you serious?"

"No, Aiko, she's not serious," Harlow said. "She fell into something and now she's trying to cover up her stupidity."

"I'm telling you," Cece said. "They wrapped around my ankles and my wrists. Built a fucking wall and—"

"Let me see," Harlow said.

"See what?"

"Your legs. Let me see."

"What do you care?"

"Because if you stumbled into poison oak, you might need something more than vodka."

Cece stared at her, calculating. She took another shot.

"Fine," she said. She stuck her right leg out in front of her.

Harlow slipped on her work gloves, knelt, and gently rolled Cece's jeans back. Blood, black and crusted, coated her ankle and shin. The skin was raw and red.

"Are those puncture wounds?"

"That's what I was talking about. The thorns—"

"You probably hit some poison sumac."

"Sumac on steroids."

"Are you allergic?"

"Not that I know of."

Aiko fished around in her cot and came up with a little brown vial.

"I've got some lavender oil."

"No, thanks."

"It'll help with the pain."

Cece rolled her eyes.

"Don't waste good vodka," Harlow said. "Take a cold shower, scrub the oil off."

Cece rubbed her neck. It was raw, but at least it didn't itch. She peeled her shirt over her head, trying not to let the fabric touch her face. Her torso was clear, but her wrists felt swollen and itched like crazy. She unbuttoned her pants and rolled them down, stopping at her knees.

Aiko gasped and put her hand to her mouth.

Every inch of skin on Cece's legs glowed red and puffy. Black puncture wounds dotted the muscles in her calves, quads, and hamstrings. Blood ran and sweated, and a few of the worst patches were already oozing pus. Cece looked at it for a moment, seemingly uncomprehending, before tipping her head back for a long pull off of her bottle of vodka.

PICK YOUR POISON

Cece tossed and turned on her cot, trying to ignore the pain and the incessant need to itch and failing at both. It got so bad that at two-thirty in the morning, Harlow sat up and said, "Jesus, Cece. Just go to the infirmary!"

"I didn't know we had one."

"Three tents down on the right."

"Does it have a nurse?"

"Does this place look like it has a nurse?"

The infirmary wasn't so much an infirmary as it was an empty yurt with a single cot and a first-aid kit sitting on an end table. Cece almost didn't bother to open it, but then, curious and in the mood for irony, she went over and flicked open the clasps. The contents of the kit made her laugh out loud. What had she been expecting? Some band-aids? A pair of scissors? Instead, all she found was three rolls of gauze, a packet of ibuprofen, and a tongue depressor.

She wrapped her oozing skin in the gauze, popped the pain relievers, and settled in for the night, most of which she spent writhing around in abject misery. Add to that the fact that the vent in the infirmary didn't work, and the most she could do was imagine what life had been like before. She tried to distract herself. The vodka had helped, hadn't it? And the shower and lavender? But challenging a rash the likes of which plagued her body was like plugging an erupting volcano with an orange.

The next morning broke as hot and as hazy as all the mornings prior. Cece sat on a box in front of the infirmary, sucking down a cigarette and watching the dawn unfold. The sky lightened, turning from purple to rose to pink, and a fine mist lifted off of the fields, feigning the appearance of a cool, English dale. But Cece knew that the only reason the temperature dropped at night was because the sun disappeared, and even then it only lowered five or ten degrees. Soon that hateful orb would rise over the ugly, cursed forest, bringing with it unbearable heat and humidity, and soon after that, she'd be out in the west field shoveling mungwort with Ben.

What the hell am I doing here? she thought.

She'd never worked harder in her life, not picking fruit, not digging trenches, not spreading asphalt. The muscles in her arms and legs ached, her back felt like a slab of concrete, and her body had been ravaged by the worst rash she'd ever known. She pressed her forearm, trying to relieve the itch. Blood and pus were already bleeding through the gauze. After a moment, she reached into her back pocket and carefully removed her father's postcard. The Chatham Bridge. The Rappahannock River. VISIT HISTORIC FREDERICKSBURG!

"Yeah," she said. "Visit Historic Fredericksburg. Where the farmers grow toxic sludge and the trees try to kill you."

She flipped it over and read the note scrawled on the back, running her fingers over her father's signature.

By the time her stomach growled, it was already five degrees hotter. She didn't want to go to breakfast. She didn't want to have to explain what happened. She didn't want to see the pity in their eyes. Especially Ben's. So she got up and made her way over to the field kitchen before anybody woke and snagged a bagel and a hard-boiled egg off the serving cart, ignoring the stares of the kitchen staff. She was heading back to her yurt when Warner and Mueller came out of the basement of the main house and stopped dead in their tracks. Cece kept walking.

"What in Sam Spade happened to you?" Warner growled.

"It's nothing. Just a few scratches."

She continued on, Warner eyeballing her.

"Stop," he ordered.

"I'm fine, Warner."

"Stop what you're doing and get your ass over here."

"No, thanks."

Warner and Mueller shared a look.

"Hey!" Warner snapped.

Watching an overweight, middle-aged man trying to run was almost as painful as being the overweight, middle-aged man trying to run. She could have stopped. She knew he was going to catch up to her. But she didn't want to. Listening to him gasp for breath as he jogged up from behind gave her a momentary feeling of satisfaction. She almost laughed out loud when he heaved his bulk in front of her.

"Stop, goddammit!"

He looked like he was on the verge of passing out. He strode a few steps away, gasping, before turning back and putting his hands on his knees.

"Man, Warner," Cece said. "You're out of shape."
"No shit."
"What do you want?"
Warner held up a finger. Cece crossed her arms.
"I need to get my gear before we head out."
"You ain't goin' nowhere."
"I told you, I'm fine."
"You look." Gasp. "Like you jumped." Gasp. "On a hand grenade."
"Look, man. I can work."
Warner stood erect, wiped the sweat off his face, and took a deep breath.
"Fuck you, you can. What is it? Ivy or sumac?"
"No idea. Probably both?"
"That shit's highly transmissible, you idiot. You so much as look at someone and they'll break out. I can't have my whole crew sidelined just because you want to prove you're the biggest butch on the block."
Cece clenched her jaw.
"Fine, I'll just sleep on my cot."
"Uh, no. We don't pay you to jerk off all day. I'm putting you on Flower Power with Rufus."

An hour later, Cece was standing in front of a flower bed next to the main house. She cast a look over at the field kitchen. Hands were heading out to the fence line in groups of three and four. Jake hopped into Aiko's four-wheeler with a whoop and kissed her before they tore away. Warner started his truck and made a U-turn, making sure Cece could see the white oval of Ben's face staring mournfully out at her as they dragged him out to shovel mungwort alone. Mueller was sitting on the wheel well in the back. He smiled like a schoolgirl and gave her a wiggly fingered wave.
Rufus, his arm in a sling, strolled up, holding a trowel.
"Holy cow. You look like a mummy."
"Thanks."
"What happened?"
"What do you think?"
"Did you swim in it?"
"Yeah. I swam in it."
"Really?"
Cece motioned at his shoulder.

"How's the wing?"
"Hurts. I think it's more than dislocated, no thanks to you."
"It'd be a lot more than dislocated if I hadn't tackled you."
"Whatever."
"You want to tell me what we're doing here?"
Rufus spread his good arm out in a dramatic arc.
"Welcome to Flower Power. The job's pretty easy."
He tapped her arm with the trowel.
"Ow! Watch it, dude."
"Six inch holes, a foot apart."
"Then what?"
He scooped up a bucket filled with bulbs.
"Put one of these in each."
"Six inch holes?"
"Six inch holes."
"A foot apart?"
"A foot apart."

Cece eyed the rich soil before her, eyed the bucket. Twenty bulbs, maybe twenty-two. Shit. She'd finish the job in a half an hour.

Fuck you, Warner, she thought. *I'll jerk off as much as I want today, you dick.*

"That's it?" she said.
"Well, she wants the whole driveway done, so…"
Rufus pointed behind her. Two dozen buckets lined the brick walkway outside the basement door.

If toiling in the blistering sun all day, cutting vines off of a fence, or hauling bundles of branches, or hacking away at endless underbrush, or digging toxic goo out of the ground was arduous, somehow planting hundreds of bulbs was worse. It must have been the monotony. Dig, scoop, dig, scoop, bulb in the hole, pack the dirt in. Repeat. Rufus mostly loafed around by the front porch, pretending now and then to plant a bulb or inspect the mulch that lined the driveway. He made himself so scarce that Cece forgot about him. That's why, about an hour into the job, she nearly jumped when a voice behind her said, "that's too deep."

She spun and yelped. Rufus loomed over her, the sun behind his head, his face strangely obscured.
"Jesus, dude! You scared the shit out of me!"
"Your holes are too deep. The shoot'll never break the surface."

Cece gritted her teeth, pushed half an inch of dirt back in the hole she'd been digging, and looked up at him.

"Much better," he said, and he wandered off to a different part of the yard.

The morning blazed onward.

Cece was five buckets in when she felt something buzz on her thigh. Thinking it was a bug or a bee or, knowing the farm, some kind of mutated death hornet, she whacked at her leg with the trowel and instantly regretted it for two reasons:

1. the pain.
2. it wasn't a murder hornet. It was her phone.

"Fuck!" she spat.

She threw the trowel down and dug her phone out of her pocket. A maze of broken glass webbed one corner, one line etched across the screen, but the rest of it was intact. A notification informed her she only had 5% of her battery left. She swiped it away, uncovering a text from Scarface.

U there?

Cece went to tap the notification, but another ad for ReGeneren popped up, and she hit the link instead. Her browser opened, and a landing page filled her screen.

"ReGeneren, by SingleCorp! Alleviate Your Anxiety, Dunk Your Depression, Forget Your Fears with ReGeneren!"

"Fuck you, ReGeneren."

She mashed the button, trying to close the ad, but the screen froze and went black.

"No!"

She mashed the button again, and the phone glowed to life. Another text from Scarface popped up.

??

Cece tapped at her screen, but her gauze-covered thumbs could only fumble over the letters. She hit send.

Fi;ader wjahsud

"Fuck!"

She ripped the bandage off her hands with her teeth and typed two letters.

Ye

Send.

Only 3% battery left.

The ellipsis blinked in and out, in and out. The battery winked down to 2%.

"C'mon, dude!"

She tapped out another text.

Call

One second. Two seconds. Three seconds.

She was in the middle of typing "call!" again when the phone vibrated. Scarface's scarred face appeared on the screen. Cece hit Accept.

"Dude, hurry up! I only have two percent."

Static greeted her in response, a high-pitched squelch of radio frequency with Scarface's voice weaving in and out of it.

"Can't… Danville… she knows…"

"I can't hear you, man. You're breaking up."

A door banged somewhere nearby, and Cece instinctively crouched and plugged a thumb in one ear.

"Tracking her… father… I…"

"Who is 'she'? What does she know?"

"… figure out… forest…"

The line went dead.

"No!" Cece barked.

She held the phone out and stared at the black screen as if she'd never seen one before, as if glaring would turn it back on. When it didn't, she slumped. A warm breeze rushed across the field, toying with her hair, drying the sweat on her skin. She stood up with a sigh and looked around. Rufus was nowhere to be seen. Yurtville was dead. Another breeze shook the lights strung between the tents. The lights! There had to be a power source somewhere. Maybe it was hooked up to the main house?

As if on cue, the door leading to the basement creaked open.

Cece's mouth dropped open. Then she chuckled.

Cece hovered in the entry, not quite ready to commit. If this wasn't B&E, it was certainly E. The basement smelled like mold and dirt and, under that, a hint of something rotten. Packed dirt floor. Cinderblock walls. Directly in front of her, a shelf laden with old power tools leaned drunkenly to one side. To the left, an old gas generator squatted in the corner. To the right, an egress window through which the sun poured. Under it stood a workbench covered with various tools, instruction manuals, and other workshop detritus. Miraculously, on top of the mess sat a power strip, its cord snaking under an old safety vest. Cece followed the cord to where it plugged into the receptacle on the wall and back to the outlets on the strip. The on/off switch blinked to life.

"Fuck. Yes."

She beelined for the workbench, whipped a power brick and cable out of her pocket, and plugged her phone in. Then she waited. Water rushed through the pipes. The white noise of the basement. Then a beep sounded from somewhere nearby. Was she hearing things? She cocked her head. Nothing but dead air. It came again. BEEP! Maybe it was an appliance? A washer or a dryer or a water heater or something.

She crept over to the stairs and peeked up. Light shone through a crack under the closed door at the top. A cabinet banged. The floorboards creaked. The shadow of a footstep interrupted the beam.

Cece scurried back to the workbench, hand hovering over her phone. She could be out of the cellar in seconds, just snatch everything up and slip out the exit. She waited for the door to open, for footsteps to start down the stairs, counted to ten, twenty, thirty. When she made it to one minute, she finally exhaled.

On the other side of the work area, a flight of antique tools hung from a pegboard: clamps and calipers, wrenches and pliers. Under that, a row of boxes stacked on top of each other. They were old and rotting, slumping to one side. She glanced at her phone. The icon glowed to life. It was going to be awhile. Might as well have a look around.

Russian letters on the box top label. Лилит Дрейк, La Casa del Porta Prestigio 68 Mérida. Mérida? Mexico? She tugged on the flap and it ripped off, so she folded it up and stuffed it in her pocket. When she tried to pull the box out, the cardboard was so old that it crumbled in her fingers. The bottom edges were wet and oily, so she shoved one hand under, grimacing at the slick feel, and gently pulled it out. The other three flaps were a little more solid than the first, and they flopped aside when she opened them up.

Sitting on top was a porn magazine with a picture of a woman wearing a cowboy hat, cowboy boots, and nothing else. She was straddling a hobby horse, firing a six-shooter into the air with one hand and whipping a lasso over her head with the other. Cece picked it up by one corner and deposited it to the side like it was a piece of diseased fruit. The next magazine was very much of the same inclination, only this one enjoyed an Arabian theme replete with camels, a man-sized sphinx, cats, and serpent spangles. Under that, more porn. And more porn. Cece picked the box back up and pushed it back into place.

Behind her, a pale face emerged from a dark corner, then darted away. Cece heard the shuffle and looked up, but all she could see was the darkness at the far end of the basement. She shook it off and returned her attention to the boxes.

The next one was sturdier but only contained basement flotsam: Zip ties, rusting chains, old locks. Disappointed, she pocketed a couple of zip ties and shoved the box back into place. A little too hard, it would seem, as the workbench shook and a manila envelope taped to the underside dropped onto the floor.

Cece looked around, expecting someone to come marching out of nowhere, demanding to know "what the hell do you think you're doing?" but it didn't happen. She unclasped the top and shook the contents out into her open hand.

Pictures. A whole stack of them. But these weren't pornographic. They were images of farmhands at various stages of work. Fixing the fence. Cutting down trees. An entire series devoted to men and women in rubber vests and shoulder-length gloves, covered in tar-like globs. A close-up of a young lady staring into the lens, dark circles under her eyes, her skin an archipelago of scars.

And finally, one taken with a telephoto lens. It was just a guy, a regular old guy. Thirty, forty, maybe older. He was shirtless, hoisting a bale of hay into the bed of Warner's truck, gritting his teeth with the effort. The muscles in his back and arms bulged, his stomach was flat and defined. Cece peered closer, disbelieving but hopeful. There. On his hip. A knife with a hand-carved antler handle.

She stared at it for a long time, her face flat, her hands shaking.

"So, you were here after all," she said.

She folded the picture and tucked it into her back pocket. Something scuffed the floor behind her. She spun around. There, not two feet away, stood an old woman. She was tall and handsome, with long, gray hair piled up in a bun on top of her head. A pair of emerald earrings hung from each ear, and a necklace with a nested doll charm rested on her bosom. She was holding Cece's phone.

"If you wanted a charge, dear," she said. "You only had to ask."

The old woman's dining room decor reminded Cece of a '70s farmhouse: mismatched chairs, distressed plank table, a worn hutch displaying antique china. An aggressive looking tulip in a pot hung from a macrame saddle. An aging AC unit chugged away in a window in the living room. It rattled to a stop, and the air in the room immediately grew warmer. Cece turned to the bay window. From there, she could see the entire property. Yurtville to the right, the field kitchen slightly off-center, and in the distance, the north pasture and the green line of the fence. Her coworkers scurried like ants around the worksite, hacking brush, chainsawing branches. The indistinct murmur of a talk show host floated out of the kitchen.

"And what are you going to do, friends, when the cabal comes for you? We're in a fight for our very country. Our souls, our children's souls, our children's children's souls are at stake."

"Pick your poison?"

Startled, Cece spun around. The old woman was standing in the dining room holding a tea service.

"Excuse me?"

"Tea, dear. What kind would you like?"

"Just regular old tea is fine."

The old woman sat the service on the dining room table, placing herself, Cece noted, between her and the living room and, beyond that, the front door.

"We don't have any 'regular old tea,' young lady. We have our own special blends." She nodded at the steeps. They looked like tiny medieval weapons. "Yellow Dream, Black Mamba, or White Bone?"

Cece considered her options.

"I'll do Black Mamba."

"Brave girl. Please, sit." Cece chose a chair as far from the old woman as possible. "We haven't properly introduced ourselves yet, I'm afraid. My name is Lilith. This is my farm."

"Cece."

"Pleased to meet you, Cece."

The radio host's voice went up an octave.

"The Deep State, with its legions of bureaucratic peons, is protecting the pedophiles!"

Lilith clucked her tongue.

"Sorry about the chatter," she said. "He was one of daddy's favorites. He got a little too into it, I'm afraid. I just like to 'enjoy the show' as they say."

She smiled at Cece as if awaiting an answer, and Cece, suddenly realizing it, said, "must be nice."

"Nice?"

"We can't even get a cell signal out here."

"We are certainly out in the boonies."

"Way out in the boonies."

Lilith placed a steep into one cup and poured hot water from the tarnished silver kettle. Steam rose into the air.

"Your phone should be ready soon. I plugged it into the kitchen outlet."

"Thanks."

"I just don't understand what you young people see in those silly devices. You're all so busy staring into them you don't even see what's going on right under your noses."

"Mm."

Lilith set the kettle down, her eyes grazing over the gauze peeking out from under Cece's sleeve.

"You're injured, I see. Farm life a little rougher than you anticipated?"

"I've had worse."

"I hardly think that's true."

The cup rattled on the saucer as the old woman handed it over the table.

"Here you are. One Black Mamba for a black mamba! I put some sweetener in there for you. It's my own special blend."

A chip marred the lip, and Cece turned the cup and sipped. Her tongue went numb, as if a wasp had stung her. She swallowed and coughed. Lilith smiled.

"Too much for you, dear?"

"No, it's good."

"Black Mamba does have a bit of a bite to it."

The window unit buzzed to life, and cold air filled the room. A yellow ribbon tied to the vent waved in the air. Cece turned her face to it, resisting the urge to open her mouth. Her throat was burning, her face flushed. A rill of sweat ran down her temple.

"That's the most hi-tech this house gets," Lilith said. "I didn't even want to put it in, but I can't really take the heat anymore. Daddy would not have approved."

"He built this place, your father?"

"From the roots up. Each beam, each pipe, each wall. His blood is in the foundation."

"Sounds like an impressive man."

"Oh, well, you know fathers. Fathers, fathers, fathers."

Cece cleared her throat again. A clock ticked somewhere nearby. The refrigerator hummed. Lilith's spoon tinkled in her cup as she stirred.

"Let's not play this silly game anymore, dear. You stole something from me, and I'd like it back."

"I didn't steal anything from you."

"You most certainly did. I saw you. In the basement."

Pinned to her chair, Cece didn't know what to say. Had she taken something of value by accident? Then it struck her.

"You mean the picture?"

"I most certainly do mean the picture."

The girl leaned to the side, took the folded-up snapshot out of her back pocket, and tossed it on the table. Lilith barely glanced at it.

"I didn't mean to take it," Cece said. "You startled me is all."

"No need to lie, dear."

"I'm not."

With a bemused smile, Lilith tapped her spoon on the edge of her cup and placed it purposefully on the folded napkin at her elbow. Then she reached out with one finger and drew the photo to her.

"Please don't misunderstand. I mean nobody harm. Workers are the lifeblood of my farm. Without them, without you, this whole place would wither and die."

She unfolded the picture and looked at it.

"This one interests you. Why?"

"No specific reason. What is that, a little something for your scrapbook? Or do you always spy on your workers?"

"I'd hardly call it spying."

"Sneaking pictures of people while they work isn't spying?"

"This is my land. I'll take pictures of whomever I please."

"That's rich."

Lilith set the photo aside.

"It just occurred to me that I don't know your last name."

"It's Stone."

"Cece Stone. Interesting. Very sibilant."

Cece smiled a tight-lipped smile.

"Let me ask you something, Ms. Stone. How many farms have you owned?"

Cece didn't understand the intent of the question, but she felt the hostility. She knew what was coming next. Condescension like that was a precursor to something worse. Almost involuntarily, she reverted to her teenage years, settled back in the chair, which creaked, and crossed her arms.

"Seasonal work draws a certain breed," Lilith explained. "Most are well-mannered enough. They just want to do their work, get paid, and move on. But some are… less savory."

"Like the guy in that picture?"

"No, no. He was very useful."

Cece's eyes danced over the photo again. Lilith saw it.

"So you *are* interested in him, aren't you?"

"Not at all."

"I told you, I don't like being lied to."

"And I don't like being called a liar."

The basement door flew open, and the strangest looking man Cece had ever seen barged in, a lab coat hanging off his bony shoulders, a potted plant clutched to his bird chest. He was both skinny and flaccid, vibrant and depleted, with a pale moon face and jet black hair. A pair of round glasses perched on the end of his pinched nose, and his hands were littered with fresh red scratches and thin white scars.

"Oh, missus!" he cried as he bumbled forward. "I'm sorry to disturb you, but the… but the…"

He caught sight of Cece and bumped into the hutch so hard that it rocked a container filled with marbles. A few spilled a few over the edge, bounced on the hardwood, and rolled into the corner. He watched them go, then looked at Lilith, helpless.

"So nice to see you this morning, Laszlo," Lilith said. To Cece: "Laszlo is our resident horticulturist."

Cece couldn't tell if the little man's eyes widened or if it was just the effect of his coke-bottle glasses. Whatever the case, he fastened them on her.

"Is this—"

"Cece Stone, Laszlo. One of the new crop."

Laszlo blinked away his confusion.

"Yes! Yes, of course! Pleasure to meet you."

He stepped forward, one limp hand extended. Cece reached out to shake it, but at the sight of the rash peeking out from under the gauze, Laszlo grabbed her wrist and pulled her arm toward him, pressing his face so close to her skin that she thought he was going to lick it.

"Goodness me, madam! Goodness me!"

Cece tried to pull her limb back, but the strange little man clamped down harder.

"Toxic vernix, radicans, diversil. Raised nodules filled with bulla, no doubt!" He fixed Cece with another wide-eyed look. "Such terrible discomfort you must be in!"

Cece finally wrenched her wrist out of his grasp.

"Touch me again, and I'll break your fingers."

"Oh, forgive me, Mistress Cecilia—"

"It's Cece."

"Forgive me Mistress Cece. I meant no harm. But your rash is so... where did this happen?"

"West field."

"West field?" Lilith asked. "Are you sure?"

"Yeah. Warner had us scooping up mungwort oil."

"Warner brought the whole crew out there? Why?"

"No, just me and Ben."

"I see. And this Ben, does he look like this, too?"

"What? No. It was... I had to take a bathroom break, so I went past the fence." Cece held up one rash-covered wrist. "Bad idea."

"Have you had any trouble breathing? Headaches? Fever?"

"No. Just the rash."

Lilith and Laszlo exchanged a look.

"What's going on?" Cece asked. "Should I be worried?"

"Evidently not, dear," Lilith said. She stood up, her chair scraping the hardwood, and started around the table, gesturing at the plant Laszlo was still hugging to his chest.

"Laszlo, my sweet. Is this the new hybrid?"

"Yes! Oh, yes! Here it is, plain as day!"

He set the plant down on the table, caressing the leaves.

"It matured this morning. Look right here. See the markings on the petiole? The red venules? The thickened blade? They're filled to bursting."

"I love the yellow orange streaks."

"Yes! I mixed it with jewelweed!"

"Be a dear and give me a leaf, will you?"

"Of course, missus! Of course!" He snapped a petal from the stem and handed it to her. "Here you are."

Lilith made a fist and crushed the petal, releasing a lotion-like sap. She held it up to her nose.

"Smells like honeysuckle." She nodded at Cece's wrist. "May I?"

Before she could respond, the old woman's fingers darted out and swiped at her raw wound with a healthy dollop of the sap. Cece gasped, first in shock, then at the immediate relief. Her wrist went numb, and the numbness crept up her arm to the crook of her elbow.

"What is that?"

"Just a little something Laszlo and I whipped up. We call it Aloesbane."

"Bane? As in wolfsbane?"

"Diluting the aconitine with aloe neutralizes the poison." Seeing Cece's uncertainty, Lilith added, "Not to worry, dear. Laszlo and I have been breeding unique combinations of plants for years, haven't we, Laszlo?"

"Oh, yes! Yes, indeed!"

Lilith frowned at Cece's arm, seeming to think about something. Then she said, "you know what? I know just the thing to aid the healing of that nasty little rash of yours."

"Missus, no!" Laszlo said.

"Oh, quiet, Laszlo."

"But—"

"There's a mineral spring a short walk through the west wood. The water has healing powers."

"I'm sure it does," Cece said.

"Laszlo here uses it all the time, don't you, my boy?"

Cece's phone buzzed to life on the counter.

"Sounds like your toy is awake," Lilith said. Notifications dinged one after the other. "I thought you said we didn't get a signal out here?"

Cece was already up. She scooted around the chairs and into the kitchen.

"We don't."

Another ding.

"You must be a popular girl."

Cece pocketed her phone without looking. Then she unplugged the brick and the cord and stashed them in her back pocket.

"Don't you even want to see who's been trying to contact you?" Lilith asked.

Cece came back into the dining room.
"I think it was just trying to update. So this pond, where is it?"
Lilith studied her.
"Laszlo, be a dear and see our guest to the path?"
Laszlo sputtered and frowned. He threw a frightened look at the front door.
"Laszlo?"
"Yes!" he said. "Of course, Missus. Of course."

Cece tramped through the woods. Sun dappled the leaves in the canopy above, birds chirped, and the air seemed to lighten the farther along she walked. She smelled the spring before she saw it, fresh and clean with a tinge of lavender and mint, and when the path opened up to the banks of the water, Cece couldn't help but laugh.

It was simply incredible.

To the right, a wall of boulders formed a fall down which fresh water trickled. A willow on the opposite bank plunged its roots into the pool, its lustrous branches shading more than half of the water's surface. Birds flitted and sang overhead. Cece half-expected a doe to creep out of the woods for a mid-morning drink.

"Oh, fuck yeah," she said.

She took off her clothes, stripped off the gauze, and crept to the edge. The dirt on the bank crumbled when she sank her toes in it, and the crumbles pattered down the incline into the water, producing perfect circles that reverberated out. With a squeal of joy, she cannonballed in.

She broke the surface with a gasp and a laugh. The water was so cold that it was hard to breathe at first, but her body adjusted as she splashed around. She backstroked in a circle, watching the sunlight flitting through the willow branches, then free-styled to the middle, flipped, and dove as far as she could. Finally, tired from her exertions, she floated on her back. She closed her eyes and listened to the sound of her breathing. She drifted to the edge, and when her head nudged a root, she opened her eyes.

A man was standing on the bank, hands in his pockets, looking down at her.

"Nice isn't it?"

"Fuck!" Cece cried.

She dropped her legs and kicked back to the middle. There she turned and treaded water.

"You've been watching me, you perv?"

"Not really. I was just looking for my dog. She likes to hang out down here."

He was younger than she initially thought. Her age, maybe? Early thirties, max. He wore a full beard and his hair high and tight, with an exaggerated part on one side. He put his fingers in his mouth and whistled.

"Sacha!"

Something stirred in the woods behind him. Bushes rattled, a few birds startled into the air, and a yellow lab burst out of the brush and knocked into the man's legs.

"Whoa there, girl!" he said, laughing. He knelt to pet the dog, which attacked his face with her tongue.

Cece was climbing out of the water when Sacha first noticed her. She barked and made as if to run forward, but her owner wrapped his arms around her chest.

"Don't turn around," Cece ordered.

"I won't."

She reached for her shirt and paused in mid-grab. Holy shit. She held her arm up to her face.

The skin was pink, healthy, and unblemished. Wrist to elbow. She felt her neck. The welts and pustules had disappeared. With wide eyes, she looked down at her legs. From the tip of her toes to her waist, her skin was clear.

"Everything okay?"

Cece looked up. Sacha was watching her, tongue lolled, but the peeping tom had his back to her. She pulled her shirt down over her head, keeping her eyes on him.

"I'm fine, thanks."

"Name's Vic."

Cece slid into her jeans and hiked them up.

"What the fuck are you doing here?"

"I should ask you the same thing. This is my property."

Cece stepped into her shoes and snatched up her socks.

"Lilith said I could swim here."

"Did she?"

A footstep in the dirt. The snap of a twig. When Vic turned around, all he saw was a branch shaking in the girl's wake.

"Nice to meet you!" he called.

MUNGWORT

Before her medicinal dip, the gauze only irritated Cece's already irritated skin. Now it was just a strange necessity. She didn't mind hiding the miracle; she would have rather kept a secret than try to explain the inexplicable. But she also didn't want to tell anybody about the spring. She didn't think Lilith would like it. Even if it wasn't true, the magic pond felt like a secret, like the old woman had let her and only her in, and opening it up to everybody else would be a betrayal. Why, if she wanted the entire crew to know about it, she would have told them already, right?

Then, of course, there was the matter of Vic. What a creep. Who was he? Where did he live? Did Lilith know about him? Did Warner or Mueller?

She spent the rest of the week avoiding everybody as best she could. She slept in the infirmary tent, woke up early and got in late, and if she ran into Ben or her yurtmates, she made small talk and pretended to be in pain.

"Yeah, I can't wait to get these things off."

"Yeah, the itching's driving me crazy."

"Yeah, it's getting a little better, but…"

Flower Power proved to be better than she could have imagined. No Harlow chewing her out, no Warner bullying her around, and no Mueller making her feel gross. Rufus made himself predictably scarce, and after the third day, he disappeared altogether. Every morning, she found the day's work spelled out for her via tools and materials left in the driveway. A trowel and a wheelbarrow? Time to weed. A shovel and peat moss? Time to freshen a bed.

She saw Lilith two more times. The first time, she was heading back to Yurtville at the end of a long day. The sun lowered itself over the trees, and the lights in the main house glowed in the gloaming. Cece glanced over and saw the old woman standing in the bay window, surveying her property. The second time, Cece was weeding a bed around the magnolia in the front yard when she sensed someone watching her. She twisted, still on her knees, and brought her gloved hand up to block the sun. Lilith was rocking in a rocking chair on the porch, waving a fan at her face. She didn't acknowledge the girl, just sat and watched, the barest hint of a smile on her lips.

Cece waited until Sunday, their only day off, to rejoin the regular population. Given the extent of her rash, explaining how it cleared up was going to be difficult, but if anybody pressed her about it, she'd mention the aloesbane Lilith had given her.

"It's been over a week," she'd say. "How much longer do you want it to last?"

The sun was barely over the oak tree when she made it to breakfast. Only the kitchen crew bustled around the line, filling bins, pouring ice, washing dishes. Another effect of her swim was the way it had improved her mood. And when her mood improved, everything improved. The coffee, usually hot but bland, zinged on her tongue. She didn't love eggs, but even the eggs tasted better than before. As she mused over this, content to be by herself, enjoying the possibilities of a day without work, Ben thundered into the space next to her.

"Hey there, burn unit!" he chortled. "Haven't seen you in a while. How's the dermatitis?"

Cece blinked up at him.

"The what?"

"The rash? The holy-shit-I-think-she's-going-to-go-into-toxic-shock rash?"

"That's not how you get toxic shock."

"Maybe."

Cece pointed at her neck.

"It was horrible for a while, but now…"

Ben leaned in like he was about to nuzzle her ear.

"I can barely see anything."

Cece laughed and pushed him away.

"Get off, weirdo."

Jake and Aiko joined them, sitting side by side.

"Oh, my god, Cece," Aiko said. "Are you… is it…?"

"Getting better. Sucks, but getting better."

"You should avoid dairy," Jake said, eyeing her eggs. "The beef here is grass-fed, so you should be okay there, but some of the veggies are GMO."

Cece spied Harlow as she grumped up to the breakfast line, holding her tray out for the morning's fuel. When a server accidentally slopped some hot grits on her hand, she yanked it back with a hiss and snapped, "watch it, you idiot!"

"Not a lot has changed, I see."

"She's pissed at you," Aiko said.

"I've been gone for a week!"

"That's the problem. She told me last night we were so far behind that we were going to have to put in an extra hour a day next week to make up for it."

"And they're paying us for it?"

"Yeah, right."

"Fuck that," Jake said. "I'm contracted to work for eight hours, I work for eight hours."

Aiko ran a hand through his hair.

"Aww, sweetie. You're cute when you peacock."

Everyone laughed, except for Jake.

After breakfast, they retired to Yurtville. Most of the workers lounged around on apple boxes, smoking, playing cards. A few of the couples traipsed off into the woods, holding hands. It was an unusually mild day for mid-summer, and while the temperature hovered in the nineties, the humidity was so low that Cece could sit in the shade and actually feel cool.

They lazed outside of her yurt, Ben lying on his back, Cece on her side, and Jake and Aiko tangled up with each other. Nobody said a word, content to enjoy each other's company in silence. After a while, Aiko sat up and stretched and yawned

"I'm gonna take a nap," she said.

Jake made a fist and said, "yes."

"Not that kind of nap, perv."

"Oh."

She gave him a quick peck on the cheek and disentangled her limbs. Jake watched her sashay into the yurt. Then he looked back at Ben, who smiled and wiggled his fingers.

"Tough luck, lover boy. Do you have any oils to help with blue balls?"

Jake lay down, linked his fingers together, and rested his head in his hands.

"You're just jealous."

"Of not getting laid? Nah. But I do have a solution to your problem."

Ben trotted over to his yurt and ducked inside, exiting a few minutes later dribbling a soccer ball. He kicked it as hard as he could, and the ball rocketed across the grass and hit Jake's feet. Jake grunted but barely moved.

"Come on, lover boy!" Ben called. "Let's work out some of that sexual energy."

Cece didn't think Jake would take the bait, but then he hopped up and dribbled the ball out to the middle of Yurtville, where the two started passing it back and forth, Jake's kicks expertly placed, Ben's stronger but less accurate. After the fifth exchange, she got up and trotted over.

"Over here."

Jake looked doubtful.

"Can you play?"

Before she could respond, he leveled a shot directly at her. Cece arched her back, bent her knees, and let it hit her in the chest. The ball bounced in the air, and she caught it in the crook of her foot. She flipped it up, planted, and kicked it with deadly accuracy right at his head. Jake ducked, his eyes wide.

"Yeah," Cece said. "I can play."

A few more hands joined them, then a few more, and soon they had enough for an honest to goodness game of five on five. They marked the boundaries with dirty laundry, the goals with apple boxes. Harlow emerged from her yurt.

"Got room for one more?"

"Sure," Ben said. "I guess."

Ben, Cece, Jake and a few others were already on one side, and when Harlow lined up with the other, Ben and Cece exchanged a knowing look. After consulting with her team, Harlow dribbled the ball up to midfield.

"First one to eleven?"

"Fine by me," Cece replied.

And the game was on.

Jake was fast and his ball-handling skillful, but he was (unsurprisingly) a ball-hog. At the first kickoff, he wove around the other team like they were in kindergarten, popped the ball over their heads, and generally made them look silly. At least until he ran into Harlow, who matched his offense with a brick-wall defense. If he dodged left, she blocked him. If he swung around, she blocked him. If he took a shot, she blocked him.

Jake and Cece's team played defense like a sieve. Ben was a somewhat functional keeper, but what he owned in size, he lacked in blocking ability. Within ten minutes, the score was two nil, Harlow's team.

"What the hell, Ben?" Jake snapped.

"Nobody's playing D!"

"We're playing D, you're just letting every shot in."

"There wouldn't be a shot if you were playing D."

"Both of you shut up," Cece said. She cast a look over her shoulder at the other team. Harlow was high-fiving one of her teammates. "Jake, Harlow's making you look stupid."

"I'd like to see you take her on."

"I would, but you're not passing the ball."

"Nobody's open."

"*I'm* open."

"No, you're not!"

"Okay, listen. I've got a plan."

She stepped closer and murmured in his ear.

"You sure?" he asked.

"Positive."

Then she went over and talked to a girl playing mid-field, who nodded.

"Alright," Cece said, trotting back to the ball. "Let's go."

She passed it back to the midfielder and sprinted forward, hand raised.

The midfielder passed it to Jake, and Cece threw up her hands.

"You got time," Ben called.

But Jake ignored it and did his usual routine. Swerve, weave, stop, go. Just like before, when he got to Harlow, she took it away from him and passed it to her forward, who streaked down the sideline and nailed a shot from the far corner.

"Sucks to suck, doesn't it, Jake?" Harlow said.

Jake had the ball stolen from him again on the next run, but Ben blocked the shot. He heaved it to the midfielder, who drove downfield, steered around the first defender, then the second. Harlow hung close to Jake, pinching his jersey, throwing her hands across his chest. The midfielder faked a pass to him and redirected it to Cece, who had posted up in the middle. The ball skipped over the grass, and Cece wheeled around and issued a hard shot at the lower right corner. The keeper leaped too late, and the ball hit the box and bounced through.

"Lucky shot, new girl," Harlow said.

"Eat me, Harlow," Cece shot back.

On the next run, Harlow guarded Cece. Cece streaked up the line as Jake dribbled straight down the middle, and she was about to get free when Harlow elbowed her in the chest. Cece rammed her with her shoulder, and Harlow took a dive. While she rolled around, holding her shin, Jake passed it to Cece, who scored again.

"Nice try," Cece said as she was jogging back. "But this isn't even rec league."

"Watch your fucking shoulders, new girl."

"Watch your fucking elbows, asshole."

It only got worse after that.

They both went up for a header, and Harlow pushed off Cece in mid-air, sending her crashing to the ground.

Harlow made a run for the middle, lining herself up for a shot, and Cece slide-tackled her.

Cece sprinted forward, stretching her leg out to intercept an errant pass, but Harlow beat her to the ball by a microsecond, reared back, and kicked Cece's foot as hard as she could.

Cece jumped into Harlow's face.

"What the fuck, Harlow?"

"Can't take it, don't dish it out."

"We're not trying out for the World Cup."

Jake jumped between the two, arms spread, chest facing Cece. He pressed her back as she pointed over his shoulder and shouted.

"That's fucking dangerous, Harlow. You could have broken my foot!"

"Soccer's a rough game, bitch!"

"Come on, Cece," Jake said. "Take it easy."

Cece shoved him away and stalked over to the sideline. Someone had brought a jug of water, and she took a long pull, poured some over her head.

"Let's call it a game, huh?" Ben said.

Both Harlow and Cece yelled, "NO!"

"Okay, okay. Halftime then. Ten minutes." Then, under his breath, "maybe you two will calm down a little."

Cece's midfielder caught Harlow's team sleeping at the beginning of the next half and pounded a twenty-yard punt that dropped in behind the keeper.

"We weren't even set!" Harlow whined.

"Three-three, Harlow," Jake said.

"Our keeper wasn't even on the field."

"Yeah, I was, Harlow," her keeper said. He kicked the ball to her. "It was a fair shot."

Harlow muttered to herself as she snatched it off the ground and set it up for kickoff.

"You mad," Cece taunted.

Back and forth the two teams went, their initial enthusiasm giving way to tired but dogged tenacity. Harlow grew more and more frustrated with every missed goal, and Cece and Jake couldn't get it past the three-quarter mark no matter how many times they passed, redirected, or cherry-picked. They pushed on for twenty more minutes before fatigue set in. Passes went wide. Strikers unchecked. Cece took a shot on goal that flew way too high, and nobody even tried to retrieve the ball.

"Okay, that's it," Ben said. "Next goal wins."

"Tired Benji?" Harlow said.

"Yeah. And this is getting too rough for me."

Harlow muttered something.

Cece saw it and said, "what was that?"

"Nothing, new girl. Next point wins."

The next point took less than a minute.

Harlow's keeper slung it to one of the faster girls, and she drove up the sideline, passed it to her midfielder, and sprinted around Jake.

"Here!" she yelled.

But Ben read the play perfectly. He came charging out of goal and intercepted the pass. Jake and Cece streaked down either side of the field. Harlow fell back and snapped onto Cece.

What happened next was like a scene from a movie.

Ben kicked the ball high into the air. It arched over the field, heading for the center. Cece tracked it coming in, adjusted her speed. Harlow boxed her out, grabbing her shirt, her arm. Cece struggled to get away as the ball sailed down toward them. She yanked her wrist out of Harlow's grip, pulling Harlow backward. Harlow fell with a WHUFF! Cece planted, timed her kick, nailed the ball inches before it landed. It spun toward the goal, hit the ground behind the keeper's outstretched hands, and bounced over the line.

Harlow snapped up off the ground.

"You fucking bitch! You could have broken my arm!"

Cece had been in plenty of fights before, and she knew there were two types of opponents: those who really wanted to throw down and those who only thought they did. The former rarely said very much before they attacked. They just attacked. The latter yelled and screamed and acted like they were out of control, but it was all for show, and Cece knew just how to put a stop to it. She just had to time the punch right.

"I'm gonna fucking kick your ass, bitch!" Harlow screamed. "You don't fuck with me, bitch!"

Cece had already begun to pull her arm back when Jake and Ben swooped in and between them, Jake facing Harlow, Ben facing Cece.

"Get the fuck offa me!" Harlow yelled.

Jake said something to her, his voice both loud and calming. All Cece could catch was "right over there."

She met Ben's eyes. He nodded to the side.

Warner and Mueller were standing in the corner of the driveway, watching the fracas, Warner's hands on his hips, Mueller leaning on the hood of the truck. Cece couldn't see his face from that far away, but she knew there was a leering smile plastered across it. Lilith appeared, strolling around the side of the wrap-around porch, her hands clasped in front of her.

"What's going on over there?" Warner shouted.

Harlow's head whipped around.

"Cool it, Harlow!" Jake hissed in her ear. "Take a walk."

Harlow, her eyes wide, her jaw clenched, swallowed her anger.

"Goddammit!" she cried.

Then she pushed him off and stomped away.

The next morning, Cece and Ben were just finishing breakfast when Warner's truck pulled up.

"Weekend's over," Ben muttered.

"Let's go, assholes!" Warner cried as he got out. "Time to embrace the suck!"

He moseyed over to the picnic tables, thumbs tucked into his belt, looking like a fat, southern lord. Mueller hung back, as usual, a grin on his face (as usual), chewing on a toothpick. Grumbling, the crew rose to drop their trays off in the dish pit. Cece slugged one last shot of orange juice and joined Ben, who was already in line.

"Boy, oh boy are you shitheels in for it today!" Warner chortled. "It's hotter'n a cooze in blender out here. Ain't that right, ET?"

"That's right."

Ben mouthed the words "cooze in a blender?" to Cece, and Cece, who was shoving a muffin in her mouth, spit half of it out.

Warner was leaning against the hood of his truck, arms crossed, as they passed by on their way to their respective assignments, Cece to Flower Power, Ben to the fields.

"Well, well, well. If it isn't Butch Rugmuncher and her gay life-partner, Whole Hog!"

"Those were three very hateful statements in a row, sir," Ben said.

"Forgive me, precious." Warner glared at Cece. "I don't know what you did to the boss lady, but you got yourself a new assignment."

"Don't fuck with me today, Warner. I'm not in the mood."

"Oh, I would never presume to lock horns with such a raging bull as yourself. You made it to the big leagues, sweetie! You are hoop-house bound."

The hoop-house was literally a greenhouse in the form of a hoop extending out of the ground. It reminded Cece of a science fiction version of the habitrail her childhood hamster, Cookie, lived in. If she flew above it, she would have seen it was shaped like a T, with the hoop-house itself forming the stem of the letter joined to a shorter, stubbier brick and mortar section at the top.

Even though it was only about a hundred yards from the main house, it might as well have been on a different planet, with its steel beams gleaming in the sun and its gray-green glass reflecting the sunlight. Solar panels lined the grass that surrounded the foundation, and a windmill whirred behind it, turning gently in a light, early morning breeze.

Cece took her time getting there. She watched Ben and the other workers head out to the fields, then pulled her phone out of her back pocket. 90% battery, but no signal. She lifted it to the sky, squinting. Still no bars.

"Damn."

Warner steered the crew to the west field, the mungwort field. The workers milled around, talking quietly in pairs or small groups. A few cast looks at the holes that Cece and Ben made when they cleared the residue, eyeing the black stains suspiciously.

Warner moved around behind a portion of a trunk set up like a demonstration. A ball of fungus hung off the side like a wet sack. Mueller stood next to him wearing a rubber apron, rubber arm-gloves, and a chest-length face shield. He leaned jauntily on a curved blade, roughly three feet long, with aggressive serrated edges, a blood channel, and a hook on the end.

"Listen up, dipshits!" Warner yelled. A few of the groups settled down. "Shut your yaps and glue your traps. You guys over there, get your asses over here."

The entire fence crew, twenty workers in all, gathered in a semi-circle around the pair, chatting lightly. Someone laughed, and Warner's face turned red.

"When I say shut up, I want to hear the sound of twenty cunts snapping closed!"

The crowd fell silent. Warner glared.

"I'm only going to explain this once. Any of you morons get your faces melted off because you weren't paying attention, that's on you." He jabbed his finger at the fungus ball. "This is triple rectified Mungotryon Morbosa, or, for those of you more comfortable with the common parlance, mungwort. It is highly toxic. It grows on tree trunks and kills the trees. That's why so many of them have been falling through the fence. Your job today is to carve this disgusting shit off of any tree you find it on within a hundred feet of the line. It is imperative that you wear the correct protective gear while you do this, as modeled by our man ET."

Mueller saluted with two fingers.

Ben raised his hand.

"Question, sir."

"Spit it out, Mooby Dick."

"Didn't you say it's hotter than a cooze in a, uh, in a.... Won't the rubber suit dehydrate us?"

Warner stared at the boy as if he'd just asked to give himself an enema. A slight shake of the head. Ben expected the man to just turn around, get in his car, and drive away. But he didn't. Instead, he said, "ET? Shed your shit. Ham Planet? Get up here and put it on."

The closer Cece got to the hoop-house, the more she realized just how science-fictiony the place was. The tinted glass walls adjusted depending on how much sunlight hit them. The panels on the top and sides were opaque, but closer to the ground, they were clear as day. The hoops into which the glass had been seated, the bones of the structure, were standard steel, American-made, anchored into the ground with cement.

A set of wooden stairs led to a thick glass door, also framed with metal. Cece marched up and peered inside, but all she could see were strips of meat-locker plastic separating the vestibule from the main section. She tried the handle. It wouldn't budge. The door didn't have a lock, but there was a bolt.

To her right was a screen about the size of a notebook. Above it, a plastic sign read "Place Hand On Screen." Cece did, and the screen glowed to life. A blue bar rolled up and down, reading her palm, she assumed. When it finished, the screen glowed green, an electric buzz sounded, the bolt thunked back.

"That's fucked up," she said.

Automatic lights switched on when she slipped through the plastic strips. She blinked around in surprise.

The place was amazing.

Rows and rows of plants grew in bins that lined the wood-planked floor. She recognized a few: geraniums, petunias, ferns. Others, however, looked like plants she should know but were strangely different. Birds of Paradise mixed with passiflora. Mimosas mixed with bougainvilleas. Angel's Trumpets mixed with chrysanthemums. The palate of colors stimulated and overwhelmed her. The humid air was alive with rich and spicy smells. It felt like she was walking into a verdant jungle instead of a greenhouse somewhere in the middle of Virginia.

She wandered down the center row, the boards creaking under her boots, her head swiveling as if on ball bearings. She resisted the urge to reach out and graze the plants with her fingertips. Knowing this place, something would strike out of a planter and rip her fingers off. Muted sunlight filtered through the panes above. Fan vents bolted into the steel hoops spun lazily overhead. A door in the back opened and out stepped Laszlo.

"Ah! Missus told me you were coming today! Yes! Yes! Please to come! Please to come!"

As Cece walked over, something at her feet caught her attention. A blinking red light blinking through the gaps in the wood planks. Laszlo frowned, looking at the gauze on her arms.

"Your arms? They aren't healed?"

"Oh, this." Cece unwrapped the length around her wrist, revealing her perfectly healthy skin. "I'm just keeping it on for a while so nobody freaks out."

"So smart you are, madam! Yes! Yes!" He inspected her arm. "There is no more pain?"

"Between the spring water and that plant goo—"

"Aloesbane."

"Right. Well, between those two, I'm ship shape."

She gave him a pained smile.

"Yes, well, yes," Laszlo said. "Follow me."

He led her to a table under a pegboard along the back wall. Goggles hung from hooks next to garden tools: trowels, hammers, screwdrivers. On the table: decapitated mannequin heads next to their lonely torsos. Someone had strapped filter masks to their faces, sleeved their arms to the elbows with thick latex gloves.

"I call this my body farm!" Laszlo said.

Then he had a stroke.

At least, that's what Cece thought had happened. He hissed and wheezed, his face scrunched up and red, his body vibrating. Then she realized that what she was experiencing was Laszlo's version of a laugh. When she didn't respond in kind, he slowly swallowed his mirth and worked his mouth, trying to regain his composure.

"Please to choose, madam. Please to choose."

Ben looked like a butcher from a horror movie. His rubber apron fit too tight around the middle, and the plexiglass face mask somehow widened his features. The gloves, stained with black mungwort residue, didn't soften the impression, nor did the long, dangerous-looking blade he was holding. He scratched his curly hair with a rubber-gloved finger.

"Is all this really necessary, Warner?"

"What do you think?"

"I think I'm boiling."

"Tough shit."

Ben held up the blade.

"I mean, we're just cutting this stuff off, right? What's the harm in doing it without all this crap on?"

"It's a lot more complex than that, Hubba Bubba. What you want to do is start the cut about three inches above—"

With a feral yell, Ben hefted the blade over his head and rushed the trunk. He brought it down with a satisfying thunk, splitting the mungwort ball right down the middle. A blast of fluorescent green gunk spewed out like a fire hydrant and hit him in the chest.

"Oh, my god! Oh, my god!" he yelled.

He ripped off the apron, which had already begun to smoke, and threw it on the ground. The mask was next, then the gloves. Warner stepped over to the mound of sizzling rubber as if making a presentation.

"If you do not wear your gear, your body will be that apron."

Laszlo steered Cece, now properly gloved and goggled, around the hoop-house floor.

"We have many babies here, madam. So many babies. Your job will be to take care of them all."

"That's it?"

"It is much work, madam! The girls are a very persnickety bunch. They require much care. So much care. You must... feed them, and trim them, and water them, and love them, and sing to them, and pet them, and, and, and—"

He stepped up to a fern and dug a finger in the soil at its base.

"And when their homes become too dry, you must transplant them so they can be happy! And when they are happy, they will thrive and reproduce, and then we take care of the new babies!"

He stopped short, blushing and holding up a finger as if he'd just told a real corker. When Cece didn't laugh, he coughed. Gathered himself.

"Ahem. Do you have any questions?"

"What's under the floor?"

"Ha!" Laszlo barked. "Under the floor?"

"Yeah. I saw lights down there."

"Oh, yes. Yes. We call that The Rendering Room. The guts of the operation, so to speak. Hahaha! I make another one! Hahaha!"

"So what's down there?"

"It is where we hide the bodies, yes? Hahaha!"

Cece stared at him, deadpan, and once again, Laszlo let the joke drop.

"In my hometown, the people called me Levin Choma after the famous comedic actor Levin Choma. 'One day, Laszlo,' they said. 'You will be a Giant of the Prairie, and perhaps even president of the nation!'."

He scanned her face for understanding and found none.

"Maybe someday you'll get used to my biting sense of humor. Shall we move on?"

He pointed out plants as they strolled.

"Rotback. Grayboil. Hanta. Anthrascae. And the pièce de résistance..."

They stopped at a table brimming with flowers. The petals were blood-red streaked with jagged black lines, and the disk was so dark that it looked like it could swallow light. They spilled out of the bed and hung over the edge of the table, forming a solid block of color. A few had even taken root in the wood floor.

"Mortifloria!"

Cece frowned, confused.

"Chrysanthemums?" she said.

"Yes! Yes! But no, no. They are so much more than 'chrysanthemums'. Allow me to demonstrate. Please to put your mask."

They both fixed the filters on their faces. Laszlo leaned over the table and inspected a plastic tube that hooked into the bed. It was so heavily stained red that Cece didn't even see it until Laszlo flicked it. He moved down the table, adjusting more, five in all, bending some, pressing others deeper into the dirt. Satisfied, he turned toward Cece, gave her a thumbs-up, and slammed his palm down on a plunger fastened to the corner of the table.

The floorboards rumbled. A mechanical whirring revved below. Dark red fluid snaked up through the tubes, rounded the hook, and squirted into the soil. Intrigued, Cece leaned forward. The flowers pulsed once, twice, three times. They tensed, went rigid, and with a muscular poof, ejaculated a cloud of yellow pollen into her face. Her eyes rolled back in her head, and she collapsed.

Ben stood next to a big, fat, juicy mungwort ball hanging from the trunk of a red maple. He was wearing a double face shield and two rubber aprons: one in the front, one in the back. He would have put two pairs of sleeve-gloves on if he could have made them fit. Jake, face shield up, apron askew, rolled up behind him, flipping his blade like he'd been born to handle it.

"What's up, Neckroll."

"Oh, great. Now he's got you doing it."

"Relax, man. It's just a joke."

He took a step toward the mungwort ball, bending over and putting his hands on his knees to get a closer look.

"This stuff is so gnarly."

"Dude, I wouldn't get so close if I was you."

Jake poked the crispy surface with the tip of his blade.

"Dude!" Ben said.

"It's fine, see? Didn't even make a scratch."

He turned and stabbed his blade into the grass.

"When did you become such a pussy?"

"You saw what it did to that apron, right?"

"Yeah. You looked like an idiot. So how's Cece doing?"

"How should I know? Fine, I guess."

"Are you two, you know?"

Jake made a fist and gave it a couple of suggestive pumps.

"What? No."

"Come on. You two were out here all alone for an entire day and you didn't even try to get it wet?"

"That's gross."

Jake worked a sleeve-glove over his hand.

"You should hit that shit, Benjamin."

"It's not like that."

"Why? She a dyke?"

"Haven't asked."

The spot where Jake poked the mungwort skin puckered. A little rill of pus slid out and dripped down the shell.

"I'm telling you," Jake said. "There's no reason not to score as much pussy as possible. We're young, this job is ass, and we'll all be gone in a month. No consequences. No mess."

"Does Aiko feel the same way?"

"What Aiko doesn't know won't hurt her."

"That's cold, dude."

"It is what it is."

The ball quivered. Jake grabbed his blade.

"Be careful, dude," Ben said.

"Okay, mom."

"I'm just saying."

"Ben," Jake said with a wink. "For once in your life, could you not be such a pussy-ass bitch?"

He turned around, face shield still up.

There was no way of telling what thoughts were running through the poor boy's head. There was no time to think very much at all. The mungwort ball exploded like a geyser, enveloping his face, his shoulders, and his chest in a deluge of luminous green pus.

Yellow haze.
Rotten teeth.
A sharpening strop.
Cece is following her father down a long flight of stairs.

He turns to her, extends a hand.
"Come on now, girl."
The laugh lines crease.

Cece opened her eyes.

All she could see at first was yellow. She swiped at her goggles, wiping off a thick coating of dust. The vent fans whirred overhead, sucking pollen out of the air and sending it out into the day. Laszlo's face appeared.

"Oh, madam! Madam! You must make sure your mask is properly fitted!"

He reached out to help her up, but she knocked his hand away.

"I did."

"Not tight enough, madam. Not tight enough. The eructations of the mortifloria can reach forty-three miles an hour. It seeks every nook, every crack, every crevice, every…" he paused and, unable to help himself, added, "orifice?"

Another deadpan stare. Cece reached up to take her mask off, but Laszlo's eyes widened and he cried, "no! Not yet, madam!"

He scanned the air, watching the fans suck the last of the yellow dust away.

"Allow me," he said.

His pale fingers reached around and unbuckled the straps of his mask. He removed it and tasted the air, suckling like a newborn.

"Ah, yes. Now we are clear."

Outside, a vehicle roared up to the entrance. The doors opened and slammed shut. The squeal of a lowering tailgate.

"Get him out! Get him out!" someone yelled.

More shouts. A gargled cry.

The glass door opened with a buzz, and Ben and Mueller stormed through the plastic strips, carrying Jake's body between them. From the stomach down, Jake looked fine. A couple of dark stains on his jeans, a few scratches on his bare arms. But black scabs patched his head and shoulders, the skin beneath swollen and red like his body had been held over a blow torch. His skull shone through bare patches of his scalp where his hair had been replaced by angry clots of blood surrounded by charred black islands.

"We got another one!" Mueller yelled.

FRESH MEAT

Evening in the summer. A trickle of sweat running down the nape of a wrinkled neck. A veined hand resting on the arm of a chair. A glass pitcher of lemonade sweating on a table.

Mueller slunk up to the front porch of the main house and leaned against the rail. Blood spattered his shirt and jeans, black fluid covered his boots, and a dark red stain bled through the bandage wrapped around his right hand. Rocking in a chair in front of the window, Lilith leveled her leonine eyes upon him. She waved her fan back and forth, back and forth.

"Hard day, my pet?"

"You ain't know the half of it. Got a minute?"

"Oh, Étienne. You know I always have a minute for you. Come. Sit."

She nodded at a second rocking chair next to the table with the lemonade on it.

"I ain't too fresh right now."

"There's nothing on you I haven't smelled before."

Mueller scoffed.

"Alright. Okay."

He took off his hat and climbed the stairs with a weary sigh. The rocking chair creaked when he sat down, and when he rocked, he couldn't help but smell himself and the smell of the rot, the mungwort, and what must have been a bit of Jake. As ripe as he was, the old woman's perfume cut through it—rosewater with a faint note of lilac. The combination made him feel green.

"Lemonade?" Lilith asked.

Mueller looked at the pitcher. Looked away.

"Pass."

"Don't be silly, child. How does Desmond put it? 'It's hotter than a cooze in a blender' out here?"

She chuckled as she poured, the ice tinkling.

"You always keep two glasses out here?"

"You never know when you're going to have company."

She squeezed an orange wedge on the rim and handed the drink to him.

"Here you go. Don't be shy."

Mueller allowed himself a little smile. He took the glass and pressed it against his forehead.

"I meant to talk to you about something," Lilith said. "Desmond left the basement door unlocked again."

"Don't surprise me. He leaves his keys in his truck all the time."

"Does he, now?"

"I'll talk to him about it."

"I can't begin to tell you how careless that is."

"I know."

"Does he think he's the only one who can drive?"

"It's a manual transmission."

"I can't see how that matters. Can you imagine it? We're not completely isolated out here. The city is only ten miles away."

"I said I'd talk to him about it."

"Perhaps he needs a new booster?"

"New batch is coming soon. Can't have him out for that long."

"Fair enough." A breath, a sigh, a reset. "The extraction is going well, I assume?"

"Well as can be."

"And what is that supposed to mean?"

"It means it's going as well as can be."

"Ètienne. Are you being curt?"

"No, ma'am."

"I think you are. Being curt."

"I ain't being 'curt'. We got a problem with the mungwort."

"And? If I'm not mistaken, here you sit before me, the man I hired to solve our mungwort problem, yes? 'Give me a team of strong backs, and I'll have it cleared up in a month.' Did you or did you not say that?"

"This is different."

"Different how?"

"Remember in the spring when you changed the formula? It's that kind of different."

"I don't see how that has anything to do—"

"That fire vine nearly burned down the hoop-house. Compared to that, this is toadstools after the rain."

"Ètienne, please be direct. I have no patience for your homespun analogies this evening."

"The new strain's spreading faster than we thought. Last week it was only on a couple of trees. It's at least a hundred yards into the woods now."

Lilith gave him a startled look.

"My, my, my."

"Mm-hm."

"So we'll acquire more help."

"We keep lining 'em up and the mungwort keeps taking 'em out. Lost another one today. Good worker, too. That's three this month. Four if you include the one who tried to run off."

"Sounds to me like you have a discipline problem."

"We lose any more, and it'll spread out of control. You know what'll happen next. I ain't taking the fall because your big boss wants to move too fast."

"Is that a threat, dear?"

Mueller swallowed his protest. He swirled the lemonade in the glass.

"It ain't a threat. It's reality."

"I don't mean to be unkind, but you are in charge of the laborers, after all."

"Warner says it's the morale. We got them pounding tail six days a week."

"The formula should take care of that." Lilith took a quick breath. "Is it really that bad?"

"You saw them two go at it on Sunday. If the boys hadn't broken it up, them two girls would've wrecked each other."

On cue, Cece stalked across the field in the distance, heading for Yurtville. Even that far away, Lilith could see the bloodstains on her clothes.

"Our dear Cecelia is quite the fireplug, is she not?"

"She walks around like she's the goddam queen of Egypt. Pardon my French."

"The mixed cliché bothers me more, my boy."

"That girl's got a bad attitude, and it infects everybody around her. I have half a mind to—"

"No, Étienne."

"You just say the word."

"I said no. The girl's off-limits. No special assignments. No 'accidents.' At least for the time-being. Do I make myself clear?"

The old woman gazed out over the driveway, stone-cold and stoic. Mueller studied her face. His eye twitched.

"Crystal."

"Delightful. Here's an idea: why not give them a day off? Throw a party."

"It's Monday. We got at least two acres to clear by the end of the week."

"Half a day, then. You'd be surprised what a little kindness can do. Give them a few cases of beer, some fresh meat for the barbecue, let them numb themselves. A little extra dusting tonight and tomorrow night should take care of the aggression. They'll even thank you for it."

Mueller listened to the night sounds swell. He shrugged.

"You're the boss, applesauce."

"I do love your colloquialisms, Ètienne." She patted his leg. "The damaged ones? Can we salvage them?"

"Laszlo says they been gumming up the works."

"Well, that won't do, will it?"

Lilith took a sip of her drink and waved her fan, thinking. Mueller watched her, waiting.

"Beer bash or not, we need some fresh meat."

"I'll place the order."

"Yeah, about that."

The City of Fredericksburg, located between two major metropolitan hubs (DC in the north and Richmond in the south) suffered the same unfettered gentrification many little towns experienced at the beginning of the 21st century. Condos and townhouses popped up downtown like weeds, bringing with them a much-desired tax base as well as unrelenting traffic. Tech workers with offices in DC, tired of the gridlock and high cost of living endemic in NOVA, brought their high salaries and electric cars south, rode the train into work every morning (or every other morning, depending on their boss's view on telecommuting), and enjoyed the slow pace of the little city on nights and weekends.

Fittingly, the laborers followed, for who was going to clean those overpriced condos and townhomes? Who was going to make Camper's Specials at Sammy T's? Who was going to wash the sheets at the Kenmore Inn?

Some of these workers came by truck and van, some arrived by sedan, but even more crossed over the city limits via Greyhound bus, something of which Karen Boemer was well aware. The Greyhound station in Fredericksburg, FRED Central to the locals, sat on the corner of Stafford Avenue and Route 1, across the street from the legendary Allman's BBQ and the Parthenon Restaurant. Boemer often parked her truck in the church lot across the street, backing into a space under a tree in the corner. There she would wait and watch, wait and watch, sometimes snoozing between runs, waking when a new bus braked to a stop at the depot. More often than not, the riders possessed inferior qualities. They were too fat or too skinny or too addicted; too lazy, too angry, too dumb. But now and then, the perfect match showed up.

Back on Lilith's front porch, Mueller clucked his tongue.
"You know Boemer's gone off the rails, don't you?"
"Oh, come now, Ètienne. How so?"
"She ain't bringing in the prime rib no more. Just picks up whatever street meat is most convenient."
"She brought us the girl, did she not?"
"Yeah, well. She also brought Rufus."

Six o'clock in the morning. The latest bus from Danville rumbled away in a cloud of diesel exhaust. Karen, snorting awake at the sound, sat up straighter. A man and a teenage girl were talking in the port. They were wearing the telltale outfits of the day laborer: cowboy hats with bandanas, worn jeans and work boots. Even more telling was their luggage, or lack thereof, for they only carried a backpack each, hers light blue, his black, both dirty and weatherbeaten, the straps thinning at the shoulders. Karen tapped on her steering wheel, a sly smile creeping up on her face.
"Gotcha."

"Miss Boemer has my trust, Ètienne."
"But—"
"That means she has yours."
Mueller took a sip of his lemonade. Then he stood up and whacked his hat on his thigh, sending dust and dirt into the air.
"Yeah. Alright."
"Good." Lilith softened. "The two of you used to be so friendly. I don't know where things went off track."
"When I realized she's one brick short of a wall."
They both looked up at the sound of a truck approaching. Karen's black Ford was motoring down the drive, kicking up dust behind it.
"Speak of the devil," Lilith said. "Ètienne, be a dear, would you?"

"Yeah, I got it."

He plonked his hat on his head and moseyed over to the top of the circular drive, where he waited with his hands on his hips. The truck circled to a stop in front of him, the gear shifted to park, and Karen shouldered the door open and hopped down.

"Hiya, boss!" she said, waving.

Lilith waved back.

"Looking good, Miss Lady!"

Mueller ambled around the front of the truck, his eyes on the pair in Karen's cab. A middle-aged man blinked awake in the center bench seat. Next to him, a young girl, thirteen or fourteen years old, rested her head on his shoulder, eyes closed, mouth open.

Smiling at Karen, Mueller said, "dropping them off in broad daylight now, huh?"

Through her own grin, Karen said, "Eat shit, ET."

Cece leaned up against the wooden planks of the outdoor shower. Pink water swirled around the drain at her feet. She let the hot water run down her body, pushed her face into the stream. She tried to block out what happened, but no matter how hard she tried, the images kept popping into her head, and she relived the entire scene again.

Mueller and Laszlo held the thrashing Jake down. Jake screamed, his lips bleeding. A piece of skin sloughed off his face.

"Grab his feet!" Mueller yelled.

Cece, still fresh from a semi-coma herself, scrambled over and grabbed Jake's ankles. She shot a look at Ben, who was trying to control Jake's arms, but Ben shook her off. Later. Aiko ran in, a panicked look on her face. When she saw Jake, she screamed and stumbled against one of the support beams.

"Any time now, doc!" Mueller called.

Laszlo bustled out of the back office holding a syringe filled with green fluid.

"Please to move! Please to move!"

Ben scooted aside to let him in. Jake's head thrashed back and forth.

"Hold the head! Hold the head!"

Mueller clamped his hands on either side, eliciting a feral scream from the wounded boy.

"That's it!" Laszlo cried.

He jammed the needle into the crispy flesh of Jake's neck, pressed the plunger until the fluid emptied. Jake stopped thrashing. His breathing slowed. Laszlo removed the needle and stowed it in his apron pocket. He looked around at everyone.

"That was exciting," he said. "Yes?"

Cece strolled across Yurtville, toweling off her hair. The air was so thick with humidity that she wasn't sure if the moisture she was wiping off her neck was sweat or water from the shower. She looked up and saw a black truck pulling into the circular driveway in front of the main house.

An image flashed into her mind.

She was sitting in a truck cab. The trees blurred past only a few feet from her window. A form next to her, the driver, a thick-bodied woman with curly blond hair.

"I guess you're going to be an asshole about it."

"Earth to Cece."

Ben was standing in front of her, waving a hand in her face.

"You there?"

"Yeah. Yeah. I was just... you know."

"I know. That was bad. Really bad. Do you think he'll be... Never mind."

Cece rolled her towel up and slung it over her neck.

"I don't know anything for sure, Ben. I hope he'll be okay."

"Me, too."

"You know it wasn't your fault, right?"

"Oh! Yeah, of course. But I was right there. I saw it happen."

He shivered.

Mueller and Warner stalked down the slope from the main house to Yurtville, Mueller jawing in Warner's ear, Warner nodding along as if he understood.

"What do you think this is going to be about?"

As the pair drew closer, Cece heard Warner snap a curt, "I didn't leave the fucking door unlocked, ET, so let that shit go."

"What's going on?" Ben called.

The men looked up, a little astonished to see Ben and Cece standing there. Warner took the lead.

"Round everybody up, you two. Staff meeting in ten."

"No fat jokes?" Ben asked as they walked away.

"Not today, Ham Hock."

When Cece entered her yurt, Aiko was curled up in bed, facing the wall, either asleep or in shock, and Harlow was sitting on her cot with her legs crossed under her, reading a paperback.

"She going to be okay?" Cece asked.

"What do you think?"

"If she wants to take a few shots of my vodka, she can."

"Noted."

"I can hear you," Aiko said.

She rolled over and sat up. Her face was puffy and red, and her hair, normally silky smooth or put up in a flawless ponytail, stood up in all directions.

"You serious about that vodka?"

"As a heart attack."

Cece went over to her bag and took out the bottle.

"Burnettes," she said. "The champagne of vodka."

Aiko snorted as she took the bottle.

"Champagne of vodka? What's that, an ad or something?"

"Something my father used to say. He was a connoisseur."

Aiko took a pull, wincing as she swallowed.

"Smooth," she said, coughing.

Cece took the bottle and tipped it back.

"He's going to be okay, you know."

Aiko bit her lip and nodded.

"I mean, he's Jake, right?" Cece added. "He's got enough vitamins and essential oils in him to cure cancer."

Aiko let out an involuntary laugh.

"I mean, it's so stupid. He's just a summer fling."

"Yeah, but you two were close. It's okay to be upset."

Harlow slammed her book down on her bed.

"Are you two really going to do this now?"

Aiko and Cece stared at her.

"God," Harlow moaned.

She got out of bed and stomped outside. A few minutes later, the smell of cigarette smoke wafted through the entrance.

"Don't pay attention to her," Cece said.

"I try not to."

A comfortable pause.

"Warner called a meeting."

Aiko groaned.

"I'm not going."

"I figured. Want another snort?"

Aiko reached for the bottle.

"No."

Cece sidled up to the back of the crowd as Warner made a perfunctory inventory of the faces.

"Anybody who ain't here, ya'll tell them what's going on. Got it?"

Solemn nods. Boots scuffing the dirt.

"I don't feel like I need to tell you about what happened this afternoon. If you wasn't there, someone probably already let you know. I think maybe we all need a little break, so the boss lady gave us the rest of the day off."

A few murmurs of approval.

"She also ordered some barbecue—"

The murmurs turned into a couple of "right on's"

"And a couple of cases of beer."

The subsequent yelling and whooping made Cece's ears ring.

Warner patted the air with his hands.

"Don't think this means anything because it doesn't. And work starts at 10am sharp tomorrow morning, so don't get so fucked up that you can't do nothing."

He would have gone on, but the celebratory din made it useless, so he threw up his hands and walked away. Behind him, Cece caught sight of Mueller escorting two passengers from the cab of the black truck. The first one was a girl, twelve or thirteen years old. She blinked in the sunlight and rubbed her eyes. An older man followed. He put a hand on the girl's shoulder and said something, and the girl looked up and nodded. Cece felt her jaw tighten.

"Oh, you've got to…"

"… be kidding me? A kid? They're letting kids work here now? What the fuck?"

She and Ben sat in front of a smoldering campfire. Ben picked up a handful of dead leaves, dunked them into a bucket of water, and threw them into the ring. They sizzled at first, then sent up a cloud of black smoke as they burned. Several other rings produced trickles and clouds of similar smoke here and there. Ben put the bucket down and sat on the ground next to her.

"It's kinda messed up."

"It's fucked up is what it is. That girl's maybe thirteen."

"Could you really tell at that distance? Maybe the guy just has a really short wife."

"A kid has no business being here."

"They'll probably give her a job in the main house."

"Great! So her dad gets his face melted off by some fungus pus leaving her to deal with that creepy old bat on her own."

"Have you eaten yet? These brats are delicious."

As if by magic, he produced a brat on a stick and took a bite.

"Not hungry."

"Suit yourself."

Somebody laughed behind them. The smell of pot filled the air, and Ben sang, "pass the dutchie on the left-hand side. It a go bun! Give me the music, make me jump and prance."

Cece glared at him, and the lyrics died on his lips.

"Sorry."

"Something fucked up is going on here," Cece said.

"Shh!" Ben hissed. He looked around, scanning for something or someone.

Cece followed suit.

"What is it?"

"Just shush, okay?"

Cece leaned in and got in his face. When she spoke again, it was with a harsh whisper.

"That's exactly what I'm talking about, Ben. What are you so scared of?"

"Nothing, I guess. I just don't want anybody telling on us, that's all."

"That's what you're worried about? This place is fucked up. I was attacked. By vines. You saw it. That's not normal."

Ben stared at her for a moment, then he broke out laughing.

"What the fuck are you talking about?"

"The vines. Out in the west field. Remember the full body rash I got?"

"Dude. You got a rash because you didn't cuff your pants like Harlow told you to."

"I got a rash because those vines attacked me in the woods."

"Right."

"Ben. You were there. You saw me get thrown out of that wall of prickers."

"Wall of prickers?"

Cece studied him. He took a swig of beer.

"Warner's an asshole and the work sucks, but there's nothing supernatural going on because supernatural shit isn't real. This place is just…"

He searched for the word, for a thread of logic that he could use to convince her, but trailed off into nothing. He took another bite of his brat.

"At least it beats telemarketing," he finally said. "Another year of that bullshit, and they'd have to lock me up in the haha house."

Cece frowned.

"I thought you said you were here on summer break."

"Okay, enough with the jokes."

"You told me you're an English major at William and Mary. You said you thought this might be something you could write about."

Ben stood up and shook his can.

"Got a dead soldier here. You want another?"

"Ben."

"I'm getting really tired of it Cece, okay? Just let it go."

She watched him wander off. Then she crushed her beer can and tossed it into the pile next to the fire ring. A couple holding hands passed by, whispering and laughing.

"Hi," the girl said.

Cece nodded, watched them amble off into the woods behind Yurtville. Lilith's house was dark except for one window, but the hoop-house glowed warmly in the distance. She imagined Laszlo bent over a formula he was working on, alternately muttering to himself and hissing with laughter.

The vent cap on her yurt turned and squeaked quietly in the night. The full moon highlighted a faint cloud floating out of the top. She looked at the vent of the yurt next to hers, and sure enough, a cloud was floating out of it, too. And the one next to it and the one next to that one. All of them, in fact. She looked at the hoop-house, her yurt, back to the hoop-house.

Cece had almost reached the entry when the lights inside cut off. She paused, listening, and when she heard the front door open, she darted around to the side of the steps and pressed herself up against the building. Laszlo scuttered out of the front door, half-singing, half-humming what sounded like a folk song.

"*I will open fields to those who love! Let them sing awake and in their rest. I do breathe and that means I'm in love. I'm in love and that means I exist.*"

The door hissed close, the lock tumbled, and he bounced down the stairs, whirling his keyring around one finger and snapping with the other, singing "do-de-do-do-do."

Cece watched him recede into the night, his white form steadily tracked by the glow of the moon. She kept expecting the darkness to swallow him up, but it never did. If there was one thing that continued to amaze her (in a positive way, at least) it was how clear the sky was out there, the marvel of the celestial lights. Did she ever know how many stars there were in the universe? They clustered so thick and full she thought it was an illusion, as if some kind of divine projector had thrown them upon the black screen of the heavens. And so bright! She stood there, gazing at it all, not minding how long it took for Laszlo to finally disappear.

The moon lit the inside of the hoop-house with pale, white light, casting shadows in the shadows. But for the whirr of a distant fan, all was quiet. Cece strolled down the middle aisle, watching the spaces between the boards, looking for the blinking red light she'd seen on her first day.

"The guts of the operation," she said to herself. "Laszlo, you freaky little creep."

A red light flashed below, and Cece stopped, looked around, grabbed a potted fern off one of the tables, and placed it at her feet. Then she retraced her steps to the vestibule, counting each one.

"Fifteen," she said.

From the fern to the back, it was twenty.

Now how to get down there? She'd crisscrossed the hoop-house floor during her brief orientation, but not once had she seen a stairway or a trapdoor or anything resembling some kind of portal someone might have cut into the floor, so either she accessed the basement from the outside, or...

She zeroed in on the door to Laszlo's office.

It was, miraculously, unlocked. All Cece had to do was turn the knob and push. The door wafted open with a little whine and then she was inside. She closed it behind her and pushed the button on the knob.

It took a moment for her eyes to adjust, but when they did, she was disappointed with what she found. She'd half-hoped for Laszlo's office to be a garden of perversity: Half-eaten bodies splayed out on examination tables, dismembered limbs attached to electrodes, faces in formaldehyde squashed up against glass jars. At the very least she thought there would be plants with swaying vines sparking with electricity and sparring with each other. Instead, all she got was what looked like a construction foreman's workroom. Bare walls, plastic blinds, a thin area rug. The only thing sitting on the shelf was an old turntable and a handful of records. Cece stepped over and inspected them. The artists were unfamiliar. The Barynya Ensemble. Don Cossack. Kitka.

She turned her attention to the desk. It was the cleanest desk she'd ever seen, completely devoid of papers, pencils, or any other office supplies, as if someone had put it together, set it up, and said, "I will never touch this again." The only item sitting on it was a foot-high statuette of a medieval monk holding a sword in one hand and a little, tiny human being in the other. A name had been printed on a bronze plate screwed into the base. She leaned over to read it.

"Paracelsus," she said aloud.

She tried to pick it up, but something anchored it to the desk. Intrigued, she pulled harder. A cord ran out of a hole on the desk's surface and into the statuette's base. When she pulled a third time, a lever clunked, and the chair behind the desk dropped out of sight. A crash, a smash, and the sound of glass shattering. Cece lowered the statuette back to its spot on the desk and scooted around to see what happened.

An empty square took the place of where the chair used to be. A trap door. Laszlo actually had a trap door. Of course he did. She peeked over the edge. A wooden ladder anchored into the cinderblock walls. The chair rested on its side below, a broken glass jar next to it. Red lights blinked in the darkness.

"Laszlo, you little Scooby Doo you," Cece said.

The ladder deposited her into another office the exact same size and shape as the one above but vastly different in decor and purpose. *The marvelous thing about mad scientists*, Cece thought, goggling at her surroundings, *is their flair for the dramatic*. While she didn't get her dueling fire-vines, the subterranean office looked like something from an evil 19th-century biologist's lab. Glass jars filled with dark green fluid. Arcane notations etched on yellowing paper. Drawings of hybrid plant-animal monstrosities. A tank populated by glowing fish sparking with red and blue electricity.

On the back wall behind the desk hung a framed picture of a severe woman staring death at whoever had been unfortunate enough to snap the photo. Everything about her was tense: her shoulders, her hair, her jaw. Her hands gripped each other like vices. On a gold plate on the bottom of the frame, a single word had been engraved.

"Mother."

A bookshelf lined the cinderblock wall, its shelves populated with jars filled with biological monstrosities. Flesh twisted with flora, a hand growing out of (or grafted to) a tree branch, a twitching heart with mushrooms sprouting all over it. And, yes! Ah, yes! There was the head in the jar. Two of them, actually. No, three. Lined up one next to the other. Cece put her nose up to the glass of the jar closest to her, frowning. The face's features were bloated and distorted, the skin lumpy and wrinkled. Five vine-like tentacles protruded from various places in its puckered scalp, waving listlessly in the green fluid. She flicked the side of the jar with her finger. The tentacles snapped awake. One shot out and struck the glass.

"Jesus!" Cece barked, jumping back.

Suckers with dozens of tiny, sharp teeth opened and closed against the jar, seeking the source of the noise. Cece put her hands on her knees and squinted, her head shaking.

"My, my, my."

A pump in the back of the sub-basement powered on, followed by an electric buzz. A fan whirred. Cece disengaged from the terror before her and exited the office through an open door at the other end. She let her eyes adjust. The rest of the basement looked more like what she had expected. Corroded water lines, sagging ceiling planks, a couple of rustic washtubs, a pile of 2x4s, waterlogged boxes. But that all proved to be just for show, for lining the far wall was a bank of computers with big-screen monitors gleaming above them.

A wire-snake extended out of a wall panel into which the computers were plugged, leading to rows of oil barrels lined up to correspond with the rows of plants above. Cables crept up the sides and over the top where the male ends connected with female receptacles in the oil drum lids. Thick, metal contraptions were bolted over the openings, themselves blinking with red, green, and blue lights. Out of the barrels ran the tubes, some clear, some flowing with the same dark red sludge that had so excited the mortifloria and knocked Cece flat on her ass a few hours before.

Most of the barrels fed tubes that ascended into the hoop-house, but Cece caught sight of three that were sending sludge in a horizontal line farther back into the basement. Green light glowed from the depths. She had to turn to the side to scoot past the barrels, and as she made it past the first one, she stepped on the pump and heard something crunch.

"Shit," she whispered.

The pump shot sparks, and she hurried on, ducking under the tubes that led to the back, hoping she didn't just start a fire.

It smelled less like a basement in the back, less moldy and musty and more pleasant. Rich. Flowery even.

And then she saw why.

Mortifloria. Dozens of plants. Sowed in perfect rows in a wide, square, raised bed. The barrels pumped the sludge into the tubes, the tubes pumped the sludge to the dirt, and the flowers pumped their yellow bounty into the air in load after pulsing load. A huge fan bolted into the cinderblock wall sucked the loads into a massive vent and shot it down a long metal duct. It seemed to be aimed toward Yurtville.

A glass jar smashed behind her, followed by two more. Pop! Pop! Pop!

Cece crouched down, her head whipping toward the noise. The fan was too loud to hear anything else, and the green grow light overhead created strange shadows. The machines continued their tireless task: the tubes pumped their red gook, the flowers pumped their yellow pollen, and the fan sucked it all away.

She'd seen enough; time to get out.

She'd just made it past the final barrel when she felt something slick drip on her neck. She put her hand up and felt around, coming away with a thick, mucus-like slime.

"What the fuck?" she said.

She looked up.

Hanging from the joist was a tentacle head. It hissed and dropped on her, landing on her back and chomping into her shoulder. The teeth-tentacles wrapped around her neck and pierced her skin. Screaming, Cece grabbed it by its oily hair and ripped it off, the mouths coming away with chunks of her flesh. The tentacles whipped around in the air, threatening to latch on again. Cece thrust the nasty thing overhead with both hands and, with all of her strength, swung it down in a muscular arch like she was throwing a medicine ball. It smashed on the dirt floor with a sick splat. The mouth worked weakly, and a single tentacle lashed around, and Cece raised her knee to her chest and stomped it. It exploded in a shower of brain and bone.

Another head scrambled toward her from under the shelf, using its tentacles as feet. Cece planted, drew her leg back, and kicked it like Mia Hamm. It scudded over the floor, through the door to Laszlo's office, and smashed into the bottles on the lower shelf. Yellow-green liquid poured over its face, melting the skin and sending up a toxic cloud. The monster screeched, the tentacles waving and lashing about. Cece's eyes watered. She covered her mouth and nose with her hand and broke for the ladder leading out of the lair.

There was no feeling like climbing a ladder and knowing something was behind you. There had been three pops, three heads, and she only got two of them. Though she practically raced out of Laszlo's evil lair, her feet pounding on each rung, with each step she expected to feel the teeth of the final head chomp into her heel, the feeling of tentacle-teeth ripping into her calf. She threw herself out of the hole in the floor and onto her stomach, pulling her feet out like a shark was about to bite them off.

But how to seal it off? The panels dropped down.

Panicked, she stood up and searched the office. The statue! She lunged for it and yanked as hard as she could. Sure enough, the panels shot back up. The lock activated with a thunk.

She waited. For what, she didn't know. When nothing happened, when no weird tentacle monster lumbered out of the nursery, when no weird fungus ball in the corner exploded in a shower of poisonous gunk, she let out a deep breath.

Then something slammed into the trap door below, and she yelped and dashed away.

CREEPER

Amana woke the next morning confused and alarmed. She sat straight up in bed... no, a cot. She sat straight up in a cot and tried to get her bearings. A tent. Not a room, but a tent. She slept in a tent. A vent in the ceiling blew cool air. A yellow ribbon waved from one of the slats. The sound of cicadas swelled outside. Oh, yeah. The farm. She was on a farm. In Virginia. She rubbed her eyes.

After a full year of traveling, she thought she'd be used to waking up in yet another unfamiliar place, but apparently not. She'd slept in some pretty horrible situations, too. A roadside ditch. The back of a brothel. A coyote's trailer. In comparison, this was paradise.

Papa?

Out here, Amana.

She crept over to the flap and peeked outside. Birds chirped in the trees, the morning sun cast everything in its bright summer light, and a warm breeze blew in from the east, bringing with it the smell of the forest. Her father, Diego, stooped over a basket filled with freshly washed clothes, picked up a shirt, and hung it over a line stretching between their tent and the one next door. Amana slipped out, letting the flap close behind her.

Good morning.

Ah, look who finally decided to wake up!

Where is everybody?

Diego nodded at a pile of beer cans littering the fire ring of the yurt next to theirs.

Boss gave them a party and the morning off.

Amana's eyes belied her understanding.

I know, Diego said. *Not the usual, is it?*

When do we head out?

Ten. Breakfast is already ready. Just over there under the oak tree.

Amana's stomach grumbled, but she didn't move. Not yet.

I don't understand why I can't go with you.

Amana, we already talked about this. The man said he wants you in the hoop-house.

Who's going to interpret for you?

I'm not an idiot, sweetie. I speak English good.

No, papa. Not good. Well. I speak English well.

Diego flapped out a shirt, laughing, and hung it on the line.

Maybe I should watch more movies. Maybe I'll take you to one after we get paid here?

Don't change the subject.

I'm not. Don't you want to go to the movies? Captain America. Mr. Iron.

Amana laughed.

Iron Man, *papa.*

"Tomato, potato." Diego smiled and pointed at himself. "See. Good English."

Amana rolled her eyes. She scanned the farm. The main house to the left, fields straight ahead. A couple of workers struggled out of their yurts, laughing and bantering.

What time will you be back?

Who knows? In time for dinner, maybe? Diego focused on his daughter. *Nervous, Amana?*

No. Yes.

How many places like this have you worked on? Don't you think—

That's the point. It's a new bed every couple of months. Every couple of weeks sometimes. Everything's always new.

Diego sighed.

We'll be done soon.

When?

Soon, I said.

You always say soon. How soon is soon? Why did we have to stop here? I thought you said your friend had a job for you.

Yes. In Pennsylvania, remember? It's two hundred miles away, sweetheart. This is the last stop, I promise.

Amana toed the dirt with her shoe. Diego flapped out another shirt.

Amana, up there—

Up there, it'll be better. I know. I still don't see why we couldn't just go to the Gulf. Uncle Miguel—

Uncle Miguel is part of the problem, Amana. You know that.

He knows people, you said. He could have made it right. We could have stayed.

That's enough, Amana.

But—
I said enough!
Diego hung a pair of socks and tried not to feel guilty.
This place isn't so bad, you know. Compared to some of the others.
Like that whorehouse?
That was a low blow.
I know. Sorry.
I know you're feeling anxious, but I'll just be right out there in the fields. If you need me, just come get me.
What do you think they'll have me doing in the hoop-house?
Probably growing marijuana.
Diego waggled his eyebrows, and finally, begrudgingly, Amana laughed.

Every job Cece ever worked had its own peculiar smell. The fryer grease and cumin of that vegetarian restaurant in Portland. The sour milk and cleaning agents of the daycare in Kansas City. And now, the overwhelming fecundity of the hoop-house on Lilith's Farm. It was like she'd been immersed in dry fertilizer.

But even the smell couldn't compete with the heat and humidity.

Outside was bad enough, but in the hoop-house, the glass doubled it, tripled it, made it unbearable. The fans helped, but after a while, all they did was blow hot air around. Then there was her uniform: long sleeves and jeans, goggles and gloves, and now and then a filter mask. Not wearing the proper gear wasn't an option. That much she'd learned already.

She stood up from trimming a vine and raised her arms over her head to stretch. Leaned to the left, leaned to the right. Her back popped, then her shoulders and neck. She let her fingers trail over the bites marks that thing had given her the night before. Even after another dip in the magic pond, the wound was still tender and bruised. The punctures made her scalp itch, but only one showed on her face. For that, Cece was grateful. Stupid tentacle head monster. Stupid vines. She looked over at Laszlo's office door then down at the spaces between the boards at her feet. No blinking lights today. No weird green glow.

The front door buzzed, and Laszlo himself bumbled through the plastic strips and into the nursery.

"Good morning to you, Madam Cece!"

"Hey, Laszlo."

"Did you have a pleasant time at the simcha? Blow off the steams?"

"It was fantastic, Laszlo. Thanks."

"So good. So good. The Mistress knows what to do, she does. You should be happy for her kindness."

Cece bit her tongue. Laszlo scanned the nursery floor.

"Everything is so clean! I see you've trimmed the tarantulas, yes?"

"Thanks. I'm about to get around to the hanta and rotback."

"No, no! Not today. Today we have the product pickups!"

He pointed at the warehouse doors.

"When the driver man comes, please to help him with the carrying and the stacking and the securing of the plants."

"Which ones?" Cece asked.

"Mr. Sorkin will tell you. He drives the biggest rigs!"

"When?"

"Oh, an hour or so? Before lunch."

He scuttled away, heading toward his office. Cece stiffened. She watched him open the door and slip inside, waiting for a yell or a shout or something to indicate he knew someone had broken in. The door closed with a click, there was a moment's silence, and Laszlo put one of his records on the turntable. The drop of the needle. The hiss and pop of the vinyl. Guitar. Flute Accordion. That was bad enough as it was, at least until the singer chimed in.

Of things I should be thankful for I've had a goodly share/And as I sit here in the comfort of my cosy chair.

"Fucking Russian folk music?" Cece said.

She was hunched over a table in the back, repotting a batch of mums, when she heard the door buzz again. The girl she'd seen the day before, the one she was so concerned about, pushed through the plastic curtains. She was shy and uncertain, her eyes wide and unblinking as she took in all the sights and smells. Cece crouched down to watch as the girl took a few tentative steps down the main aisle. She was smart enough not to touch or smell anything, kept her hands in the pockets of her jeans, in fact. Sweat formed on her brow almost immediately, and she wiped it away with the cuff of her long-sleeved work shirt.

"Hello?" she called.

Cece nodded to herself. Decided. Stood up.

"Back here."

The girl looked around, frowning, unable to find the source of the voice. Cece waved.

"Here. Back left."
"Oh, hi. I didn't see you."
"It's alright. Come on back. I'm Cece."
"Amana."
"Nice to meet you, Amana."
Amana strolled down the main aisle and hung left toward Cece.
"This place is amazing."
"Sure is. Until it isn't anymore. Let me show you around."
Cece led her up the nearest row, pointing out the plants.
"Over here we have mums, mums, and more mums."
Amana seemed to take everything in at once, her eyes rolling left to right, up and down.
"I wouldn't do that if I were you," Cece said.
"Do what?"
"Look around like that. Your eyes will keep focusing and unfocusing. It's a surefire way to get a headache."
"Got it."
"Are you sure? Because you're still doing it."
"I'm fine."
Cece shook her head.
"Suit yourself."
She steered around to the next aisle.
"You've got to be careful with the flowers on this one."
"Why?"
"Because some of them are toxic."
"They don't look poisonous."
"I didn't say poisonous. I said toxic."
"What's the difference?"
"Here, let me show…"
She turned to see Amana standing on her tiptoes, trying to smell the white flowers on a vine swaying from a hanging pot.
"Don't!"
Amana backed off, her hands up, her eyes wide.
"I was just—"
Cece stomped over and yanked Amana back by the shoulder.
"Ow!" Amana yelped.
"What the fuck are you doing?"
"Smelling the flowers."
"I told you. That's not a flower. It's fucking rotback."
"What's rotback?"

"It's like poison ivy times ten. Don't touch it, don't smell it, don't go anywhere near it. In fact, don't do or touch anything unless I tell you to."

Amana cocked her hip and crossed her arms.

"I've worked on farms before."

"Not like this one."

"Gimme a break. Me and my dad—"

"Your dad shouldn't have brought you here."

"What's that supposed to mean?"

"This place is dangerous."

"I bet. Should we have stayed on our side of the wall?"

Stunned, Cece blinked.

"That's not what I meant."

"Sure it isn't."

Cece struggled for words.

"You know what?"

She went over to a hose hanging from a rack in the middle of the aisle, hefted it over her shoulder, and brought it to the girl.

"You're on water duty," she said, and she dropped the hose on the planks between them.

The morning whiled away. Amana watered the plants while Cece did the rest, all to the soundtrack of Laszlo's weird Russian folk music. She snipped thorns, pruned plants, replaced dry soil. Up and down the rows. Over and over. The monotony had a rhythm to it, and even though she was sweating and uncomfortable, and even though all she could think about was what happened to her the night before, the distraction of the work helped to get out of her head. Soon she lost herself in the toil, so much so that she didn't even think to check on Amana until she heard a pained yelp.

"Ah, shit. What happened?"

She stalked out of her row and saw the girl on the other side of the nursery, looking at her arm, her face a mask of pure terror. Cece rushed over.

"I didn't touch anything," Amana said as Cece pulled up. "I did exactly like you said."

Cece grabbed the girl's wrist and turned it over. An ugly black puncture wound marred her forearm. Angry red lines had already formed on its periphery, racing, it seemed, toward the crook of her elbow. Amana's already wide eyes widened even more.

"What's happening!"

"Calm down. Tell me what happened."

"I-I don't know. I was just watering these things and something struck out like a sn—"

Cece plucked the girl's camisole strap.

"What the fuck is this?"

"W-what?"

"You had long sleeves on when you came in here." She looked around and spied Amana's shirt hanging from a peg on the backboard.

"Why'd you take off that off?"

"It's like a million degrees in here. Oh, my god, that hurts."

"I told you to keep your shirt on."

Through gritted teeth, Amana said, "you told me not to touch anything, not to keep my shirt on!"

"A little common sense goes a long fucking way. Come on."

Cece grabbed Amana by the back of the arm and steered her to the first-aid box hanging on the wall. As expected, there was nothing inside except for a few rolls of gauze, a half-empty box of latex gloves, and a bottle of rubbing alcohol. Cece took a roll and doused it with the alcohol.

"This is going to hurt."

Amana pulled her arm away.

"Wait."

"You want this to spread or what?"

"No, but—"

"Then give me your arm."

Amana's eyes shook over Cece's shoulder just as a voice spoke up behind her.

"Ain't even lunch yet and you already got a man down?"

Cece closed her eyes.

Fuck. Mueller.

She turned. Mueller was standing in the middle of the aisle, thumbs hooked in his pockets. She fixed him with a glare.

"Cut the shit, man. She got into the hanta."

Mueller sleazed down the row, his eyes pinned on Amana. He pinched the brim of his hat, gave her a nod.

"Little lady."

"Why is every first aid box in this place empty?" Cece demanded.

"That ain't hanta," Mueller said. "That's a grayboil burn."

"So?"

"So alcohol ain't gonna do shit for that."

Mueller addressed Amana.

"May I?"

Amana sent a glare at Cece and held her arm out to him. Mueller took her wrist and gently turned it over.

"Painful, ain't it, honey?"

Cece stepped up to him.

"Mueller, just let me—"

"I said I got it."

They stared at each other, but it was Cece who blinked.

"All she needs is—"

"I know what she needs. You go on back to whatever it was you was doing. I'll have her fixed up in no time. Ain't that right, darling?"

"Yeah," Amana said. She cocked her head and looked Cece right in the eyes. "I'm fine."

Cece opened her mouth. Closed it. Held up her hands.

"Fine," she said, and retreated a few rows away and snatched up a pH vial and pretended to work.

Mueller pulled a hanky out of one pocket and a tube of something out of the other. Then he got down on one knee, spread the hanky over it, and lay Amana's wrist down.

"This ain't gonna hurt one bit," he said.

"What is it?"

"It's kinda like numbing cream and disinfectant all in one. Gets rid of the oil."

He squeezed a healthy dollop into the puncture wound on Amana's forearm. She gasped, then laughed.

"It's cold."

"Feels good, don't it?"

Mueller rubbed it in, working his way up from her wrist to her elbow.

"Looks like you got some on your shoulder." He pulled her camisole strap down and caressed her skin. "How's that feel?"

"Okay."

"It's spreading on your collarbone, too."

Amana squirmed as he rubbed the cream into the skin on her chest.

"I think I'm okay now."

She tried to pull away, but he tightened his grip.

"Hold on a minute. Just a little longer."

"Let me go."

Mueller looked deep into her eyes. Pulled her closer. Murmured something low and easy.

"I-I don't know," Amana said.

She cast a panicked look around the hoop-house. When she tried to pull her arm away again, Mueller yanked her back.

"Just a little longer, I said."

Cece was suddenly there.

"Let her go, Mueller," she said.

Startled, Mueller turned, easing his grip just enough for Amana to pull it away. He stood up and put his hands on his hips, a crooked grin spreading across his face.

"Hooweee! We got ourselves a wildcat!"

Cece squared up to him, and even though he stood a good three inches taller, she looked him right in the eye and poked her finger at his face.

"You don't put a finger on her again, you hear me?"

"She didn't seem to mind."

"She's just a kid, you creep."

Mueller leaned in.

"I'll put my fingers on anybody I damn well please."

"You put them on her, and I'll cut them off."

Cece's hand trailed down to the knife on her hip.

"Oh, you're a tough one, huh?"

"Yeah, I'm a tough one."

"You like to tussle?"

"No. But my daddy taught me how to deal with guys like you."

"Did he, now?"

"Oh, yeah. All this posturing? That's all you have."

"I got a whole lot more than that, darlin'."

"I'm sure you do. That's why you never leave this place, isn't it? Because off this farm, you've got nothing. Off this farm, if you tried this shit with somebody, they'd shove your teeth down your throat. And you know it."

Mueller's sleazy smile turned into a sneer. He leaned in a little more. Cece unbuckled her knife.

"That's right," Mueller muttered. "Let's see what you got."

They were standing there, toe to toe, nose to nose, when the warehouse door rolled up, sending a blinding wave of sunlight into the open space. Vic stood on the other side, a box in one hand, Sacha beside him, wagging her tail. Behind him, a pickup truck with the tailgate down. Sacha's tail froze the moment she saw Mueller. A low growl rumbled in her chest.

"Quiet, girl," Vic said.

He sized up the situation. Mueller towering over Cece, a sneer on his face. Cece's hand on her knife. A girl he'd never seen before looking at both of them with wide, scared eyes.

"Everything okay in here?"

"Just peachy, Vic," Mueller replied.

"Uh-huh. You wanna take a step back then?"

"I don't need your help," Cece said.

She never took her eyes off of Mueller's.

"I didn't say you did."

"You heard the girl, Vic. Why don't you toddle off and pick up your flowers?"

Sacha's growl deepened.

Laszlo's music cut off, the door to his office opened, and out stepped the little man himself, humming and content.

"Ah, Mr. Mueller! How fortuitous!"

He hurried forward and squeezed between the angry pair, looking straight up at the still seething Mueller.

"I'm so glad you're here. One of the beep-beeps requires your mechanical prowess. Shall we?"

Mueller waited a long beat before looking down at the strange little man wedged between him and Cece.

"Sure, doc," he said. "Whatever you need."

"I swear to God," Cece said, pointing her fork at Ben's face. "If Laszlo hadn't shown up, I would have killed the creepy shit."

Ben lowered her fork with two fingers.

"Mueller's gross, but holding onto a little girl's wrist isn't a murderable offense."

"He didn't just... If you'd seen it, you would have had the same reaction."

"It doesn't sound all that terrible. Are you sure he was—"

"Yeah. I was there. I saw it."

"Because, I mean, you're right. Mueller's a creep, but he's not freakin' pedophile."

Cece pressed her lips together, a slow boil working up inside of her.

"I can see him being gross with you or Aiko," Ben said. "Maybe even Harlow, although I don't really see anybody being brave enough to try anything like that with Harlow. Who knows, maybe he's gay. It wouldn't be so unusual for a guy like that to be repressing something. But little girls? I just don't see it."

"Oh, really? Like grown men hitting on little girls hasn't ever happened before?"

"That's not what I said."

"Do you know what grade I was in when an old guy first hit on me?"

"Cece—"

"Sixth."

Ben remained wisely silent.

"I was eleven years old, Ben. My dad collected vinyl albums, and he took me to a used record store in Culpeper. I used to like it. He'd let me wander around and look at all the album covers while he did a deep dive in the rarities bin."

"Cece, you don't have to do this."

"Shut up. I'm telling you. There was a case up front behind the counter where they kept the really expensive stuff. First issues, signed copies. There was an album in it with a girl holding an airplane. She was topless. I was looking at it, trying to figure out what I was looking at when the guy who worked there came up behind me.

"'You like that one?' he asked.

"I almost jumped out of my skin. He was right behind me. I think I stammered something about the plane, but the guy wasn't interested in a conversation. He cut me off in the middle of it.

"'She's about your age in that picture,' he said.

"Then he went behind me to get back around the counter, and when he did, he grazed my ass with his finger. Didn't grab it, grazed it."

"Oh, gross."

"That's what I'm talking about, Ben. It's not that 'Mueller wouldn't do something like that', or, 'I think you're blowing it out of proportion'. He did it, and I'm not exaggerating. This shit happens to girls all the time." She stabbed her fork into the chicken breast on her plate. "All the time."

The field kitchen buzzed with the easy banter of the workers. Laughter decorated the air. It was a rare, cool evening. A gentle breeze blew, shaking the leaves of the oak tree.

"Blind Faith," Ben said.

"What?"

"The album you were talking about. It was a Blind Faith album."

Cece stared at him.

"My dad was into vinyl too."

"Awesome. Good for him."

Cece ducked her head and looked over her shoulder. Aiko was sitting at a table close to the buffet line, staring at the untouched food on her plate. Her hair hung lank and unwashed, and she had dark circles under her eyes. She looked up at Cece. Her face was blank. Makeup ran down her cheeks.

"Oh, shit," Ben said. "Speak of the devil."

Cece turned the other way. Mueller was strolling through the field kitchen, a jaunty pep to his walk, a toothpick resting in one corner of his mouth. He appeared to be heading for Diego and Amana's table. She half-stood, fork in fist, but Ben stopped her with a hand on her forearm.

"Wait."

Mueller changed course and went over to Aiko. He put a foot up on the bench, rested his elbows on his knee, and leaned in to talk. Aiko listened but wouldn't, or couldn't, meet his eyes. Cece grabbed her plate.

"I'm getting seconds. Want anything?"

"Beans," Ben said. "And uh, yeah. Beans."

At the buffet, Cece moved slowly down the line, pretending to survey the food under the sneeze guard, head cocked as she strained to hear was Mueller was saying. He spoke low and steady, the bass tone of his voice making it difficult to make anything out. Then Aiko snapped, "I don't care! I want to see him!"

"Lower your voice, little girl."

"Don't talk to me like that."

Cece tried to make eye contact with Aiko, but the girl wouldn't look in her direction. She was two seconds from stomping over when someone tapped her on the shoulder.

"Excuse me?"

Diego, balancing two plates in his right hand, was standing behind her. He nodded at the fruit bin.

"Please?"

Cece stepped aside.

"Oh, sorry."

"Gracias." Diego tonged some strawberries and apple slices onto the plates. "Good food, yes? Fresh?"

"The best."

"You work with Amana in the…"

He jerked his head in the direction of the hoop-house.

"Yeah," Cece said, half-listening.

Mueller murmured to Aiko, who stared at her hands.

"But you said he was going to be okay," she said. "I don't understand why I can't see him."

"You can."

"When?"

"When he's out of trouble."

Aiko glanced in Cece's direction, saw her staring. Shook her off.

Diego tapped Cece on her shoulder again, and Cece spun around with an irritated, "what?"

"Lo siento," Diego said. "Amana? You work with her?"

"What about it?"

Back to Mueller and Aiko.

Mueller stood up and took his foot off the bench.

"If you think it's more important to bring your boyfriend a teddy bear and a bouquet of flowers than carry your load here, far be it for me to—"

"I do."

Mueller nodded. Switched the toothpick from one side of his mouth to the other.

"Okay, then. Come on."

"Wait. Really?"

"Do it or don't, little girl," Mueller said as he walked away. "Either way, I still get paid."

Aiko swung her legs off the bench and headed after him, staying a few paces behind. Cece watched them go, frowning.

"She give you any problem?"

Diego again. She looked at him as if she finally realized who he was.

"Who, Amana? No. No problems."

"She work good for you?"

"Yeah. She's a good kid. Good worker."

Cece swung around in time to see Mueller hop into the bed of Warner's truck. Aiko stared straight ahead from the passenger seat, her jaw set. Warner put the truck in gear and puttered out of the driveway. Amana came up behind her father and nudged him.

I told you I'd get it for you, Diego said.

You're not, though. You're talking to the white girl.

Amana took her plate and tonged up a sausage link, casting furtive glances at Cece.

What were you two talking about?
She is a woman of few words.
She didn't say anything about work today?
Diego stopped to look at his daughter.
What would she have to tell me, hija?
Nothing. She's just not very nice is all.
The first days are the hardest. Getting used to new things, new people. Give it time.
I don't want to give it time. I think we should leave. This place is bad.
You remember when we went to Six Flags? Diego said, chuckling. *You said the same thing about the Batman ride.*
They moved down the line.
How long do we have to stay here?
This again, Amana?
Can't you just give me a date?
I don't know. One paycheck? Maybe two?
A whole month?
Amana reached out for a pancake, and her father spotted the remnants of the rash on her wrist.
What's that?
Amana pulled her sleeve down.
Nothing.
Let me see.
It's nothing. Some of the flowers make me itch is all.
If it's nothing, why can't I see it?
Because it's nothing, that's why.
Amana—
Just leave it alone, papa! I'm fine.
Amana chucked the pair of tongs she was holding back in the bin and walked back to the table. Diego watched her go, allowing himself a weary sigh.
"She's upset," Cece said.
"Oh, you know," Diego replied. "I'm her dad. I'm *estúpido*."

It always amazed Cece how in Virginia the heat of the day carried over into the night. She preferred the desert so much more. It was less capricious, easier to read. If she stood in the sun, she got hot. If she stood in the shade, she cooled down. But in Virginia, shade accounted for very little, and even when the sun finally set, the humidity made sure its effects stuck around. When she was little, and the heat and humidity made it impossible to sleep, her father let her and her brother bunk down on the screened-in back deck. The screens helped with the bugs, but trying to sleep outside wasn't much better than trying to sleep inside. Sometimes a warm breeze cooled the sweat on their skin, but more often or not they found that the only difference between sleeping on the back deck and sleeping in their rooms was that instead of sweating through their sheets on their beds they sweat through their sheets on their cots.

Yurtville didn't have any decks, screened-in or not, and the bugs, so pervasive and irritating during the day, seemed to increase at night. Nighttime bugs were a joke mother nature liked to play on anybody who sought relief from the heat by sleeping outdoors. You think gnats suck? Get a load of my chiggers! To keep the insects at bay, the farmhands either had to slather themselves in bug spray or keep a low-burning fire going or both.

That night was no different.

The temperature was somewhere in the low eighties, the humidity up around 60%, and the bugs were out in full force. Little fires were burning all over Yurtville, fires so smokey that it reminded Cece of the summer she spent in L.A.

She hung out with Ben for a while at his ring, but then, seeing Diego and Amana exit their yurt, she punched him on the arm as a farewell and walked over to talk.

Diego teepeed three branches over a litter of kindling.

You'll have your own room there, I promise. The schools are good. They have a futbol team.

I never thought I'd say it, Amana said. *But I miss school.*

You get that from your mom. She was the smart one.

I miss her.

I miss her, too. Every day. Diego looked up as Cece approached. *Look who it is.* Hi there!

Amana focused on lighting the fire.

"Hey, you two," Cece said. "Sorry if I'm interrupting."

"No, no," Diego said. He half-stood to offer his box. "Sit?"

"Oh, no. Please. Thank you. I'll just sit on the ground."

She lowered herself next to Amana and crossed her legs.

"Hey, Amana. I just wanted to apologize to your dad for brushing him off earlier. I had something on my mind."

Diego looked at his daughter, and she translated.

"*She says she wants to apologize for being such a flaming asshole to you before.*"

"Language, Amana!"

She shrugged.

"*It's true.*"

"*Tell her it's fine. I've gotten far worse treatment from far worse people.*"

To Cece, Amana said, "he says you're not the first jerk he's had to deal with."

Cece nodded.

"I suppose I deserve that. But look, I know you guys gotta do what you gotta do. You wouldn't be here if you didn't need to be. But just keep your eye on the exit plan, okay? The people who run this place... I don't trust them."

Amana's face went through several emotions. Surprise, mainly, followed by confusion, ending with something akin to respect.

What did she say? Diego asked.

She said we need to be careful. That she doesn't trust the people in charge.

Diego studied on that. Poked at the fire.

And we can trust her?

Amana scoffed, unsure if her father wanted her to translate, but then Cece spoke up. In perfect Spanish.

You can trust me, she said. *I promise you that.*

Diego and Amana shared a stunned look. Then they both broke out into laughter.

THIS DOES NOT MEET OSHA WORKPLACE SAFETY STANDARDS

That night, Cece slept peacefully for the first time since she arrived. No weird dreams. No fungus rash. Just blissful, untroubled sleep. She slept so well that when first call sounded and she opened her eyes, for a moment, she didn't exactly know where she was.

Harlow was already up and pulling on her work jeans. Cece yawned and stretched her arms over her head. Her eyes fell on Aiko's empty cot.

"Did Aiko sleep here last night?"

Harlow pulled her shirt over her head, shook out her hair.

"Not my night to watch her."

"The only reason I'm asking is because I saw her go off with Mueller."

"She's not fucking Mueller."

"That's not what I meant."

Harlow rolled her eyes as she headed for the exit.

"Jake's probably in the ER right now."

"You think he took her to the hospital?"

"You figure it out."

The morning broke overcast and humid, more humid than usual. Mosquitos and gnats clouded the grass as Cece tromped her way to the field kitchen. She recognized this kind of weather, and for once she was grateful that she was working in the hoop-house. If it didn't pour buckets at some point, it was going to remain unbearable all day.

Ben greeted her with a nod as she sat down to eat breakfast. His curly hair flopped on his head like a mop. The spaces next to him where Jake and Aiko usually sat were conspicuously empty.

"Sleep well?" Ben asked.

"Topping."

"It is friggin' miserable out. I just want the storm to come already. You think they're going to make us work hard today?"

"What do you think?"

"Doesn't matter to you, I guess. You got yourself a prime position."

"It's a greenhouse, Ben. It's always humid in there."

"At least you're out of the sun. Don't pretend it's not easier."

"I'm not. It's just as hot is all I'm saying."

"Yeah. Right. A regular jungle in there."

"That's the idea."

"How'd you get that job, anyway? What makes you better than us?"

"I got injured, remember?"

Ben shot her a glance.

"Oh, yeah. The shoulder thing."

"Shoulder thing? That was Rufus."

Ben laughed.

"Yeah, right. 'Rufus'." Then, seeing she was serious, he added, "I mean, right. Rufus."

He forked a sausage and took a nibble. Cece watched him, concerned. Warner's truck rattled up to the oak tree, brakes whining as it stopped. Warner pounded on the door.

"Let's go, let's go! West field today, people! New breach."

The hands moaned and groused as they stood up.

"Wah, wah, wah," Warner said.

Cece took a slug of orange juice and got up to leave.

"That's my cue. See ya, Ben. We'll meet up after, okay?"

She chucked his shoulder and went over to the dish-pit to dump her tray, then headed off toward the hoop-house, keeping her head down as she drew a wide bead around Warner's truck.

"Not so fast, Butch," Warner called. "You're back on fence duty."

Cece stopped in her tracks.

"According to who?"

"According to me."

Mueller leered at her from the passenger seat.

"Does Laszlo know about this?" Cece asked. "He's expecting me to—"

"Who do you think made the change? One assistant is all he needs. Plus, if you haven't noticed, we're a little short-handed today."

Cece put her hands on her hips and ducked her head. She spat on the grass. Fucking Laszlo. She wondered if he knew she'd broken into his little house of horrors.

"Sucks to suck, don't it?" Warner said. "Now if you don't mind?"

The sun burned off a little of the mist rising from the grass, but the relative cool of the forest left twirling rills of smokey fog that hovered a foot off the ground. The field was so wet with dew that Cece's jeans were soaked through by the time they reached the job site. A familiar scene greeted them: fallen trees, black mung burns, and a fence carpeted with vines, weeds, and other heady growth. That didn't bother Cece so much as the notable loss of manpower. The crew had been decimated. Chainsaws no longer buzzed in the air, machetes no longer thwacked at the brush. What noise the remaining workers made felt muted and impotent, like throwing a sandbag on the shore and expecting it to stop the waves. Shit. They'd started with at least twenty people. Now they were down to twelve.

"Where the fuck is everybody?" she asked.

"Gone," Ben said.

"Does this always happen?"

"There'll be more."

"That's not the point. Where do they go?"

"Oh, you know. Some of them get hurt, like Jake. The rest just leave the way anybody does." He whacked into the thicket covering the fence. A vine whipped out and sliced his arm. "It's not exactly glamorous work."

Cece thought about the two voices she heard outside her yurt the first night she arrived.

"Where's OSHA in all this?"

Ben laughed.

WHACK! WHACK!

"Does this place look like it follows OSHA guidelines? Look at who they hire."

WHACK! WHACK!

Cece looked over at Diego. He was on tree duty, hauling the severed branches over to the pile he'd later douse with chemicals and cover with a tarp.

"Do you know when I got here, me and Harlow were the only white people?" Ben said. "Everybody else on the crew was from south of the border. Ecuador. El Salvador. Guatemala."

"So what happened?"

Ben stopped and looked at her.

"Do I really have to explain it to you?"

"Sorry I'm not as smart as you, professor."

"The election, Cece. The election happened."

WHACK! WHACK!

"Now it's the recession. Ever since then, it's been people like me and you. And Jake and Aiko. And Harlow. And let me tell you, we don't last very long out here."

"You have."

"Yeah, well—"

WHACK! WHACK!

"I don't exactly have any better offers."

By eight, the heat index reached 110 degrees. By nine, as if in on some cruel joke, the sun burned off the clouds and beat, and beat, and beat. Everybody stopped taking scheduled water breaks and drank whenever they felt the need. Cece felt like she was swimming in her clothes. She downed as much water as she could handle, but she just seemed to sweat it right out. At one point, she held up the water jug she'd been drinking from and said, "this is almost empty, and I haven't had to pee yet."

At ten, they all slogged back to the field kitchen to eat and rest in oak tree's shade, trying not to think about the heat, the work, or that they still had four hours to go. Cece sat with her back on the trunk, taking healthy bites out of a ham sandwich. Ben lay next to her, snoring lightly. She let her head roll to the side and saw Laszlo and Mueller arguing in front of the hoop-house. Laszlo gestured. Mueller gestured back. Laszlo jabbed an angry finger at the workers and stomped away. Mueller watched him go, hands on hips. He spat on the ground. Then he headed for the field kitchen.

"Ben, wake up."

"Sleepin'."

"Mueller's coming this way."

"So?"

It took Mueller less than five minutes to get there. When he did, he took off his hat and rubbed down his shiny pate with a bandana, glaring at the crew lying around the oak tree.

"Goddammit! Get up off your asses. We don't pay you people to sit around."

Ben snorted and sat up, dazed. He started to get to his feet, but Cece pulled on his sleeve.

"It's our lunch hour, Mueller," she said.

"What'd you say?"

She slowed it down for him.

"It's. Our. Lunch. Hour. Who cares if we're sitting or laying down?"

"*I* care. We're way behind schedule."

"An hour for lunch means an hour for lunch."
Mueller's left eye twitched.
"Lunch is over."
"No, it's not."
"It's over when I say it's over. Get up."
"Warner know about this?"
"Fuck Warner and fuck you. Get back to work."
Nobody moved.
"Move it, people!"
All it took was one person to break ranks, and that person was Ben. He stood up with a groan, and the rest followed.
"Come on, Ben," Cece said, still sitting. "This is bullshit."
"I don't want to get in trouble," Ben replied.
"You should listen to him, little girl," Mueller called.
Cece appealed to Harlow, who had been sitting by herself at one of the picnic tables.
"You gonna let him do this?"
"Above my pay-grade, princess."
Cece watched as the rest of the workers shambled away from the tree, her head shaking.
"Oh, I see," Mueller said. "We got ourselves a little predicament."
"You have yourself a predicament," Cece said. She took a bite of her sandwich. "I'm eating lunch."
Everybody froze, their eyes flicking back and forth between Mueller, imperious, glaring down at Cece, and Cece, legs crossed, trying to appear nonchalant. Mueller looked around. Saw them all watching. He nudged Cece's foot.
"Get up."
"No."
"Get up or I'll get you up."
"No."
Mueller leaned over and snatched her sandwich out of her hand. Cece was on her feet before he could blink, standing nose to nose with him. He grabbed her by the throat. Her hand flashed to the knife on her hip. Mueller let out a shuddery breath.
"Go ahead. Do it."
Cece didn't even see him. Didn't see anybody around her. Not Harlow, smirking by the dish-pit. Not Ben, rushing to her side. She was somewhere else entirely. Her thumb flicked the buckle on the sheath. Mueller's eyes widened.
"ET!"

It was Warner, stalking toward them.

The spell broke. The world rushed in.

"ET!" Warner yelled again.

He'd stopped several feet away. His eyes flicked to Cece's hand resting on the handle of her knife.

"What the fuck is going on?"

Mueller and Cece continued their standoff.

"You hear me, ET?"

Mueller blinked. He released Cece's throat and backed away, hands up, a slick smile playing across his lips.

"That's two," he said.

Warner watched him, scowling. Then he addressed the crowd.

"All you get back to work!" he barked.

The crowd dispersed slowly, and soon the field kitchen had emptied, leaving all but Cece and Warner. Cece hadn't moved from her spot under the tree. Her hand was still hovering over her knife handle, but it was shaking now. She looked over at Warner.

"You waiting for a written invitation, Butch?" he snapped.

Cece slashed her way through the brush, possessed with the residual anger and adrenaline she wasn't able to get rid of during her confrontation with Mueller. Thorns dug channels on the back of her hands, cut her neck, ripped her shirt. Sparks flew when her machete hit the links on the fence. She cleared a whole section by herself, then turned her attention to the branches of the tree trunk. Ben, who had been watching her, first amused, then concerned, then exasperated, said, "hey, Cece, wait…"

Cece whacked her way down the trunk, and when she ran out of branches, hacked into the saplings and brush to the side, then cut her way into the forest.

"That's not helping!" Ben called. "Where are you going?"

A strong, cool wind blew his hair out of his eyes. Black clouds were rolling in from the west.

"Cece! There's a storm coming!"

She'd already moved into the woods, a branch shaking in her wake. Behind him, workers shouted and gathered up what gear they could carry. Some covered the heavier equipment with tarps. Warner's truck sped by, bouncing across the fields toward the main house. A jagged bolt of lightning shot down from above. Ben started to count. He reached eleven when the thunder boomed.

"CECE!"

Another gust of wind rushed through the trees. Another flash in the sky, followed by the distant rumble of thunder. Then he heard it: Cece's voice. Faint, farther away than he expected, but definitely her voice.

"Ah, shit. Goddammit. Fine."

Gripping his machete, he ran into the forest.

Everything inside him wanted to find shelter, but the point was moot. Running through the woods in the middle of a thunderstorm might have been stupid, but at least it wasn't as stupid as running across an open field in the middle of a thunderstorm.

"Cece!" he cried. "Where the fuck did you go?"

A clap of thunder answered him.

"CE! CE!"

Something struck him behind his right knee, and he screamed as he went down. A hand slapped over his mouth, a harsh whisper in his ear.

"Shut up."

Ben bit the hand and screamed.

"OH MY GOD! OH MY GOD!"

"BEN IT'S ME, YOU IDIOT."

It was Cece. She was squatting next to a fallen tree, her face and arms covered in dirt and mud.

"Cece?"

"Shh!"

"What are you doing down—"

Cece put him in a headlock and re-clamped her dirty hand over his mouth, then motioned with her eyes.

On your right.

Ben followed the look. At first, he saw nothing. Tree trunks. Underbrush. Vines and thicket. Rain patted on the leaves above.

"What am I looking at?" he whispered.

"Shrub. Ten yards."

Ben narrowed his eyes. Focused.

The rain picked up. The wind picked up. Another bolt of lightning flashed in the sky, and in the strobe-light effect, a round thing with tentacles sticking out of it scurried out of the bush and zipped across his field of vision.

Ben backpedaled, throwing Cece off and holding his machete out in front of him.

"What the fuck was that!"

"Shut up and follow me!"

Cece threw herself down on her belly and wiggled under the fallen tree. When he didn't follow her, she stuck her head out.

"Ben!"

She'd discovered a kind of makeshift shelter. It was little more than a depression in the ground bordered on one side by the tree's thick trunk and a wall of dirt on the other. A litter of branches crisscrossed overhead, just thick enough to block the rain. Ben almost felt safe.

They squatted in the hole, facing each other, gripping their machetes, eyes searching the cracks between the sticks overhead. The outline of the trees swayed back and forth as the storm passed through. It was gone in a few minutes, an unnerving peace settling in its wake. Birds tweeted as they flitted from branch to branch. Thunder rumbled in the distance. When they spoke, it was in muted whispers.

"What are we doing?" Ben asked.

"Hiding from that thing!"

"I know, but… what are we going to do when it finds us?"

"Kill it, you idiot."

"Okay. Maybe we won't have to. Maybe it's gone."

"Maybe."

"What is it?"

"I think it's something Laszlo made."

"Something Laszlo made?"

Cece side-eyed him.

"I'll explain later."

"It looked like a face with tentacles."

"That pretty much describes it."

"ARE YOU FUCKING KIDDING M—"

She clamped her hand over his mouth a third time. Ben huffed through her fingers. They stared at each other with wide eyes. Something was shifting in the leaves around their hideout. Dirt sifted through the entry where Cece had dragged Ben, and a tentacle slithered after. Ben's breathing grew heavier. The tentacle perked up at the sound. Another followed.

Cece held up her machete with her free hand, tilted her head at the blade, and removed the hand she'd clamped over Ben's mouth. Ben nodded and raised his machete, but the tip scraped a rock pushing out of the dirt. The tentacles struck. Ben fell back and lashed out with his blade, cutting one clean in half. Fluid sprayed out of the severed end. A garbled scream. The second tentacle zipped back up.

The dead leaves on the branches above them rattled. A tentacle darted down to Ben's left. He dodged to the right. Another shot straight down towards his head. He shrank aside. A third jutted down at his foot. Ben kicked it out of the way. The fourth one got him. It pierced the canopy and punctured his shoulder with a wet splat. A fifth tentacle shot through and latched onto his cheek. A sixth planted itself in his chest. They pulsed and pumped. Black fluid spilled out of the corners of each orifice, ugly and viscous, and rolled down his skin, leaving sizzling red trails.

Ben cut the one in his chest in half, grabbed the one in his cheek and ripped it away. Cece whipped out her knife and slashed the one in his shoulder. The thing above them squealed. The ends wiggled in the air, spraying their dark mischief. Cece launched herself out of the makeshift cover, dead branches cracking, dead leaves flying. The monster was already rolling away, spraying black bile, but she brought her knife down swift and sure and spiked it through the skull. It squealed again, weaker this time. A lame tentacle waved at her. Cece held her machete up, holding the monster in place with her knife. She lifted the machete high in the air and paused, letting the monster track the blade.

"You see this?"

The beast mewled.

Cece brought the machete down as hard as she could. It chunked into the monster's skull with a splat.

In the moments that followed, all she could hear was the dripping of the rain as it fell from the limbs above and Ben's gasping breaths as he struggled to take air.

"Ben!" she cried.

He'd collapsed against the dirt wall, legs splayed out before him, hands shaking in his lap. A portion of a tentacle hung limply from his cheek.

"I don't feel good."

Leaves crunched out in the woods. The sound of something rolling across the forest bed. No. More than one thing. Several.

"Ben, come on. We've got to go."

"I can't move."

The rolling things grew nearer.

"Get up!"

Cece hopped down behind him and tried to haul him up by the armpits.

"Fuck, Ben. You've got to help me."

Ben's eyes rolled white. Cece tore out the piece of tentacle still stuck to his cheek. His eyes flew open and he let out a weak moan.

"Get up."

"Dude," he rasped. "That fucking hurt."

"It's going to hurt a whole lot more if you don't get up."

She peeked out over the top of the shelter. Movement in the bush surrounding them. A head popped up in the distance. More were on the way.

They stumbled through the woods, Ben leaning heavily on Cece, Cece scanning the area, looking for the familiar path. The heads rolled on behind them.

"Ben come ON!"

"I can't."

A head bounced out of the brush to Cece's right and sailed over them. Another one snapped a tentacle at her foot and caught her ankle. Cece whipped it forward as she ran, smashing it against a stump. Ben swatted a third out of the air with his machete, knocking it into a pricker bush.

"Cece," Ben gasped. "I have to stop."

"Just a little farther, man, come on!"

Ben's legs gave out, and he fell flat on his face.

"Shit!"

Cece pulled on his arm.

"BEN COME ON!"

He lay there, motionless.

She stepped over him and straddled his body, knives out.

A trio of heads rolled up the path, tentacles whipping as they sped for them.

Cece didn't have time to get scared. She didn't have time to laugh at the ridiculousness of the situation. She only had time to react.

The heads streaked forward.

Cece bounced on her toes.

They were a foot away when, with a growl, a furry form jumped out of the bush and tore into them. Cece took a startled step back. It was a dog, a golden dog with sharp teeth and muscular jaws. It took a moment for her to realize who it was.

"Sacha?"

Sacha chomped down on one head and shook it, growling. The thing squealed, and its tentacles flailed, and Sacha threw it up in the air and pounced on the second one, and mauled it to a pulp. When she finished, she snapped her bloody muzzle up from the morass of brain and bone, ears perked, to look for the third head, but it was long gone.

Sacha danced around Cece as she dragged a still unconscious Ben to the edge of the mineral pool, nipping at her heels.
"Ow! Stop it, girl."
Sacha barked and sneezed.
"Did you get bit, too?"
Another bark.
"Well, go on then."
With a snort, Sacha sprinted down the path. A few seconds later, Cece heard the telltale splash as the dog jumped into the pool. When she finally dragged Ben to the edge, she didn't even pause. She pulled his arm over her head, spun him around, and shoved. He sank like a tank. She jumped in after.
Later.
Ben stretched out on the bank on his back, eyes staring blankly at the canopy above. The water lapped up against the dirt with hypnotic repetition. Birds sang in the trees. Cece sat next to him, water dripping from her hair. Sacha lazed nearby, her head on her paws.
"What's in that pool?" Ben asked.
"I don't know."
He put his fingers up to his neck and felt around the place where he'd been bitten.
"You should have brought me here earlier. My hemorrhoids have been killing me."
Cece laughed out loud.
"No, seriously. Why haven't you told anybody about this place?"
"I don't know. I didn't think anybody'd believe me, I guess."
"But Jake."
Cece picked at a tuft of grass between her legs, flicked it into the brush.
"I don't think it would have helped. He needed to go to the hospital."
"Are you sure?"
"No."

"What were those things?"

"The heads?"

"No, the trees. Yes, the heads! I mean, what the fuck?"

"You're actually surprised?"

"That I was attacked by heads with tentacles sprouting out of them? Yeah."

"You do know how fucked up this place is, right?"

Ben propped himself up on his elbow.

"I worked at a pizza place one summer in high school. It was hot, the customers blew. My manager was an ass. It was kind of like working here, except for one thing. THERE WEREN'T ANY TENTACLE HEAD MONSTERS TRYING TO BITE MY FACE OFF."

"I know. That's what I'm talking about."

"I don't know what that means. What are you talking about?"

"I fought two of them off before. Down in the basement of the hoop-house."

"What? Why didn't you tell anyone?"

"Oh, sure. Like anybody'd listen to me. 'Hey guys. How was your day? Oh, by the way, Laszlo's growing tentacle heads in the hoop-house'."

"Good point."

"I'm just saying. The mungwort? What the fuck is mungwort? Have you ever heard of something called mungwort?"

"I've heard of mugwort."

"That's tea. Tea doesn't leave toxic burns on the ground or melt people's faces."

"As far as we know."

Cece's face fell flat.

"Sorry," Ben added.

"I need you to take this seriously."

"I am taking it seriously. This is how I take things seriously."

"It doesn't feel like it."

"I am."

Cece glanced at him.

"Ben, you said you were here for a while before I showed up?"

"Feels like years ago now."

"How long though? How long were you actually here?"

"Who knows? At least a month."

"The other workers. The ones who were here before. Did you know any of them?"

"Yeah, a few. I came in at the tail end of a new crew, though, so there weren't many I got to know real well."

"Did you... did you know a guy named Eddie?"

"Eddie?"

"Yeah. Eddie Edwards. Tall. Kind of lanky. Mid-forties."

"That's awfully specific."

"I'm looking for him."

"Why?"

Cece took a moment to consider what she was going to say next. Should she lie? Tell the truth? How should she go about either? In the end, she chose the latter, albeit an abbreviated version.

"He's my father. He went missing. The last thing I got from him was a postcard postmarked from Fredericksburg. He said he was 'working on a magic farm'." She snorted.

Ben turned his head to look at her, appraising her expression.

"I can't remember anybody named Eddie Edwards, sorry."

"It's okay. Shot in the dark."

"You could ask Harlow. She got here a month before I did."

Cece's jaw tightened.

"How much longer are you going to stay here now?" she asked. "You know, after this?"

"I don't know. I guess I can leave whenever I want. I should have about five grand saved up. They haven't paid me for the second half of the month yet, though."

"You just got attacked by a face with tentacles." Cece jabbed her finger at the pond. "I saved your life by pushing you into a magic pond. You really want to stick around for a paycheck?"

"It's a couple thousand bucks."

"If I was you," she said. "I'd get out of here as fast as I could."

Sacha, who'd been dozing in a patch of sun with her chin on her paws, snapped awake, alert, ears pointed. With a growl, she popped up off the ground and jumped away into the brush.

Ben clapped the dirt off his hands and stood up.

"Maybe we should—"

"Yeah."

AREN'T YOU JUST A LITTLE VELMA DINKLEY?

Harlow was sitting on an apple box outside her yurt when she spied Cece and Ben coming in from the fields. The sun kissed the tops of the trees, and she spat in the dirt at her feet and squinted. What were they about? Trying to pull overtime to look good to Warner and Mueller? Fat chance. Warner didn't care whether they worked one minute longer than they were supposed to work or six hours. The job was done when the job was done. And Mueller obviously felt the same way about Cece as Harlow did. She watched the pair stop at the field kitchen to snag some leftovers before heading back to Yurtville.

Harlow could have gotten up and left. She had no desire to even look at that bitch. But in the end, she stayed put. This was her yurt, too, and she'd be damned if she let a mouth-breather like Cece intimidate her.

Cece and Ben parted ways with a fist bump at the main fire ring, and Harlow waited until Cece had almost reached the yurt before lighting a cigarette and blowing it in her direction.

"You're not getting paid to bone Ben on the job."

Cece paused. A flicker of anger flashed across her face, leaving as fast as it came.

"Bum a smoke?"

Harlow took a drag, held Cece's gaze, and flicked the cigarette away, half-finished.

"Fine," Cece said.

She pushed through the entrance and disappeared inside.

When she was sure Cece wasn't coming out, Harlow took another cigarette out of the pack in her breast pocket and lit it. God, she hated girls like that. Overconfident, full of ego. If she had ever gone to therapy, her therapist would have explained why: girls like Cece reminded her of the way she used to be, and if there was something Harlow tried to forget, it was any reminder of the person she used to be.

When had it all gone wrong for her? She grew up in a nice family. Firmly upper-middle class. She went to summer camps when she was a kid, did swim team in the summer. School was a breeze. Getting straight-A's was as natural to her as breathing.

But when she was sixteen, she met Otis. Otis Bailey.

Harlow didn't have the words or the wisdom to explain what happened to her after she met Otis, but if she did, she'd realize that her downfall came as a result of the two things that had plagued adolescents since the dawn of humanity: horniness and bad boys.

Otis introduced her to a lot of things. Sex and alcohol at first, then weed, then coke. More was soon to follow. She barely scraped by her junior year. An objective observer could describe her senior year as ridiculous, not to mention cut short by a drinking problem that metastasized into a pain pill problem that culminated in a near-fatal fentanyl overdose a week before Christmas.

The first time she finished rehab, her mother and father picked her up from the center, tearful and happy. They took her out to brunch, asked her about what she was going to do "now that she was clean." But she soon found out that rehab helped only when she was in rehab. She relapsed. Went back to rehab. Embarked on a short-lived career as a phone jockey at GEICO, followed by a second relapse, a third stint in rehab, and the endless cycle was well underway.

Upon her fourth discharge, she walked out of the front door, lit a cigarette, and scanned the parking lot. Rita, one of her counselors, strolled up to her car. When she spotted Harlow standing in the entrance, she picked up her pace, jamming her thumb on her key fob so many times that her car chirped and blinked like it was having a seizure. Harlow watched, bemused, as the old bat's shoe got wedged in the door as she practically threw herself into her calico Corolla, blew a cloud of smoke out of the side of her mouth as the car squealed away. Twenty minutes later, the lot remained empty, and Harlow had to borrow the intake nurse's phone to order an Uber home.

Her mother didn't say a word when she showed up at the door. Her father wouldn't even come out of the basement. They kicked her out a month later. Cue the cliché: homelessness, prostitution, a string of arrests. One night, she found herself drinking shitty coffee in a shitty diner just outside of town. There were only a few people in the dining room. An old woman muttering to herself at a table by the door, a dyke in flannel in a booth in the back, and a creep in a hoody sitting at the counter. At least the stupid server finally left her alone, but only after demanding she pre-pay for her coffee (the slag). She was trying to decide whether she was going to rob the creep at the counter or ask him if he needed a date or both when the woman from the back appeared at her elbow. Harlow couldn't remember who it was or what she wanted.

"Can I help you?" she remembered saying, and the next thing she knew, she was on Lilith's Farm, dealing with a shitty job, shitty people, and even shittier bosses.

But at least she was off drugs.

She took a drag of her cigarette and shifted her butt on the apple box. Apple boxes made for shitty furniture. Cots made for shitty beds. Tents made for shitty houses. Fuck. Get out of your head, Harlow. She pulled her wallet out of her back pocket and flipped it open. She kept a photo of herself in the front plastic display. She was twelve years old, kneeling in the grass in her soccer uniform, smiling and pig-tailed. She turned to the next one. Eight years old. A camping trip with her dad. She was sitting in front of a fire, eating a roasted marshmallow. The last picture was of when she was a baby. Her mother was holding her on her lap, feeding her a bottle.

When it got too dark to see, she put the wallet back in her pocket and took another drag off her cigarette. Over by the main house, Warner's truck pulled up to the basement door, and Warner and Mueller got out. They jawed a little, said their farewells, and then Mueller hopped in the driver's side, slammed the door, and drove away, heading for the hoop-house. Warner watched the only working tail light recede into the evening, his hands on his hips. Then he ambled away, heading for the boss's quarters.

Decisions, decisions.

If Harlow could have gone back in time, she would have gone back to her sixteen-year-old self, grabbed her by the shoulders, and shook all the hormones out of her.

"There are plenty of other boys out there," she would have said. "Pick a better one to ride."

In that imaginary scenario, the rest of her life unfolded like a beautiful flower:

Finishing eleventh grade with a 4.0.

A senior year internship with a marketing company.

Winning the Jefferson Scholarship for a full ride at UVA.

B.A. in Business.

This fall would be the start of her second year in the Darden School, an M.B.A two semesters away.

Decisions, decisions.

Laughter a few yurts over. It was the newbies, the DILF and his skinny-ass daughter. Who the fuck brings a kid to work on a farm like this? She watched them for a while. The girl laughed at something her father said, and her father rubbed her head. Another drag, another thought, another cloud in the air.

Harlow shifted her gaze back to the hoop-house glowing in the distance. Brake lights flared as Mueller parked.

Decisions, decisions.

With a quick breath, she flicked her cigarette into the dirt at her feet, the red coal still burning, stood up, and aimed for the hoop-house.

Mueller squatted down in front of a barrel in the hoop-house sub-basement and shook his head at the broken mung pump.

"Goddamn motherfucker," he said.

Like it would help. Damn things were always going down for one reason or another. Most of the time it was the mung itself. Mung was thick and goopy, inclined to clogging the tubes and mucking up the works. If there was a loose bolt or a crack in the pump housing, the stuff squirted out and corroded the switches. And when it leaked onto the motherboard, call it a day. Fried the whole thing. There was no way to repair something like that, which meant they had to order a replacement, which took forever because the only supplier they could find was out of the country. Worse than that was when circumstances forced them to use subpar sources. Lilith might call it scientific method. Laszlo might call it a part of the process. Well, they could call it whatever they wanted; inferior sources made for chunky mung, filled with globs of derma and black impurities, and he was the one who had to clean it all up. At least they had a reliable prime at the moment. Made the mung smooth and creamy.

He inspected the pump beneath him. The cracked housing exposed a nest of bent wires and twisted sockets. Someone had probably stepped on it. Probably that idiot Laszlo, checking on "his babies" in the back. He tried to loosen the input nut, and the unit sparked, and he snatched his hand back with a hiss.

Friggin' Laszlo, he thought, sucking his finger. *How's it possible for someone to be so smart and so dumb at the same time?*

In the end, it didn't matter who broke the damn thing, he still had to fix it, and fixing a mung pump meant disconnecting all the ingress and egress hoses, and doing that meant he had to ream them out, and cleaning them out exposed him to all the disgusting shit they stored in the barrels. It squirted out of the hoses, leaked out of the washers, got all over his clothes and hands. Once, a cracked washer gave way as he tightened a nut, and mung sprayed him in the mouth and eyes. He barfed and dry-heaved for an hour after.

He was reaming out a connecting hose with a wire brush when he heard the pneumatic hiss of the hoop-house door followed by footsteps on the boards overhead. He stopped and looked up, tracing the footsteps as they clomped from one side of the nursery to the other. Had to be Laszlo, checking on his babies.

"Goddammit, Laszlo!" Mueller yelled. "How many times I gotta tell you this defective shit gums up the works?"

The footsteps paused. Mueller resumed his work.

"Why's Boemer keep scrounging in the gutter for scraps? How hard is it for her to pick up some prime rib now and then?"

Laszlo hurried over to the office. The creak of the ladder as the little kook climbed down. Shoes crunched on gravel. Mueller pulled the brush out of the hose and twisted around to show the weird little fuck the red muck and knotted hair clotting the tines.

"You see what this shit d—"

Harlow stood in the middle of the basement, her eyes sparkling as she took in her surroundings.

"I knew you guys were into some weird shit, but this? This is like the X-files."

Mueller stood up so fast that he hit his head on a low-hanging support beam.

"Fuck!"

"Watch yourself now, ET."

Rubbing his head, Mueller scowled and pointed the wire brush at the trapdoor.

"Get back up that ladder. Now."

"What's in all those jars back there?"

"Get out, girl."

"But I just got here."

"Ladder! Now!"

Harlow leaned to the side to peek behind him, and he stepped in her way.

"What is all this stuff?" she asked.

Mueller threw the brush down and reached out to grab Harlow's arm. But Harlow wasn't some teenage girl. She'd dealt with plenty of guys like him, starting with good old Otis. She swatted his hand away and punched him in the face. While he recovered from the shock of the blow, she stepped around, brought her knee up to her chest, and kicked him in the back as hard as she could. Mueller stumbled forward a few steps, catching himself before he hit his head on another beam. He whipped around, one hand rubbing his jaw, the other rubbing his back. Harlow was waving her finger at him.

"Taekwondo since I was twelve," she said. "Only made it to red belt, but it's still red belt."

"This is the last time I'm gonna tell you. Get out."

"No. That's not how this works."

Mueller started for her again, but Harlow shifted her stance, balled up one fist. Mueller considered it. He relaxed.

"Okay. I'll play. What do you want?"

"Depends. I thought you guys were running drugs. Meth, actually." She pointed at Laszlo's jar room. "But after what I saw in there? Oh, man!"

Mueller rolled his eyes.

"That shit's just Laszlo's sick little hobby. We ain't got nothing to do with it."

"You got a bridge you wanna sell me, too?"

"Spit it out. I'm busy."

Harlow softened her stance a speck.

"How long have I been working with you guys?"

"You've been working *for* us for about six months, and you're fucking it up right now."

"Oh, I don't have much to fuck up, do I? I'm just a worker. One in a long line, too. You and Warner on the other hand… You know how many crews I've seen turn over?"

"I don't keep track."

"Three. Three *entire* turn-overs. Considering there's at least twenty hands on each crew, that's a lot of people coming and going. Mainly going. That does not bode well for your employee satisfaction surveys. Any other place'd be struggling if that many people didn't want to work here."

"Good. I'll bring that up to the boss-lady. Now if you don't mind—"

"I *was* just going to take whatever money you had and run. I know, I know. Robbing meth dealers doesn't sound like the greatest plan in the world, but I had a good one. Airtight."

Mueller laughed despite himself.

"Oh, little girl. You have no idea how stupid that sounds."

Harlow held his gaze for a moment, then backed up to the first barrel and inspected the lid. Tapped the side.

"Don't do that," Mueller said.

"What is this stuff?"

"None of your business."

"Laszlo calls it the 'guts of the operation,' doesn't he?"

She knelt and dabbed a finger in a puddle of mung, rubbed it between her thumb and forefinger, smelled it.

"I think I got it now."

"Is that so?"

"I know you're dumping bodies in the woods. I'm guessing that's where you took Jake. Probably Aiko now, too. At first, I thought maybe they'd crossed you somehow. Stole product or shorted you a few bucks. But those two weren't the dealer-types, and it didn't jibe with that yellow shit you're blowing through our vents."

Mueller stood up a little straighter, his droopy eyes belying his shock.

"Oh, shit! I was right?"

"Listen, Harlow—"

"I knew it! I've been sleeping with a filter mask on for a couple of weeks. Don't worry. I told everybody it was for sleep apnea."

Mueller gathered himself. Wagged a finger at her.

"Aren't you just a little Velma Dinkley?"

"I want in."

"In? On what?"

Harlow gestured around her.

"Whatever you've got going on here."

"That's it?"

"That's it."

"If I say yes, will you go away?"

"Maybe."

Mueller stared at her, thinking. Then he dropped his head and laughed a short little laugh.

"Fine, Velma. Here's what I'm willing to do. I'll run it by Warner. If he's okay with it, we gotta run it by the boss lady. I wouldn't get your hopes up, but I think I've got a way we can use you."

"Well, okay then." Harlow eyed the exit. "I guess I'm just going to —"

"No, no, no. Stick around. You said you wanted in, so let me show you what all this is about."

She squinted, calculated. Mueller pressed on.

"The barrel you was muckin' around in holds the refined product."

"What product?"

"Can't tell you that. Not yet." He nodded to the area behind her. "But them on the wall behind you is where the cool shit is."

"Back there?"

"Just a bit."

Harlow cocked her head to look, curious but uninterested in going any farther into the dark shadows of the basement. Mueller snuck a sly foot forward, his hand resting on his belt.

"It's just three barrels down. Go on."

Harlow put out her hand as a warning.

"You stay back there."

"Okay."

"I'm serious."

Mueller put his hands up. Harlow took a few tentative steps in.

The tanks anchored to the wall were dirty and patched with rust, but the pipes leading out of them and into the ground were pristine and shining. Even the inflow apparatus looked clean. Each tank had a spigot, and from each spigot, a hose ran along the floor and up into the barrels.

"Do they hook up to the sewer lines?" Harlow asked.

"That's kind of how it works. We got our own dedicated system out here, though."

"Where's it come from?"

"Main house. We pump the tea over here. Takes a couple weeks for the solids to settle. That's what them tanks is for."

"Solid what?"

"This and that. Anything that ain't broke down by the composting process."

"So the composting starts at the main house?"

A whisper of a footstep, a quiet shush of sound, and Mueller was behind her. He plunged his knife into her neck before she could even scream. Her eyes went wide. Blood spurted out over his hand and splatted on the floor.

"Sometimes," he said.

PHYTOVIRAL SPILLOVER

Cece woke up with a start. She sat there, thinking, listening, trying to remember. What had she been dreaming about? Mutated faces pressing against a window, a woman dead in a tub, an overwhelming sense of dread. The tendrils of the dream slipped just beyond her grasp, and the harder she tried to remember, the faster they escaped. All she could hold on to was the dread, and soon that dissipated as well.

Aiko's cot was still a mound of blankets and clothes. Harlow's cot still neatly made. The vent blew lukewarm air down from above. Unnerved, she tossed the damp sheet off of her body and put her feet on the cool earth. It wasn't like Harlow to stay out all night. If anything, the girl was a stickler for routine. Cece looked at the entrance.

"Harlow? You out there?"

No response.

She stood up and padded outside.

"Harlow?"

Yurtville stood silent. The moon rose full. And Harlow was nowhere to be seen. A half-smoked cigarette sat in the dirt. Cece knelt and looked at it, shaking her head.

"Way to go, Harlow."

Never one to let good tobacco go to waste, she pinched off the ends and stowed the remnants in the watch pocket of her jeans. She took one last look around, wondering if perhaps she'd catch Harlow sneaking out of one of the other yurts, doing the walk of shame after an ill-advised hookup. The trees formed a solid wall in the distance. The stars twinkled overhead. The black shadow of Lilith's house hulked nearby.

Back in the yurt. Harlow's bag lay prim and proper on the ground. Cece sat down on her cot, leaned her elbows on her knees, and thought about going through it. Harlow would come back. Of course she would. And if she entered the yurt and caught Cece ransacking her bag, what was the worst that could happen? They'd get in a fight?

Cece had been in fights before. Hell, she'd fought Harlow before. She templed her fingers and tapped them against her lips.

"Oh, what the hell."

In one swift movement, Cece scooped the bag toward her, unzipped it, and probed around inside. After a second, she pulled out a large tube with the words VITAMIN B PASTE written in blocky black font on a white field. Under that: FOR GOATS.

"Perfect for you, Special H."

She flipped it away, meaning for it to land on Harlow's cot, but it hit the top pillow instead. The pillow tumbled forward, revealing Harlow's black filter mask. Cece frowned. She'd always assumed it was some kind of CPAC device, but now that she thought about it, where were the tubes? The annoying machine? She leaned over and picked the mask up by the strap to get a better look. Nope. Just a filter mask.

Aiko's cot, empty. Harlow's cot, empty.

The mask. The paste.

She looked up at the vent, the ever-blowing vent.

"Worth a shot," she said.

She strapped the mask on and lay down on her cot. She thought it would be uncomfortable at first, but it was surprisingly light, and though it took a while for her to fall back asleep, when she finally drifted off, her slumber was deep and dreamless.

The next morning broke hot and clear without an ounce of humidity. Perhaps that helped. It didn't seem to matter when the temperature soared up over one hundred degrees. Ben joined Cece at breakfast, setting his overloaded tray down with a hearty "morning!" Cece pointed at it with her fork.

"You're really avoiding the lash today, aren't you?"

"What can I say. I'm a growing boy."

"You probably need it with all that blood you lost."

"Yeah," Ben laughed. "Good one."

"How's your neck?"

"Fine."

"Can I see it?"

"What? No."

Cece grabbed his face in her hands and tried to turn his head. He pulled back, irritated.

"Stop!"

"Just let me see your neck."

"Why?"

"I want to see the bite."

"What bite?"

She grabbed his head again and, with more effort than he thought he'd need, Ben pulled away.

"Sheesh. You're like Charles Atlas."

"You don't remember?"

"Remember what?"

"The forest? Yesterday?"

"Of course I remember."

"Oh, yeah? What did we do?"

"Same as we always do. Slash, pile, burn. Slash, pile burn."

He forked half a sausage into his mouth and chewed. When he saw her staring at him, he said, "what?"

"Nothing."

They ate in silence, Ben scooping bite after bite, focused on his meal, Cece stirring her scrambled eggs, quiet, pensive.

"Harlow didn't sleep in the yurt last night."

"Mm. Maybe she finally got lucky."

"With who?"

"I don't know. There's plenty of guys here. One of them has to be desperate enough. She's not bad looking."

Another quiet pause.

"I'm thinking of going for another dip later," Cece said. "Maybe you should come along."

"Sure. Sounds good. You find a creek or something?"

She watched Ben eat, wondering if he was messing with her or not. When he didn't laugh or say anything, she turned her attention back to her breakfast.

"Yeah. Something like that."

On the way out to the west field, Cece put her hand on her belt and stopped.

"I gotta go back to the yurt," she said. "Left my knife."

"Okay," Ben called as she trotted away. "I'll see you out there."

A girl she hadn't seen before was wandering around Yurtville when she arrived. She was taller than Cece, with long, blond hair that ran in a braid down her back and a flat look of confusion painted across her face. Cece scoffed at her outfit: tight designer jeans, a sleeveless top with spaghetti straps, pink flats.

"Who the fuck are you?" Cece asked.

The girl shot her a startled look.

"Huh?"

"Your name? What is it?"

The girl seemed to search her mind.

"Stephanie," she finally said. "I was just..."

She turned around and looked at Cece's yurt.

"You were in there?"

"I think so."

Panicked, Cece trotted across the grounds and ducked inside. The sheet on Harlow's cot stretched over the mattress just as tight as before, but her bag and personal things were gone. Cece's bed looked exactly as she'd left it, with the sheet thrown hastily over the pillow and her bag leaning up against one leg. She hurried over to it and thrust her hand inside. Her knife was still resting on top, still in its sheath. Cece knelt and closed her eyes. She pulled the knife out and pressed it against her forehead. How could she be so—

Someone snorted in her sleep. Cece's eyes popped open.

Aiko was lying in her cot, her black hair flowing out over her sheet, her brown shoulder peeking out from underneath.

"Aiko!" Cece said.

When Aiko didn't move, Cece got up and shook her by the shoulder.

"Hey, Aiko, when did you get ba—"

Aiko rolled over, and Cece sucked in her breath.

The girl on the bed wasn't Aiko. Same color hair, same color skin, but a completely different person.

"What?" the girl moaned.

Cece stood up, mouth ajar.

"Nothing. I'm sorry. I—"

The girl rolled back over.

"Can't a girl get some sleep?"

There were other new workers out in the west field, too. A lot of men speaking Spanish. A few girls with hollow eyes and stringy hair. A boy with a high-top fade. But still no Aiko. Still no Harlow. Cece and Ben grabbed their machetes and headed over to a section of the fence Cece swore they'd cleared the week before. The sun beat down on them as mercilessly as ever.

"Harlow's stuff's gone," Cece said.

"Doesn't surprise me. Probably quit."

"Are you kidding? She loved this shit job. She got to tell everybody what to do."

"It takes its toll, you know. She wouldn't be the first to just up and leave."

"Without getting her pay?"

"Who said she didn't get paid?" Ben ripped a bundle of thicket out of the fence and tossed it behind him. "Gonna suck not having her around. She was a pretty good supervisor."

Cece stopped working to stare at him.

"Are we talking about the same Harlow?"

"I know you hated her, but she had her shit together."

"She was a bully."

"She was a manager. Good managers aren't supposed to be nice. They get walked all over if they are."

"That's a load of garbage, and you know it."

"Oh, really?" Ben nodded toward Warner and Mueller, who were leaning up against the hood of Warner's truck, watching the crew work. "You think people would work hard if Warner wasn't so intimidating?"

"Are you saying the only way to earn respect is by acting like an ass?"

"No, but—"

"Have you ever taken a class on a subject you loved with a teacher you hated?"

"Ha! Yeah. Mrs. Mosby. Trig and Math Analysis. Senior year. That woman was a flaming bundle of pig shit."

"And that's all you remember, isn't it?"

"Pretty much, yeah."

"I had the opposite experience. Mr. Mosconi. AP Physics. I was a humanities kid, never earned higher than a C in any of my science classes. But that man was the kindest, funniest, gentlest teacher I'd ever met. I busted my ass for him. Earned a B-."

"True, but this isn't school. This is real life."

"What's the fucking difference, Ben?"

Something caught Cece's attention. It was one of the new girls. The one who'd been sleeping in Aiko's cot. She was waving her machete around like a drum majorette next to a tree trunk with a mungwort sack drooping off it, ready to burst. Stephanie watched her, laughing.

"Here," Cece told Ben. "Watch."

She marched over to the girls.

"Hey!" she yelled.

The girl didn't hear her and kept waving the machete.

"Hey! Stop!"

The new girl stopped twirling the blade and leveled a deadpan stare at her.

"What?"

"What's your name?"

A roll of the eyes.

"Sorarya."

Cece paused, trying to figure out the best way to respond. She wanted, with every fiber of her being, to prove Ben right and say something curt and nasty, but she fought against it. She took a deep breath, reset, and smiled.

"I'm Cece. Nice to meet you."

Sorarya said nothing. Cece pressed on. She pointed at the tree trunk.

"You see that?"

"Yeah."

"That's a mungwort ball."

"So?"

Cece held out her hand for the machete.

"Can I?"

"Sure. Whatever."

Sorarya handed it over, and Cece took it. She flipped it a couple of times, adjusted her grip.

"Get behind me," she said.

Sorarya rolled her eyes.

"Seriously, you don't want to be in front of this."

She waited for the pair to move behind her, then approached the mungwort ball from the side. Gripping the handle with both hands, she brought it up over her head, took a step forward, and brought it down, slicing the mungwort ball in half. Green fluid burst forward like a hydrant and splatted onto the ground. It hissed and spit and sizzled, burning a black hole into the dirt. When she turned back around, Sorarya and Stephanie looked like they were going to be sick.

"You've got to be careful with this stuff, okay? I don't want that shit to melt you to the bone."

Sorarya and Stephanie shared an uncertain look.

"You'll be fine if you don't fuck around, alright?" Cece said. "Also, you need sleeves and gloves, and you need to tuck your pants into your socks."

"I don't have any gloves," Stephanie said.

Cece took hers off and handed them over.

"You can have mine."

"Thanks."

"No worries."

"I can't pay you back for these," Stephanie said as Cece trudged away.

"Don't sweat it. I have an extra pair."

On her way back to Ben, Cece glanced at Warner and Mueller. Warner leaned over and muttered something in Mueller's ear, and Mueller nodded.

It continued not to rain the next day. And the day after that. And the day after that. The grass browned and grew crunchy; the dirt in Yurtville swirled in the hot afternoon breeze. On the fifth day after the storm, Cece awoke to the smell of smoke. She left her yurt, expecting to see workers burning brush in barrels or maybe even some idiot burning piles of poison ivy, but instead, she saw black smudges rising in the pink dawn.

Warner and Mueller were in the field kitchen, hunched over a table, drinking coffee and sharing an intense conversation. Warner cleared his throat as Cece drew near, and they both stopped talking. Cece thought about ignoring it and heading for the chow line, but to do so was not in her nature. So she strolled right up to the table they were sitting at and stood there and waited.

"What do you want, Kiki?" Mueller said.

"Eat shit, Mueller."

Mueller managed to sneer and smile at the same time. He started to get up, but Warner said, "sit the fuck down, ET."

Mueller hovered there, his eyes leveled on Cece's.

"Now!"

But he didn't.

He got up, and Cece put her hand on her knife, and he snorted, shook his head, and wandered over to the oak tree to smoke a cigarette. When he was certain Mueller couldn't hear them, Warner turned to Cece.

"You listen to me. I need you to cool it with him."

"You tell him the same thing?"

"I'm talking to you now."

"He backs off, I back off."

Warner banged his fist on the table.

"Goddammit!"

Cece jumped a little. Even Mueller's eyes snapped up.

"I can't have this middle school bullshit going on with my crew. I don't know if you've noticed, but we got ourselves a little natural disaster to contend with."

"You mean the wildfire?"

"No shit the wildfire."

"It's heading our way, then."

Warner stood up.

"Ya'll fill up. We got ourselves a long couple of days in front of us."

He moved to a table and sat by himself while the rest of the crew came over from Yurtville, their voices muted but lively. Cece noted more Spanish being spoken than when she first arrived. She kept her eyes out for Amana and Diego, noting where they sat (apart from everyone) and whether Amana seemed distressed (she didn't). Ben slumped onto the bench next to Cece, his plate not as piled high as usual. His curly hair stood akimbo, and dark circles had formed under his eyes.

"Tough night?" Cece asked.

Ben grunted. He plugged a biscuit into his mouth.

"Couldn't sleep. Friggin' vent conked out on me. I must have sweated three gallons."

"You better hydrate then. I have a feeling we're in for some heat today."

Ben grunted. Sorarya and Stephanie strolled by, trays in hand. They said "hi" to Cece and nodded at Ben.

"How are the new yurtmates?" Ben asked.

"Hard to say. They're out cold most of the time."

"First couple of days are brutal."

Warner scanned Yurtville for any stragglers. Seeing none, he nodded to himself, downed the last dregs of his coffee, and stood up.

"Everybody listen up now."

Some of the din died down. Warner climbed up on his table and spread his arms.

"I said shut up!"

The crew fell silent.

"Mueller, you ready?"

"Ready as I'll ever be."

He pitched his cigarette and moseyed over to the table.

"Alright," Warner said. "As many of you have already guessed, we got ourselves a wildfire."

To Cece's vast surprise, Mueller interpreted Warner's speech into Spanish.

As many of you have already guessed, we have a wildfire on the way.

A murmur from the crew. Warner and Mueller proceeded as a team, Warner speaking first, Mueller picking up the gist.

"The bulk of the fire's southwest of the property, but the wind's kicking up north by northeast, so it'll be heading our way."

"How soon?" somebody asked.

"Depends on the wind and the ground cover. That storm helped wet things down quite a bit, but it's been dry for almost a week. Some of them firs'll go up like tinder… I'd say we got about twenty-four hours."

More murmurs from the crew.

"Settle down, settle down," Warner said.

Tranquilo. Tranquilo.

"Right now it looks like it'll hook around to the south and miss us. But there's a good chance the wind'll shift back North north west and send it up into the east fields. So here's what we're going to do."

We need five crews: four for the homestead, one to take the lead. Homestead crews'll take the east and southeast fields, two to a section. We will be clearing a road, cutting brush and wetting it.

"That's the easy part. Me and Mueller'll be out here directing. But we also need an advance team to take the west field on their own. We got a neighbor who's done some time fighting wildfires out west, but we need people with experience to help him out."

Any of you ever do anything like that?

Cece looked around. Most of the workers stared at the ground or slowly shook their heads, but Diego raised his hand.

"Papa," Amana said. "No."

Quiet, Amana.

"That's it?" Warner asked.

"I can do it," Cece said.

Warner's eyes fell on her.

"You serious?"

"Yeah."

Mueller chimed in.

"Horseshit, Butch. The only jump you got in you is rabbit."

"Who said I was smoke jumping, Mueller? I didn't parachute in anywhere. Just fought wild fires."

"Where?"

"Did a season in Cali. Four in Colorado."

"Come on, Warner," Mueller scoffed.

"Shut up, ET," Warner said. To Cece, he said, "you better not be lying to me."

"Fine. Don't put me out there. The fuck do I care?"

Warner stared at her, jaw clenched.

"Alright, Mary Sue. You and Diego go out with Vic."

"We need shovels, axes, and rakes," Cece said. "Coms. Shelters. You guys have any of that stuff?"

"Vic's got some." A truck poked its way up from the southeast. "Here he comes now. We still need at least three more out there. Any volunteers?"

"Ben'll go," Cece said.

Ben shot her a look.

"What?"

"Of course he will," Warner said. "Couldn't break up the dream team now, could I? Anybody else?"

Vic rolled up next to Warner's truck and parked. He got out, holding the door for Sacha, and rolled his shoulders back, biceps bulging. He flashed a smile at the group.

"Hola, muchachos. Muchachas."

Sorarya and Stephanie sat straight up.

"We'll go," they said.

The new girls hopped in the cab before Ben could even reach the truck, so he sat in the back next to Cece, leaning on her shoulder with his eyes closed and trying to take deep breaths without vomiting. Vic's truck was bigger than Warner's, and as a result, he drove across the fields a lot faster. At one point, they hit a dip at about thirty miles an hour, and even Cece got a little queasy. Ben hiccuped and she stiffened.

"If you puke on me, Ben, I'm throwing you over the side."

"Do it. Anything's better than this."

He gets carsick? Diego asked.

"Yeah."

His name's Ben?

"Yeah."

Tell Ben to give me his feet.

Cece shrugged her shoulder, making Ben's head bounce.

"What?"

"Diego wants to see your feet."

"What?"

Diego motioned to his feet.

"Ben, your boot," he said. "Off."

Ben rolled his eyes up at Cece, who shrugged.

"What the hell," Ben said.

He took his boots off.

"Lie down," Diego said.

Ben scooted forward and lay flat on the bed. Diego picked up his right foot and pressed on the gap between his big toe and the toe next to it.

"Oh, that's good," Ben said.

Diego moved a little farther up his foot, putting pressure between the tendons. Ben closed his eyes again.

"Oh, that's really good. I actually feel better. What is he, some kind of karate magic guy?"

He wants to know if you're a karate magic guy, Cece said.

Haha. No, no karate magic. Mexican voodoo.

He pressed down hard, and Ben yelped.

"Dude, do you know what you're doing?"

I'm a chiropractor, Diego told Cece.

Really?

Licensed and insured. Well, I used to be insured.

"What is he saying?" Ben asked.

"Our buddy Diego here is a chiropractor."

Ben's eyes flew open.

"He's not going to hit some pressure point and make me get a boner or something, is he?"

"Probably."

"Okay, whatever works."

"You're not feeling sick anymore, are you?"

Ben shook his head.

"No. No more sick."

They bumped along for a while. Diego switched feet.

"You need to clean socks," he said.

Ben snorted.

"Tell me about it." After another minute, Ben sat up and reclaimed his foot. "Holy shit. I feel tons better. Gracias, senior."

"De nada."

Ben laced up his boots, casting a glance at Cece.

"You going to tell him or should I?"

"About what?"

"What do you mean about what? Those heads out in the woods."

"You remember them?"

"Of course I remember them. One of them took a chunk out of my neck."

Cece watched him for a long moment, thinking.

"Your vent conked out last night?" she asked.

"Yeah. It was hot as balls."

"Maybe right now isn't the best time to tell him about weird tentacle heads."

"Why not? We're heading out there. No pun intended."

"Yeah, but. I don't know. I don't think he'll believe us. Not yet."

"They're out there. He'll find out one way or another."

"Maybe the fire will drive them away."

"Yeah. Maybe."

Vic pointed his truck at the west field, aiming for a breach at the southern end. The smoke had increased so much that it blocked out the sun, and the sky took on an ominous orange tone. They pushed through the breach and into the woods, and the light dimmed even more.

They made it to an access road soon after. At one point, it looked like someone had paved it with gravel, but time and neglect had worn it away, and what had once been a road was little more than two ruts carved into the ground. Trees spanned the gap overhead, locking limbs so long entwined that they melded into one. Vines hung down like swinging creepers. Firs lined either side, so overgrown that they formed a wall, and brush spilled out under them onto the road.

Vic slowed to a crawl once he hit the road, and he ambled up the path until he came upon the remains of a fallen trunk blocking the way. He stopped, put the truck in park, and cut the engine. The trees seemed devoid of birds. Even the bugs had gone silent. Cece hopped over the edge of the bed as Vic got out of the cab. He squinted up at the canopy, calculating.

"Do you think they know it was like this?"

"What do you think?" Cece replied.

"Well, shit. What the fuck do we do then?"

Cece reached into the bed of the truck and pulled out an axe.

"We do the best we can do."

Vic spread a map over the hood of his truck and marked their area with a Sharpie.

"Here's the road," he said, drawing a thick line. "This is our anchor. We'll need to cut back the firs and rake the brush on either side. I'll take that."

"Me, too," Sorarya said.

"And me," Stephanie added.

"We need a scratch line farther out," Cece said. She pointed at a blue line on the map. "Is this bed dry?"

"Kipp's Run?" Vic said. "Sometimes."

"Is it now?"

"Hard to say. Last week's rain should have had it running well enough."

"We'll start there and move east."

"Sounds like a plan. You doing any controls?"

"Probably."

He dug a Zippo out of his pocket and flipped it to her. It was old, maybe antique, the steel black from years of handling, the edges worn and chipped from use.

"That was my grandfather's," Vic said. "Don't lose it."

Cece, Ben, and Diego tramped through the woods, kicking up dead leaves and snapping sticks. Vic had equipped them with a single Pulaski each, and Ben swung his cavalierly as they walked, hacking at vines and branches, anything, really, that he passed.

"Are you sure you know where you're going?" he asked.

"Yeah. South south west is this way."

"How can you tell? All of this looks like the same direction to me."

"Relax. I've done this before."

A minute passed, then five. Ben snuck a look at Diego.

"I still think we should tell him."

"The only thing I'm focused on right now is setting up the scratch line. Besides, if one of those things shows up, I'm pretty sure he'll know what to do."

They reached the run in about thirty minutes, stopping at a switchback bank that overlooked a dry bed strewn with rocks and leaves. Cece dropped into it and dug around with the toe of her boot.

"It's plenty wet underneath."

She climbed the opposite bank.

"But we're at the top of a hill over here."

"Gotcha," Ben said.

Cece dropped back down and crossed the bed, and Ben reached out to haul her up.

"You don't have any idea what that means, do you?" she asked.

"Not the slightest."

"Fire runs faster up."

This was Diego.

"That's what it means." Cece said. She pointed in both directions. "You two spread out along the bank. Walk for about ten minutes. Follow the bed. Cut back anything you see within ten feet of the bank. Rake the ground down to the dirt. We'll meet back here."

She repeated the instructions for Diego in Spanish. He nodded and struck off.

"What are you going to do?" Ben asked.

"I'm going to rake the leaves in the bed back to the bank and burn them." She clocked his skepticism. "Don't worry. It'll be a controlled burn."

"If you say so."

Raking leaves out of a creek bed might have been hard work, but Cece chose her job for a reason: it was at least five degrees cooler in the bed. She got to work, raking, piling, raking, piling. Once she had a thin line of old leaves stored up under the bank, she flicked Vic's grandfather's Zippo open, sparked the flame, and set it to the leaves. The fire smoldered rather than burned, and soon the bed was so full of smoke that Cece had to jump up onto the near bank to avoid inhaling it.

She worked that way for a full hour, clearing and burning a good hundred yards before taking a break to wait for Ben and Diego. Her gear lay up against an old tree with roots that formed a bowl. She lowered herself down into it with a groan, took a swig from her water bottle. It was warm. Her power bar was not much more than a mass of chocolate goo, but she was too hungry to care. When she was done, she wiped her hands off on the roots, considered lighting up a cigarette, then realized how stupid that would be. The root pocket allowed her to lean back against the trunk, and she rested against the bark and closed her eyes.

Just a few minutes, she thought. *Just a few minutes and I'll*—

Cece's eyes flew open.

How long had she been out? It couldn't have been over ten minutes, right? Judging by the stiffness in her limbs and the sore spot on the back of her head where it had been resting on the tree, she'd been asleep for over ten minutes. Thirty, at least.

Shit. Shit.

She unfolded herself from the root bowl, knees popping, and stood up. Her right foot was asleep, so she limped to the edge of the bank and looked down into the bed.

Phew.

The leaves had burned down to ash. Those that weren't must have been too wet. Still. Falling asleep was stupid. She put her hands on her hips and scanned left and right. Where the fuck were Ben and Diego? The memory of the tentacle-head surfaced, an image of teeth taking a chunk out of Ben's neck.

This time, she said it aloud:

"Shit."

Cece jogged along the edge of the bank, trying not to panic.

"Ben! Where you at?"

Nothing.

She followed the line of cleared dirt, finally stopping at the spot where he had stopped working.

"BEN!"

Still nothing.

"You better not be fucking around, man!"

She searched the ground, seeing if she could find any signs of a struggle. Trampled earth. Blood. She found a pair of ruts instead, ruts that looked like someone had slid down into the bed. She jumped down into it, landing on an island of rocks. A tree loomed high on the other side, its roots bulging out of the side of the bank. Someone could have easily used them to climb up.

"Ben! This isn't a time to go exploring!"

The walk back to the truck took twenty minutes. She would have done it in half that time if she'd run, but she didn't want to panic. She could see the scene unfold as she hurried back:

Low-slung branches whip her body as she sprints through the woods. She ducks under one, dodges another. The only sounds she hears are her heavy breaths and her footsteps thumping on the ground.

"Ben!" she yells. "Vic! Anybody?"

A noise up ahead. Was that a shout of alarm or someone laughing? A cry of pain or a cry of joy?

She unbuckles the sheath on her hip, whips her knife out. The firs that line the access road link together like linemen. With a warrior's yawp, she bursts through, face streaked with grime, hair tangled with cobwebs, eyes wide and wild, only to see everyone sitting in the bed of Vic's truck eating lunch and staring at her like she was a crazy person.

So she walked.

Fast.

But soon panic overwhelmed her, and the fast-walk turned into a trot, the trot to a jog, and then she was running. The branches whipped, the cobwebs tangled. When the firs appeared fifty yards away, she slowed to a stop and knelt, listening. Nobody laughing. Nobody bantering. Just the sound of the wind in the trees.

Cece crept toward the road and pushed through the firs to the other side. Vic's truck was about ten yards in front of her. The driver's side door stood ajar and the tailgate was down, but that wasn't what freaked her out. What freaked her out was the hood. It had been shredded to ribbons. Metal blossomed out of the block like a blooming flower. Cracked engine parts lay strewn all over the road.

Motion to her right.

A man stood in the middle of the road about a hundred yards away. Was that Vic?

Urgent whispers from the left.

"Cece! Cece!"

It was Ben and Diego. They were lying flat on their stomachs under the truck, motioning desperately. Cece knelt, her knees popping.

"What the fuck are you guys doing down there?"

Ben's eyes fixed on something behind her.

"Oh, my god."

Diego was already scrambling backward, his Pulaski raking the gravel.

"Cece Run!" Ben yelled.

It was too late.

Something grabbed her from behind, wrapped a rope around her throat, and heaved her into the air. Cece kicked and pinwheeled to no effect. The pressure on her windpipe increased. Her eyes bulged. Her face felt full. She tried to grab at whoever was choking her, but her hands only found vines and branches. The rope tightened around her neck. She fumbled with her sheath and unbuckled it, but before she could pull her knife out, she was whipped back and forth like a doll in a feral dog's jaws.

Then it stopped. Like whoever or whatever it was had just run out of strength.

Cece yanked her knife out of the sheath and thrust behind her as hard as she could. She was expecting for it to thud into something solid, for her attacker to scream in pain, but she only felt a thick thatch of leaves. A thorny vine wound around her wrist, puncturing her skin. She tried to rip it off, but the vine wound tighter and yanked her hand away. She screamed. The pressure on her throat increased and cut the scream off. Her eyes went dark.

Then Diego was there. He rushed across the road, his Pulaski over his head, and with a scream, hacked into her attacker. An otherworldly screech deafened Cece's ears, but the force on her throat lessened.

"*Rip it off! Rip it off!*" Diego yelled.

Cece clutched at her throat and ripped a branch away. Another screech. Then Ben was on her other side, hewing into the thing with his axe. The screeching weakened. Cece brought her knife up to the thorny ropes squeezing her neck and sawed into them. Someone else ran up behind Ben. Vic. He was holding a shotgun. He thrust it into the mass behind her.

"Cover your ear," he said.

Her hand flew up to her head and he pulled the trigger. The blast deafened her nonetheless, but the grip around her neck disappeared, and she dropped to the ground. Her foot hit a divot at a weird angle, and her ankle kissed the dirt. She rose to her knees, retching and coughing, the ringing in her head blocking all other sounds. She couldn't stop shaking.

To her left, Diego and Ben were still hacking at a mound of sticks and vines. It shook and shifted with each blow, seemed to ripple as it rolled for the forest. Branches reached out like an arm and tried to pull the mass forward. Vic reloaded his shotgun, stomped over to the thing, jammed the barrel into its center, and fired. With a final screech, the heap shuddered, shook, and collapsed.

The man Cece saw in the middle of the road was not a man. It was a statue made of sticks and leaves fashioned into the shape of a person. They approached it slowly at first, Cece included (despite Ben telling her to take it easy), weapons at the ready, but when it became apparent that it wasn't a threat, they relaxed. Cece limped around, poking here and there with her knife. The figure had frozen in a pose of agony: head thrown back, fingers intertwined with the vines that made up the neck. Depressions formed the eyes and ears, but the mouth was open wide. Cece stood on her tiptoes to peer inside.

"Who would do something like this?"

"*What* would do something like this?" Ben countered.

"It's a distraction," Vic said.

"How do you know?"

"Distracted you, didn't it?"

Ben brought his axe up over his head, intending to hack into it, but as he brought his arm down, Diego stepped in and caught his wrist.

"Dude, what the fuck!" Ben snapped. "I could have killed you."

When he spoke, Diego addressed Cece.

Where are the girls?

Cece's eyes went wide. She looked at the strange statue before her and took a step back.

"What?" Vic said. "What'd he say?"

"What'd you say the newbies were doing?"

"Cutting down firs on the side of the road."

"Where?"

"Sorarya's about a half mile that way."

"What about Stephanie?"

Vic suddenly knew what she meant. He took a step back, too, looking at the statue with both fear and disgust.

"She started out here."

They found Sorarya lying halfway on the road and halfway off, as if something had dragged her into the woods. Her back arched from the balls of her feet to the bun of her skull, and her fingers twined through the vines around her neck, pointlessly pulling. They carried her back to the truck and lay her in the bed next to her friend, then started the long walk back to the farm.

ED IS DEAD

The group overshot the farm and ended up emerging from the woods next to Lilith's house. Farmhands dotted Yurtville, lounging, hanging laundry, kicking around a soccer ball. The smoke cloud was a black smudge hanging over the tree line, but it had moved off to the west. Warner and Mueller were leaning on the hood of the truck in the circular driveway, their backs to Cece and crew, and as soon as Vic saw them, he broke into a jog, Sacha right on his heels.

"Hey!" he yelled.

Sacha barked.

Warner popped off the truck. Mueller twisted around.

"What the hell is going on?" Vic cried.

Cece lost the rest of what he said in the distance, but his body language was clear. He jogged up to the pair, jabbing his finger at the woods, leaning in as he loosed a string of abuse. Warner and Mueller absorbed it at first, their arms folded over their chests. Then Mueller jerked off the truck, stepped up to Vic, and poked him in the shoulder. Vic grabbed him by the lapels and shoved him backward. Sacha zeroed in, hackles raised as Mueller raised his hands, palms out.

With a final bark, Vic marched away, heading, Cece thought, back to his house. Warner watched him for a moment, then stomped through the grass toward Cece and her friends.

"What the fuck happened out there?"

"Don't fuck with me right now, man," Cece said. "I'm not in the mood."

Warner stepped right up and got in her face.

"You don't tell me what to do."

What's wrong with you? Diego said. *Can't you see she's hurt?*

"I don't speak spic."

"Lay off him, Warner. He's just sticking up for me."

"Oh, you understand him? Tell him if I wanted any shit out of him, I'd squeeze his head."

Diego clenched his jaw and white-knuckled his Pulaski. Warner raised his eyebrows.

"You got something you want to say?"

"I speak English well, pendejo."

"Good to know."

Warner refocused on Cece.

"You gonna tell me what happened?"

"What did Vic say?"

For a moment, Warner looked uncertain.

"Vic said a lot of shit."

"Then that's what happened."

Cece tried to step around him, but Warner pushed his not inconsiderable belly in her way.

"I'm not playing with you, Butch."

"Oh, but I think you are Warner."

"What the fuck's that supposed to mean?"

Cece scooted by him for real this time.

"It means what it means."

He watched as she limped back to Yurtville, Ben and Diego right behind her. They gave Mueller a wide berth.

Nobody spoke until they reached the dirt border that separated Yurtville from the rest of the property.

Diego, you know the vent in your ceiling? Block it tonight.

Why?

Just a hunch.

He nodded, a quizzical expression on his face. Amana came out of their yurt and ran for him.

"Papa!"

Diego tipped his hat at Cece and Ben and went over to hug his daughter.

"What'd you tell him?" Ben asked.

"Same thing I'm telling you. Block your vent tonight."

"Are you kidding? I'll roast."

"You feel better today, don't you?"

"Yeah."

"Less foggy? Like you can remember stuff?"

Ben contemplated the idea.

"I guess."

"Trust me on this, okay?"

The next morning, they were out along the north line doing what they'd done for weeks. Another fallen tree, another section down, another thick thatch of brush and thorns. Cece waited for Ben to get into the rhythm of his work before she asked.

"Did you do it?"

"Do what?"

"Stuff your vent?"

Ben hacked at the brush on the fence, seeming to think.

"Well?" Cece asked.

"You're right. This place is fucked up."

"That's it? That's all you got?"

"Why haven't you left yet?"

"It's hard to explain. There's something I've gotta—"

Her phone buzzed in her back pocket. For a second, she didn't know what it was. She was so accustomed to not even thinking about it, she truly forgot she was still carrying it around.

"Something you've gotta what?" Ben asked.

Cece pointed to the breach

"I've gotta take a piss."

Ben frowned, skeptical.

"Ben, I know. But I've gotta take a piss, okay? I promise I'll tell you everything."

"When?"

She was already walking away.

"When I can."

Cece went even deeper into the woods this time, mindful of the vines and underbrush. She found a stump and pulled out her phone as she sat down.

Another notification from SCARFACE was on her screen.

U there?

She tapped her response.

Call.

A few tense seconds later, her phone vibrated, and Scarface's face showed up. Cece hit accept and put the phone up to her ear.

"Dude, where the fuck have you been?"

"Boemer made me in Sussex, so I had to lie low for a couple of weeks."

"Couple of weeks? What are you talking about, man? The last time we talked was, like, three days ago."

"Three days? Try twenty."

"Haha. Good one."

Scarface cleared his throat.

"You've got to get out of there, Cece. That shit's rotting your brain."

"I'm not going anywhere until I find him."

"If you stay there any longer, you won't be able to."

"I've got it under control."

"The only person who has anything under control there is that crazy bitch."

"Did you call just to scold me, or do you have something I can use?"

"Something you can use? Like what? I told you everything."

"He wasn't there."

"You found the basement, right?"

"Yeah, I did. Why didn't you warn me about the tentacle-head monsters?"

"Tentacle-head monsters?"

"Tentacle-head monsters. That freak Laszlo's got 'em in jars."

"Cece, what the fuck are you talking about?"

"What the fuck are *you* talking about? You said I'd find him down there. I didn't find anything but those fucking heads, a vent system, and a bunch of mortifloria."

"I said you'd find something. I didn't know what. I just know they kept toting barrels in and out of the hoop-house."

Cece stood up and paced.

"No. You said you knew my father. You said you worked with him for a full month. You said they asked him to go over to the basement and then he never came back."

"Right."

"Fuck me, dude! There's nothing there! What the fuck do I do now?"

"I told you before, Cece. That place is a deathtrap. If you stay, they're going to kill you. I barely escaped, and look what they did to my face on the way out."

A chain saw started up from the direction of the fence line. Some of the workers barked orders in Spanish.

"Get out," Scarface added. "Get out as soon as you can."

Later that night, Cece was sitting on the apple box outside her yurt, smoking a cigarette. She kept playing the conversation with Scarface over and over in her head.

Three weeks. Had it really been three weeks since they last spoke? It couldn't have been three weeks. She remembered when she first got there, standing out in the middle of Yurtville like an idiot until Ben rescued her. How long was it between that point and getting attacked by the vines? A day? Two days?

Fuck. She really couldn't remember, could she? Every day ran into the next out there. Eat. Work. Eat. Sleep. Repeat. Scarface was right. She was losing it. One of the vent tops squeaked across the commons, and Cece could see flecks of dust shooting out. This fucking place.

She took a drag, blew out a cloud.

How could she have been so stupid to listen to a guy like Scarface in the first place? She'd been so hell-bent on finding her father that she didn't pay attention to the red flags. But he wasn't wrong, was he? He said she'd find "something" in the basement. In her excitement, she assumed that meant the "something" was her father.

Another drag. Another cloud.

She went back into the yurt, grabbed her bag, and brought it out. After a moment of digging around, she pulled out a stack of postcards bound with a rubber band. She shucked the band and slid the one on the bottom up. Her father's spiky handwriting scrawled across it, slanted and heavy.

No closing. No signature.

They all pretty much ended that way, some of them more or less angry, all of them postmarked from Fredericksburg.

Until a few months before she arrived. Three months, to be exact. Then the postmark, which varied from card to card, switched to Richmond and stayed there, and the tone of the messages changed, first a little ("Two months sober. Found a new job.") then drastically ("I'd love to see you again. I think you'd like it here.") He signed the very last one "Love, Dad."

Somebody closed a window in the main house, the crack of the sash, the rattle of the panes. How old was that place? Judging by the moldy smell in the basement and those tools on the pegboard, it must have been built in the late 19th century—early 20th at the latest. Man. Cece had seen horror movies before, and that basement...

Cece stood up. Locked her eyes on the main house.

Ten minutes later, she found herself standing in front of the basement door. There was no place for her to hide, no bushes to duck behind, no retaining wall, nothing. At least it was dark. Judging by the cobwebs that covered the light fixture over the jamb, nobody had changed the bulb in years. If anybody approached, Warner or Mueller, for instance, she'd just say she lost something or heard a noise. Warner'd chew her out, make some kind of stupid gay joke, Mueller would try to start a fight, but that would be it. She reached for the knob but stopped abruptly, letting her hand hover above it.

"You don't have to do this."

She didn't. She could just turn around, grab her things, and leave. Who cared if Ben was still here? Who cared about Amana or Diego or anybody else? She was nobody's hero. She was—

A crack like the report of a rifle echoed in the night, followed by the whine and groan of a tree falling. The ground shook.

Another one down.

She put her hand on the knob.

"If it's locked, it's locked," she said. "You'll just go back to the yurt and go to sleep."

She closed her eyes. Twisted the knob. It turned.

The door opened on creaking hinges. Cece stepped in and closed it behind her with a gentle click. Locked it. Moonlight filtered in through the window over the workbench, illuminating the area with an ethereal glow. The smell hit her again: mold, dirt, and under that, something rotten. She tried to stand as still as she could and cocked her head, listening. The white noise of the open space. Water rushing through a pipe. The creak of a floorboard.

There!

That digital beep. Coming from the back, the section beyond the stairs.

When creeping through a basement, one must adopt a certain posture, and so Cece proceeded to investigate like a cartoon character: knees bent, hands out, walking heel to toe, heel to toe. A quick look up the stairs. The door was closed, no light shined from under the crack. The beep sounded again, louder now. The area beyond that point was darker than dark, blacker than black. She took her phone out and clicked on the flashlight app.

The basement was bigger than any she'd seen, the part beyond the stairs extending well beyond the main section. A warm glow emanated from the back corner. Cece made her way to it, and as she grew closer, she saw the same plastic meat-locker strips in the hoop-house covering the entrance to another room. The rotten smell was overwhelming there, filtering out through the spaces between the strips. The machine beeped a third time.

She pushed through.

When Cece was fourteen years old, she went to a haunted house with her friends. It was terrifying. Mostly because of the jump scares and the pitch blackness. She remembered pinching the shirt of the boy in front of her. She didn't know who he was and she didn't care. She didn't think she was going to get out of there alive. At some point, though, the boy pulled away to catch up to his family, and Cece's friends were hanging back, having been cornered by a gigantic hairy thing carrying a butcher's knife. She found herself all alone in a set piece designed to look like a slasher flick operating room. She crept across the gore-streak threshold, stepping over a slick patch of black blood. The overhead lights blinked in and out, just enough to let her see the savagery she'd walked into while simultaneously making it difficult for her to move forward. A body lay on a slate stone table a few feet away, covered in a bloody sheet.

Cece squeezed past, stretching her arms out to feel along the wall, her eyes rolling everywhere. She inched along, facing the body the whole time, waiting for the inevitable, and then she was halfway to the exit, then three-quarters of the way, and then the doorway was right there, a black hole leading to what promised to be yet another horrific scene, and she turned to make her escape and ran into the chest of a hulking surgeon in a white smock soaked with blood.

That was nothing compared to the body horror nightmare she found in the back part of Lilith's basement.

To the right, meat hooks anchored into a cinderblock wall.

Above, naked lightbulbs swinging on lines.

In front, two corpses chained to rusty bedsprings.

Sunken cheeks, hollow eyes, emaciated limbs. But they weren't corpses, were they? Because if they were, what was the point of the IVs and the heart monitors? She took a few steps closer, noting the burns on the body closest to her, the shallow breathing, the long, blond hair—

Oh, my god.

Jake.

Cece swept forward, jamming her phone into her back pocket. Her foot struck something metal as she pulled up to the spring Jake was on. A metal pan lay under him, catching fluid that dripped off of his body. A hose led out from under the bed to a barrel a few feet away. An electric click, a whir, and a pump powered on. The hose sucked the rot out of the pan, viscous and black, and fed it to the barrel.

They were melting him.

Cece put a gentle hand on Jake's shoulder.

"Jake?"

He didn't stir.

The heart monitor next to the bed continued to beep. Oxygen hissed through an oxygen clip fastened to his septum. She wanted to unhook him, carry him away, but what if these were the things keeping him alive?

"Jake," she whispered. "Come on, man."

His chest rose and fell. Rose and fell.

"Shit. Shit."

The other body shifted, and a creaking moan escaped its mouth. Cece looked up, and her breath caught in her chest. She stepped around Jake's deathbed.

This body was in much worse condition. Skeletal, concave, the life nearly drained from it. Its torso sank into the rusty springs as if it was melting through, and the right leg jutted off the bedsprings, severed at the knee. White bone stuck out of the open wound, peeking from under the fray of a pair of cut-off jeans.

Cece cast a quick look back at the plastic strips, took a deep breath, and leaned over so that her face was a mere foot away from its dry, cracked lips.

"I almost left, you know," she said. "I thought to myself, 'there's no way. No way he could still be here'." She snorted. "But there's nothing Eddie Edwards can't fuck up, is there?"

The corpse's eyes flew open.

Cece lurched back, bumping the IV stand with her elbow. The catheter straightened, threatening to pull out of the emaciated limb. She grabbed the stand and settled it, looked over at the heart monitor, waiting for the frantic beeping to die down. The creature beneath her wheezed for breath, eyes rolling, and Cece couldn't tell if it was in pain or just trying to figure out who, what, or where it was or all three. After a moment, its eyes settled on her. The wheezing turned into a cough, the cough into sputtering laughter. It leaned to the side and spit a wad of blood on the floor at Cece's feet.

"Jesus fuck. Of all the people, it had to be you."

"Nice to see you too, Eddie."

"You gonna stand there like an idiot, girl? Get the cops."

"First time I've heard that come out of your mouth."

"Cecelia Stone, I swear to god, little girl. If you don't hup to, I'm gonna—"

"You're gonna what? Doesn't look like you're able to do much of anything from where I'm standing."

A sneer. A breath.

"We'll just see about that."

Eddie planted his palms on the side of the bedspring, chains rattling, and tried to sit up. Cece watched him strain, his useless arms shaking. He lasted longer than she thought possible before he collapsed.

"Aw, hell," he said. "Look at what they done to me."

He grunted, trying to lift his right leg, but the springs merged with the muscle.

"That looks terrible, Ed," Cece said. She squinted at the limb. A hunk of his hamstring had pulled off like chicken meat. "You oughta get that checked out."

"Cecelia, you gotta help me. I'm in a terrible mess."

"Oh, sure. I'll do it guerrilla style. Like that time you wired my jaw shut. Remember that?"

"Cecelia Anne—"

"Cece. My name is Cece."

"I know your damn name! I'm the one who give it to you."

Eddie grimaced as a wave of pain washed through his body.

"How'd you find me?"

"Wasn't that hard."

"Bullshit. You got the mental authority of a slug."

"You're not exactly a supervillain, Eddie. You sent me postcards, remember?"

"They wouldn't've led you here." His face lit up. "I bet it was that scar-faced motherfucker, Quentin, wasn't it?"

Cece blinked. Eddie rasped out a laugh that ended in a gurgling cough.

"Oh, shit!" he said through the fit. "It really was him? Damn! I knew I couldn't trust that faggot."

The two fell into a silent stand-off. Cece staring, horrified, Eddie wincing as his cough subsided. Cece wriggled, fought the urge to look away, held firm. Another wave of pain washed over Eddie's face.

"So you're not going to get help, huh?"

"You've always been an asshole, Eddie, but I never pegged you for an idiot."

"So why are you here?"

"Aw, Eddie. You know why."

Another long pause.

"You ain't got the balls."

Cece snorted.

"Even now, you can't help yourself."

"Yeah. You always were weak. You and your brother. I tried to toughen him up—"

Cece reached out and stuck her thumb in Eddie's stump. He howled so loudly that she had to clamp a hand over his mouth.

"Don't you talk about him," she hissed. "Don't you *ever* talk about him, got it?"

When he didn't respond, she shoved her thumb deeper into his stump

"Got it?"

Eddie, his eyes squeezed shut, nodded. Cece removed her thumb. Took her hand off his mouth. Eddie took a moment to swallow the pain.

"So, what is it? What the fuck do you want?" he asked.

"An apology."

"A what?"

"I want you to apologize. For what you did. To me. To Walt."

Eddie stared at her, his mouth dropping slightly open.

"That's it?"

"Yeah. That's it."

"Okay. Here's your apology: Fuck you."

Cece's jaw tightened. Eddie continued.

"Because *you* should be apologizing to *me*. I put a roof over your head, food on your plate, but all I ever got in return was a bunch of crybaby bullshit. 'Oh, you're hurting my feelings. Oh, you're too hard on me.' Especially Walt, that little—"

Cece lurched forward and put her hands around his neck, pressing down on his throat with her thumbs. His eyes bulged, his mouth went wide, blasting her in the face with a foul stench. He thrashed as best he could, but Cece muscled down.

"Look at me," she said. "Look at me."

Eddie's eyes locked on hers.

Little by little, the light behind them faded. The thrashing stopped. His body went limp. Cece relaxed her grip. She couldn't hear anything, couldn't feel anything, didn't even know she'd let go until she saw her hands shaking in front of her. A ringing sound filled her head. She blinked. The monster under her was dead. Finally.

She shoved herself off the bedspring, and the world rushed back in. The ringing turned into the heart monitor singing its single note song. Panicked, she turned and strode away. As she passed Jake, his hand flashed out and grabbed her wrist. Cece squealed and clapped a hand over her mouth.

Jake was awake, his one good eye pinning her down.

"Please," he whispered. "Please…"

Back in her yurt, Cece jammed her belongings in her backpack, zipped it up, and threw it over her shoulder. The need to run filled her limbs. Her heart thrummed in her chest. Blood surged through her veins. Adrenaline flooded her muscles. She turned to go, remembered something, and spun back to her cot. Harlow's filter mask hung from a post. She whipped it off and shoved it in her bag.

She was about to barge out of the yurt and make a run for it when she made herself stop. There was nothing that made someone look guiltier than running.

Okay.
Calm down.
Close your eyes.
Flex your muscles.
Hold them.
Let it go.
A calming breath.
She opened her eyes.
Much better.

Yurtville was still asleep when she stepped back out. A few tents glowed with warm light, but that was it. She took one step forward.

Going somewhere?

Cece spun.

Diego stood outside his yurt, hands in his pockets.

Oh, hi. I, uh, no. I'm not going anywhere.

Diego's eyes flickered over her backpack.

It looks like you're going somewhere.

Cece didn't answer. She didn't know what to say. Diego rocked on his heels.

Nice night, huh? he said.

It's a great night.

That's the first thing Amana and I noticed when we got out of the city. No more noise pollution. The crickets. Such a beautiful sound. That and the stars.

Diego, I really don't feel like shooting the shit.

We're from Juárez, Amana and me.

Cece scanned the darkness. The lights in the main house were out. No sign of Warner's truck.

I've never been, she said.

But you travel a lot.

Here and there.

You work a lot of places like this, don't you?

An image of Eddie Edwards melting into the bed spring popped into Cece's head.

Not quite like this.

That's what I thought.

What's that supposed to mean?

Just an observation. The only white people I meet who can speak Spanish like you are migrant workers or college professors.

You know a lot of college professors?

Yes, actually. My wife.

Where is she, your wife?

Dead.

I'm sorry to hear that.

It's okay. It was a long time ago. Where'd you work before this? Salinas? Lubbock?

Around about there, yeah.

Me and Amana, we were down in Naranja first, picking citrus. Oranges. Limes. Before that, it was string beans in San Antonio. And before that, and before that...

Peanuts, Cece said.

What?

They grow peanuts in San Antonio, not string beans.

Diego smiled.

I know.

An owl hooted nearby.

You think I'm a bad father, Diego said.

What?

When I first got here, you said, 'you shouldn't have brought her here'.

Holy cow, man. I don't have time for this.

Cece made like she was going to leave, but then she spun around, angry.

Do you want to know why Amana was so upset the other day? Because that creep Mueller came on to her in the hoop-house.

Diego shot her a sharp look.

So that's why she wanted to leave.

Yeah, well, kinda hard for a kid to work at a place where grown men treat her like a piece of ass.

Amana can take care of herself.

Are you kidding me?

You ever work in Mexico?

How did someone respond to a question like that? If she told the truth, she was a racist. If she lied, he'd know. Cece went with the middle ground.

More work north of the border.

Yeah? Ever work in Canada?

Cece clenched her jaw.

That's what I thought, Diego said. *Juárez is not the best place in the world. We knew that, Araceli and me. Big city. Gangs. But we had good jobs. Amana went to a good school.*

Cool. Good for you. Listen, I really do have to—

Amana's thirteen. She'll be fourteen in a month. Not that it matters down there, not to the assholes in the gangs, not the police.

Okay. I get it.

No, you don't. But that's okay. I don't expect you to. A pause. *We're going up north after this. I've got a job, and she can go back to school.*

Cece closed her eyes. Silently cursed herself.

I'm leaving.

I figured.

Why don't you and Amana come with me?

Come on, Cece. We can't just hitchhike around the country like you.

Two headlights appeared in the distance, bouncing over the west field. Warner's truck. At first, it looked like it was heading toward the main house, but then it veered toward them. Cece fought the urge to run. She put her backpack down, kicked it behind her legs. The truck sped forward, bouncing along the grass and dirt, and skidded to a stop in front of them, pinpointing the pair in its headlights. Cece and Diego winced and held up their hands. The truck idled for a long moment, and then Mueller's voice floated out of the cab.

"The fuck you two idiots still doing up?"

"Christ, Mueller," Cece said. "Kill the lights, will ya?"

Mueller didn't respond. Cece imagined him switching his toothpick from one corner of his mouth to the other. The headlights continued to blare.

"You two get yourselves back inside. Got a job of work to do tomorrow. You're going to need the rack time. Bosslady don't pay you to sleep on your feet."

He waited a beat. Cece and Diego exchanged a look. Then Mueller put the truck into gear and pulled away. They watched it turn onto the gravel drive and head for the front gate. The screen door to the main house banged, and Lilith, dressed in a flowing nightgown, stepped out onto the front porch. She leaned on the rail and looked out over at Yurtville, a queen surveying her property. Cece felt a pit of ice form in her stomach.

"That's my cue," she said, turning to Diego.

He'd already retreated into his tent, the flap flapping in his wake. Cece sighed.

"Fuck."

After another long moment, she picked up her backpack and slipped back into her yurt.

PENDEJO

The next morning at breakfast, Diego put his dishes and tray in the dish pit and joined Amana where she was standing under the big oak tree. He winced at the mournful despair with which she looked at the hoop-house.

Everything okay? he asked.
I'm fine.
You get enough to eat?
I'm fine, papa.

The workers started their long walk out to the north field, chatting and laughing.

"Holy shit, it's already a hundred degrees out," someone said.

Papa? I don't like it here.

Diego sighed.

I know, Amana.
Can't we just leave?
I told you. We'll leave when they pay us.

He ruffled her hair, and she ducked away and headed for the hoop-house.

See you after work! Diego called.
Okay.
Right here.
Okaaaay.
Three o'clock sharp.
DAD!

Diego didn't think the weather would be hotter in Virginia than it was in Juárez or Houston or even Mobile, but there he stood in the middle of the Old Dominion, sweating through his clothes at seven in the morning. Ninety-five degrees anywhere was ninety-five degrees, but Juárez was a desert. Virginia was closer to sea level. Ninety-five degrees plus ninety-five percent humidity felt like Juárez times two. How did these gringos take it? Most of the white boys he worked with could barely stand a morning picking fruit in the heat, but these guys (and girls) seemed unfazed.

He wiped the sweat from his brow with the back of his hand as he marched through the tall grass, slapped at the mosquitos, waved away the gnats. The sun blazed in the sky. One more week, he told himself. One more week and he'd take his pay, buy a bus ticket, and he and Amana were home free. Warner wouldn't like it, but Diego didn't care. Guys like Warner were gruff. No-nonsense. Racist. He'd make threats, refuse to pay, but Diego knew how to put a stop to that kind of nonsense.

Speaking of the devil, the big man was already at the job site, standing in the bed of his pickup as the crew trudged up to the fence. His belly bulged out of his button-up, and sweat was already forming around his collar and spreading out under his arms.

"Get your asses over here! You lazy sumbitches walk any slower you'll go backwards!"

"Okay, man. So, you've got to make sure you start the cut up high and curve it under the ball. The shell's pretty hard unless you pierce it between the bark. There's like, veins or something in it."

Diego nodded at Ben as if he understood. Pointed at the ball.

"Show me?"

"Right."

Ben flipped his face mask down and hoisted his saw. In addition to his usual garb (two aprons, front and back, a face shield, shoulder gloves) he'd somehow found a pair of hip-waders.

A mungwort ball the size of a hog drooped low off the trunk, ensuring a heavy load of toxic juice. Ben made the first cut half a foot above the ball and started to saw. Soon, his face was red, his curly hair sopping and flopping, and Diego was sure he'd pass out if he didn't say anything.

"I get it, buddy."

Ben carefully removed the saw and flipped up his face shield.

"I think I'm going to die," he said. "Where's Cece?"

"Warner put her on saws."

"Chainsaws?" Ben looked around, trying not to look jealous. "Okay, well, you ever see *Aliens*?"

No entiendo.

"Oh, um. Well…" Ben slowed down his speech and raised his voice. "YOU'RE IN FOR A REAL TREAT."

He pointed at the mungwort ball.

"Most of the time, the ball'll just hit the ground and we're good. But if one of these things explodes?" He made a wild gesture, mimicking an explosion. "BOOOSH!"

He rolled his eyes and dragged his fingers down his face.

"Ahhhhhh my face is melting."

He stopped. Diego winced at the performance.

"I speak *un poco* English."

"Oh! Okay. Awesome. So that's basically it. Cut the balls off with these blades, but make sure you cut behind it or it'll explode and melt your face."

"It always takes long?"

"Good point. This blade is *un poco* dull. Hey, Warner. I need another mungwort machine. This one's shit."

"Maybe if you wasn't so fat, you'd be able to cut better."

"That makes no sense at all."

"So?"

"So. Man. I'm getting awfully tired of the fat jokes."

"Sorry to hear that, mayonnaise."

"There's like, fifty more balls since yesterday."

"Uh-oh. Looks like Lieutenant Lardass is turning into a wah-wah."

Ben stared at Warner as the big man laughed at his own joke.

"Can I just get another blade, man?"

"Alright, alright." Warner raised his chin at Diego. "Sanchez!"

"Not cool, dude."

"It's his name, idiot."

¿Sí? Diego said.

"Give your blade to Chunky the Hutt here, take his back to the hoop-house, and sharpen it up."

"The house?"

"Yeah. *A la casa.*"

Lilith had worked with Laszlo for quite some time. They met in Biology 101 as undergrads. Lilith, a fresh-faced farm girl with an IQ in the high 120's, and Laszlo, a refugee of Videla's purges with a similar, if slightly lower, intelligence score. Lilith didn't know why she liked him so much. He was strange and barely spoke English, but she hated the rich boys and girls who populated their school, and the two bonded over their mutual status as outcasts.

It allowed more time to study, for one, and they quickly mastered the mysteries of the world and scaled up everything the science department offered. Soon they found themselves the sole students in the fabled Professor Jason Lee Riddle's Experimental Bioengineering class. Then it was on to SingleCorp, where they served their time as lab rats in the company's sterile basement confines, their working relationship firmly established once again by a disdain for the other scientists, none of whom recognized their genius. Now, forty years after they first met, they served their muse on the very farm her daddy founded, planted, and harvested all by himself all those years ago.

Like a marriage, their relationship had followed the predictable arc, from early infatuation, to growing familiarity, to the early pangs of disillusionment (oh the fights, the fights!), ending not with full-blown romantic love but the final decision to stick around.

Hm.

Romantic love.

Perhaps Laszlo had once considered it an option, but Lilith certainly had not. As much respect as she felt for the man, he was a bizarre little person through and through, as bizarre as a person could be without tripping over the line that demarcated the difference between adorable eccentricity and unbearable weirdness. From his odd mannerisms to the foreign lilt in his voice—an affectation as far as Lilith was concerned, for Laszlo should have long overcome his native accent—he was the very definition of an iconoclast. And he was so frail, so birdlike! She was sure his bones were hollow. How had he mustered the strength to escape Argentina?

She watched him now as he poked around Eddie Edwards' body, alternately whispering and muttering to himself. With her hand on her hip and slightly bored mien, she looked like an older sister forced to babysit for the afternoon.

"Ligature marks around the wrists boulla boulla boulla," Laszlo whispered. "Necrosis of the lower extremities as predicted. Man tea properly vetted and purified, yesssssss. Oh and… and what's this then? Bruising on the esophagus? Heh heh heh. Naughty boy, but to be expected."

"Laszlo, dear," Lilith said. "I have to pack for my trip to the peninsula. Please stop prattling and tell me what happened."

Laszlo snapped erect, his wide eyes further widened by his glasses.

"Yes, Missus! Yes! It makes little sense."

"Could it have been another heart attack?"

"Dual heart attacks minutes apart? No, madam. No."

He scurried over to one of the computer monitors and read the screen.

"Their vitals show no anomalies, no fluctuations, no vexations from my last check-in. Then, BOOM! Elevated heart rate, high blood pressure, followed by nothing. Poof."

Lilith held her palm out to the corpses on the rusty bed springs.

"Do their vitals look unvexed now?"

Laszlo blinked.

"Please to please, Missus. It isn't like I haven't warned you. The human body can only take so much trauma before—"

"I have no desire to place blame, my pet."

Undeterred, Laszlo inspected Jake's body.

"How many times? How many times did I say it?" He pointed out the exaggerated bulge in Jake's carotid artery. "The mungotryon coagulates the blood, it does. Mungles the blungles, so to speak."

"Such poetry you spout, my dear."

"Yes! Yes!"

He leaned closer to Jake's crispy skin and sniffed.

"Smells like chicken," he said, his hoarse hiccup of a laugh following soon after.

Lilith winced. Laszlo suddenly became interested in something on Jake's neck. He leaned in close.

"Oh, and what's this now? What's this? Oh!" He stood up again. "A phalanx on his larynx!"

"Let me see."

Lilith pulled her flowing robe back to kneel next to the corpse, pushing her glasses back on the bridge of her nose.

"Right here," Laszlo said. His breath was pleasantly minty. The man always took good care of his teeth. "On the border between the —"

"Don't talk to me like I'm one of your pathetic tutees, Laszlo."

"My apologies, Missus."

Lilith studied the markings on the boy's throat, sniffed, and stood, unconvinced.

"He was murdered, Missus!"

"Your sense of irony is lacking, my dear." She turned to look out of the exit. "Where is Étienne? Did I not tell him this was of utmost importance?"

Laszlo worried his fingers.

"But Missus. The mungwort in the forest multiplies daily. Messers Warner and Mueller inform me that their subjects cannot keep pace. If we don't have a prime, how will we—"

"We have a new prime, Laszlo. She's stronger. And better."

Laszlo's head was already shaking.

"No, no. No, no. We can't be sure."

"You saw the rash on her body. Anybody else would have died from the shock. And Karen said it took two blasts to knock her out in the car."

"But Missus—"

"You doubt my probity yet, dear Laszlo?"

"Even if you're right, it still won't suffice." He pointed at Eddie's corpse. "His was barely enough. Barely enough! And our line is already dangerously congenital. We need more variety. Fresh tea from a new source."

"Perhaps. Or perhaps she's the key to stop the deformities. If we can put a stop to the outbreak, imagine how much more mortifloria we can sell."

Behind them, the basement door whined open. Footsteps on the gravel floor angled past the stairs, heading for them. Lilith and Laszlo stood, paralyzed, watching the plastic curtains. A form appeared on the other side, and Diego pushed through.

"Hello?" he said, looking around.

The meat hooks on the walls. The computer monitors. Lilith moved to block his view of the bodies, and Laszlo stepped in front of Jake's head.

"Can we help you, my dear?" Lilith asked.

Diego held up his dull blade.

"Senior Warner tell to go to the house?"

"Did he?"

Si.

Diego's eyes fell on the blood-stained floor, the bodies lying on the rusty bedsprings.

Dios mio.

He turned to run, but Mueller was already looming out of the darkness behind him.

The relief Amana felt at not having to see Mueller or Laszlo all morning surprised her. She knew she disliked them. She just hadn't realized how much. That relief turned to discomfort by midmorning, when the only thing that punctuated the silence was the sound of the scissors she used to trim the plants, the hose she used to water the flowers, and the sound of her own breathing. By lunch, she was pretty creeped out.

The end of her shift couldn't have come soon enough. She left five minutes early, bounced down the steps and out into the humid Virginia evening. It was hard not to run to meet her father. She wanted to tell him about how weird everything was at work, sure, but the silence of the day had unnerved her; anxiety tickled her stomach.

The first thirty minutes of waiting were easy enough. She didn't expect him to be on time. That was always the case with this kind of work. They were done when the man said they were done. She watched the exhausted workers trundling through the fields, passing her one by one on their way back to Yurtville to wash up before dinner.

She didn't panic until dinner was well-underway and her father still hadn't shown up. The skyline turned yellow, then orange, then red. The tops of the trees in the forest looked like crooked fingers. Someone said, *see you later!* and Amana spun around, expecting to catch him among the last group of workers coming in, smiling, arms already spread, but it was just some random man she'd never seen before.

Warner's truck bumped in from the fields, Warner at the wheel, Mueller in the back, the curly-haired boy Cece hung out with in the passenger seat. The window was down, and she heard him saying, "… why else do you think the Orcs didn't have a single commanding officer? Because they were brainwashed brown shirts, good little fascists just like their leader."

"Oh, bullshit!" Warner replied. "This is just a bunch of neckbeards sitting around jerking each other off about fairies and elves."

Mueller watched her, dead-eyed, as the truck puttered away.

"Hey, everything okay?"

Amana jumped. Cece had sneaked up behind her.

"Relax," Cece said. "It's me."

"Have you seen my dad?"

"Not since this morning, actually."

"He was supposed to meet me here."

Cece squinted out at the fence line, suddenly concerned. Nothing but the steadily darkening sky and the black outlines of the trees. Behind them, Ben slammed the door with a jaunty "smell ya later, man!" but the truck stayed where it was, idling as Mueller jawed at Warner through the sliding back window.

"Hey, Ben!" Cece called. He looked up, and she waved him over.

"What's up?"

"You seen Amana's dad?"

"Who's Amana's dad?"

"Ben. You fought a fire with him, and the you-know-what."

"Fire guy. Diego, right?"

"Did you see him today, Ben?"

"Oh! Well. I was showing him how to cut off the mungwort balls earlier."

"Where is he?" Amana demanded.

Ben acted like he was looking for the man, like he could see in the growing darkness.

"I'm not sure. Oh! Warner sent him to get a new blade this morning."

"He come back?" Cece asked.

"Yeah. Of course. I mean, I think he came back."

Cece's faced hardened.

Warner's truck headed back the other way, aiming for the hoophouse. Cece jogged over to flag it down, but it sped up. She jumped in front of it at the last safe second, and Warner slammed on the brakes. He jerked his head out of the window.

"You fuckin' stupid?"

"Amana's looking for her dad. You see where he went?"

"Aw, for fuck's sake, Butch. I ain't got time to babysit."

"You talking about Sanchez?" Mueller called from the bed.

Amana perked up.

Cece said, "yeah."

"He had himself a little accident out in the west field this morning."

"What?" Amana said. "What happened?"

"Oh, just a little accident."

"Tell me where he is."

Warner pulled the cab window aside and said something. Mueller leaned in, listening and nodding.

"I asked you where my father is," Amana said.

Warner draped his arm out the window.

"You wanna sink your shrill a few decibels?"

"Don't talk to me like that. Tell me what happened to my father."

"Butch, get a clamp down on your girlfriend."

"Why don't you tell her what happened to her dad?"

"Mueller? You wanna take this?"

"We took him up to Spotsy Hospital, okay?" Mueller said.

"What?" Amana said. "Is it serious?"

She approached the truck as Warner steered around Cece and pulled away.

"He'll be fine," Mueller called. "Go get yourself some dinner and some rack time. He'll be back before you know it."

Amana tried not to curl her lip as she watched them go.

"Pendejo."

When she first got back to Virginia, Cece marveled at the swell of the insects at night. Bobby's rig had just rumbled away, heading back to the interstate, leaving her in a podunk truck stop parking lot in the middle of a state she'd vowed never to return to, and there she stood, taking in the sound of the crickets and thinking about her childhood, her father and her brother. The mix of emotions was overwhelming.

If she knew then what she knew now, would she even have bothered to enter that diner? She hadn't been to the Outer Banks since her mother died. Maybe she could have hitched a ride to the coast, camped out at Hatteras, waited tables and surfed for a few months before taking the ferry back to the mainland and thumbing it down to Florida.

Now, standing in the dark in front of the door to Lilith's basement, the yearning for that alternate reality struck Cece so hard that she felt dizzy. She could smell the salt air and the steamed shrimp, feel the sand between her toes. Then thunder rumbled in the distance and a flash of heat lightning snapped her back to Virginia and the farm and all the danger and weirdness she'd gotten herself into.

The door was only a few feet away, yet she couldn't open it. She knew Diego was in there. She knew what they'd done to him. She knew how scared he must have been. How his final thoughts must have turned toward Amana.

Cece took a long look around the property. Behind her, Yurtville, the black spires of the tents standing out against a midnight blue sky. To the north, the field kitchen with the grand old oak watching over the property. To the west, the caterpillar back of the hoop-house. Other than the bugs, all was still and silent.

She screwed up her courage. Don't worry about the door this time. Don't worry about getting caught. Just stride right up, grab the knob, and turn. So she did.

And it was locked.

She tried the knob again, thinking maybe it stuck.

It didn't move. Not even a rattle.

Fuck. Fuuuuuck.

Then she remembered the window over the workbench.

In the basement it had seemed impossibly high; she would have had to stand on the bench to reach it. But outside, it was a mere foot off the ground. She pulled on the handle, not expecting it to be unlocked but hoping it would be. It was.

Aside from a dim light glowing to her right and the light of the moon coming in behind her, the basement remained inky black. She searched the workbench for something she could use as a weapon, but all the tools had been removed, even the screwdrivers.

Shit.

How was she going to free Diego from those rusty bedsprings?

No time to worry about that now. She'd just have to improvise. Seconds later, she pushed through the plastic curtains and into the antechamber where Eddie Edwards had met his end. And Jake. She couldn't forget Jake. She expected to see Diego strapped down to a bedspring, IV pumping poison into his arm, heart monitor beeping, his body in the early stages of melting into the pan underneath him.

But the place was empty.

No rusty bed springs.

No Diego.

No heart monitor, no IV stand, nothing.

Just the meat hooks bolted into the wall to her right and an empty space before her. A naked bulb swayed over where she'd killed Eddie, casting shadows in brown light.

Cece beelined for Yurtville, barely able to contain her anxiety. She threw a nervous look over her shoulder, expecting to see Mueller leaning against the old oak tree, leering at her, or Warner sitting in his truck, the red coal of a cigarette lighting up his wrinkled face.

But she didn't.

Miraculously, all was clear.

She trotted to her yurt and ducked inside.

She exited a few seconds later, her bag on her back, heading for Ben's yurt.

Ben's yurt smelled only like an enclosed area occupied by Ben could smell: sour socks and food with an undercurrent of sweat. The air was heavy, too, as if with every one of his labored exhalations he expelled a fine mist comprised of the deepest secrets of his innermost Ben-ness.

Cece wavered in the entrance. To her left, an empty cot. Had that been Rufus's? To her right, another empty cot. Must have been Jake's. Ben was sleeping on his back, right arm flung over his head, left hand resting on his bare belly. A sheet covered his lower half, though both legs were sticking out of the bottom. He snorted and smacked his lips.

"Ben," Cece whispered. He didn't move. "Ben." Louder this time. Still nothing.

She waded farther in, kicking aside balled-up socks, his (probably still-moist) work pants, and a pair of boxers, and stopped just shy of his cot. What if he slept in the nude? Leaning over, she pinched a corner of his sheet between her fingers and pulled it up to have a peek.

"Cece?"

Cece gasped and stepped back.

"I'm not. I wasn't."

Ben was awake, looking at her quizzically. He looked down at his waist.

"What are you doing?"

Cece realized she didn't know what she was going to tell him. So she just told him the truth.

"Warner and Mueller are killing everybody and turning them into compost."

Ben stared at her, comprehending and not comprehending. He wiped his face with his hand.

"Let's say, for the sake of argument, I believed you. What then?"

"What do you mean 'what then'? I'm getting the fuck out of here, and so should you."

"You're not going to kill them?"

"What? Kill them? No. Why?"

Ben thought about it. He looked like he was about to argue, thought better about it, and with sudden indifference, said, "fuck it. I'm in."

If she'd been a few years older, Amana would have already run. But she wasn't a few years older. She was thirteen. A child. No matter how many awful situations she'd survived, no matter how many dangerous predicaments the past year had thrown her way, there was no way she could have known what to do. Her father had made all the decisions up to that point, and her father was missing. He'd told her to wait for him, and even though she knew it was stupid, she was going to wait for him.

That didn't mean she couldn't be upset, though. And she waited like any child in this situation would wait: curled up on her cot, trying, and failing, not to cry. She was in this position when Cece burst into her yurt. Amana sat up like a catapult.

"Get out!"

"Grab your shit, Amana. We're leaving."

"I'm not going anywhere with you. My father—"

"Your father's gone."

"Yeah. He's in the hospital."

Irritated, Cece scanned the room, snatched up a shirt and a stray sock. A black backpack hung from a cot post.

"Is that your dad's bag?"

"Don't touch that!"

"Amana! Diego told me you wanted to get out of here, so let's get out of here."

Mueller said—

Christ, Amana. Your dad's not in the hospital.

But he said Papa'd be back soon.

"Really? You're going to believe that creep?"

Amana clamped her mouth shut. Cece snapped her fingers.

"Grab your bag. Let's go."

"I want to see my dad."

"I told you—"

"In the hospital."

Cece shook her head, eyes wide.

"Fine. If I take you to the hospital, will you come with me?"

Heat lightning etched across the southern sky. Clouds gathered, hanging like a thing alive, a nucleus core of silent energy. Cece adjusted her backpack as she and Amana trotted through Yurtville. They made it onto the gravel drive and fairly ran up to the gate. Ben was standing in the shadows, wearing a yellow rain slicker and cargo shorts.

"Where the fuck have you guys been?"

"Take that jacket off," Cece hissed. "I can spot you a mile away."

"No way, dude." Ben nodded at the clouds in the distance. "I'm not getting caught in that."

"Why is the gate closed?"

"It's—"

Cece tried the handle. It rattled but didn't budge.

"Fuck, Ben! We need to go!"

"Unless you want me to use my mind powers on it, I suggest you stop yelling at me."

Cece grabbed the rusty iron rungs and shook.

"You mean to tell me you didn't plan for this?" Ben said. "Oh, this is great. Just great."

Cece ran to the post where the chain-link fence was welded tight. Though the fence was higher than the gate, it was certainly scalable. They'd need something to throw over the top where the links stuck up like knives.

"Give me your jacket."

"What?" Ben followed her gaze. "No way, man. That's like fifteen feet high."

"It's the only way out."

"Those links are like shanks, dude."

"That's what the jacket's for."

"This is a raincoat. They'll cut right through it."

Cece spun on him.

"Do you have a better idea?"

"I do," Amana said.

She was standing at the opposite post, pulling a section of the chain-link open with one hand.

"Damn," Ben said. "She's better at this than you."

Now it was Amana's turn to take the lead. First, she was just walking fast, then she started trotting between spates of fast-walking, then she was trotting, and then she was finally outright running. Cece kept up at first, but the girl soon outpaced her by at least twenty yards. Ben lagged even farther.

"What's she doing?"

"Amana, slow down!"

"No!" Amana yelled.

The forest, tight on either side of the gravel road, was alive with fireflies. They passed through odd pockets of cold air and hot envelopes of swampy rot. Amana disappeared around a bend, and Cece yelled, "Amana!"

The girl popped back into view.

"Hurry!"

"Wait!"

Ben groaned. Breathing heavily, he said, "just let her go, dude."

"We're not splitting up. I've seen that movie."

"Good point."

Amana was vibrating by the time they reached her. She struck out as soon as Cece was within arm's reach. The wind kicked up, and she stopped abruptly, grimacing.

"What is that smell?"

It hit Cece and Ben at the same time. Cece was about to say "just swamp rot" when the sound of an engine echoed in the night. All three of them turned toward the gate, waiting, listening. The engine grew louder. Headlights flickered in the trees.

"Fuck, it's Warner," Cece said.

There was no moment when Cece didn't know what to do, no moment when she froze, no moment when she asked herself, "where do I hide?" She pushed Amana toward the edge of the road. "Go!"

The road was at least five feet higher than the forest below, with a graded gravel decline leading into a weedy ditch. The stench grew stronger. Amana pushed back on the brink.

"I'm not going in there."

Warner's headlights hit the trees at the curve.

"It smells like something died in there."

"No," Ben said. "Something did die in there."

Mueller's truck banged over a pothole, and the three of them turned as one and jumped into the ditch. For the split second between the moment when she thought she was going to hit the ground and didn't, Cece thought that she had pushed them into an endless pit. Then her feet struck the earth, jolting her knees and forcing the breath out of her with a huff.

The truck grew closer, loud rock music blaring from the cab. Cece hoped it would speed by as Warner or Mueller or whoever was driving headed out to do whatever horrible thing evil henchmen did. But to her horror, the stupid thing slowed.

"Get down!" she hissed.

She needn't have bothered. Amana was already crouching in the tall grass between the ditch and the woods, and Ben had already hit the deck like someone had thrown a grenade.

"Oh, what did I land in?" he moaned.

"The smell," Amana said.

"It's gooey. And crunchy."

"I think I'm gonna puke."

"I think *I'm* gonna puke."

"Shut up, both of you!" Cece snapped. She pulled Harlow's filter mask out of her backpack and thrust it at Amana. "Here."

"That's not going to make me feel better," Amana said.

"Just put it on."

"Why?"

Cece's next sentence came out all at once.

"Amana-can-just-do-one-thing-I-tell-you-to-do-for-once-without-an-interrogation!"

Amana pulled her head back, eyebrows raised.

"Okay, okay."

She slipped the mask over her face and presented it to Cece with a gesture that said "satisfied?"

"You got another one of those in there?" Ben asked.

"Shh!"

Warner's truck stopped exactly where they'd been standing moments before, the wheels right above their heads. From that vantage point, they could see the undercarriage and the headlights piercing the darkness. A turn of the key, the engine died, and the driver's side door creaked open. A pair of old work boots stepped out onto the road.

"So apparently the whole thing was a metaphor for WWII."

Warner.

On the opposite side, another creaking door, another pair of work boots. Mueller.

"I don't see it. The watchamacallits. The morks?"

"Orcs."

"If the orcs is Nazis, shouldn't they be perfect? Like, not ugly? Better fighters and such?"

Ben tugged on Cece's shirt. His wide eyes said it all.

"You're missing the point. They was an unstoppable force rolling across Middle-earth, killing everybody that got in their way and enslaving the rest. Ergo, Nazis."

The scent of tobacco smoke. Mueller's boots joined Warner's.

"I guess that makes sense."

"I'm just telling you what the kid told me. Come on. Time to get to work."

Mueller took a final puff and flicked the cigarette away. It flipped through the air, landed on the back of Ben's neck, and slipped down his jacket. Ben jolted into action, his arms flapping against his back. Cece tried to shove a hand down and snatch it out, but Ben was twisting and writhing too much. She half-mouthed, half-whispered the word "STOP."

Ben rolled over and pressed his back into the ground, a pained squeal squeaking out of his throat. Mueller's boots stopped and turned toward the woods.

"You hear that?"

"Hear what?"

"I heard something."

"Fuck's sake, ET. We're outside."

"Sounded like a whisper."

"The only whisper you're gonna hear out here is the sound of my foot whispering up your ass. Now get over here and let's get this done."

Mueller's boots didn't move. Cece squeezed her eyes shut. She could imagine him standing there, peering into the darkness, listening.

"Mueller!" Warner barked.

"Alright, alright."

The tailgate lowered with a squeal and a thunk.

"You get the top, I'll get the bottom."

"Why do I always gotta get the top?"

"Because that's the part you get."

"Top part's the heaviest part."

"Get your ass up in that bed."

Ben rolled back onto his stomach.

"We need to run," he whispered.

Amana nodded in agreement.

"No," Cece whispered back. "They'll hear us."

"Mueller already heard us."

Amana pointed at Ben, nodding again.

Warner and Mueller grunted as they removed whatever it was they were removing from the bed. Their boots scraped the road.

"Shoowee! it stinks out here," Mueller said. "We've got to find a different place to do this."

Warner grunted in assent.

"I read somewhere that these things have a couple bag's worth of nitrogen in them when they break down."

They were only a foot away from the edge. Ben flattened his body. Cece curled into herself. Amana leaned back and, with a strange crunch, planted her hand in something soft and squishy. She stifled a squeal.

"Maybe we could put them in the boss lady's garden? Give her a little October surprise."

"Not funny, ET. I like her pumpkin pie."

Amana craned her neck to see what her hand had landed in. Her already terrified eyes grew wider. A little moan escaped her lips, muffled behind the mask. Cece reached out and grabbed her by the shoulder. A finger to the lips. A tight shake of the head. Then she saw the girl trembling, her heaving chest. Amana's eyes rolled to the side. Cece followed them.

It was Aiko's dead body.

Her eyes were wide and unseeing, a splash of blood had dried on her crushed skull. Amana's arm had disappeared into her chest cavity.

Warner and Mueller were at the edge of the road.

"On three," Warner said. "One—"

"Wait. Throw it on three or three and then throw it?"

"Same way we've always done it, idiot. One. Two. Three!"

Warner threw on three, but Mueller waited for a beat too long, sending the bundle spinning into the woods. It crashed into a tree and hit the ground behind Amana.

Amana yelped, muted but audible. Cece clapped a sympathetic hand over her mouth. It was another body. Long black hair was covering the face, but Cece could recognize that tattoo anywhere. Sexy tomato in the hammock.

"The fuck I say?" Warner snarled. "On three means on three!"

"Shh! This time I really did hear something."

"Jesus Christ, ET."

Boots at the edge of the road.

"Something squawked, I'm telling you."

"Probably a mouse or an opossum."

Mueller stepped onto the verge.

"Wasn't no mouse, and it sure as shit wasn't no opossum."

All he had to do was look down and he'd see Amana's hand plunged into Aiko's chest. Another inch and he'd see her face. He stared out into the darkness.

"Who's out there?"

"You really think someone'd answer that?" Warner snapped.

Ben picked his head up off the ground and looked Cece in the eye.

"Follow my lead," he whispered.

Then he popped up and yelled, "ah HA!"

Warner and Mueller jumped back with two startled grunts.

"Sucks to suck!" Ben yelled.

He grabbed Warner's leg and yanked it out from underneath him. Warner pinwheeled and fell back. His head hit the ground with a sick crack.

"Run!" Ben screamed.

Amana sprinted into the forest. Cece jumped up and followed. Ben turned to join them, but Mueller leaped forward and took him down with a flying tackle.

"You fat motherfucker!" he yelled.

"Ben!" Cece yelled.

"I'm coming! I'm—"

Mueller reared up, his knife glinting in the moon, and sank it into Ben's calf. Ben cried out and flipped onto his back. With a strength Cece didn't think he had in him, he grabbed Mueller by the lapels and threw him off.

Cece cast a look at Amana, scampering through the woods, then back to Ben. They locked eyes.

"Go!" he cried.

So she did.

She tried to catch up to Amana, but the girl scurried like a rabbit. She ducked under branches, leaped over fallen tree trunks. She caught sight of her once, lost her again, pushed forward. There! A break in the forest up ahead. Were those headlights? No. Just fireflies. Amana jumped across the threshold of the forest and disappeared into the darkness. Thirty seconds later, Cece breached the forest's edge and sprinted into a field of wildflowers. She'd made it almost twenty yards before she realized what she'd stumbled into.

Mortifloria.

Acres of it.

Pollen misted the air, and she felt woozy. Ahead, Amana plowed a course through the field, kicking up dirt, dust, and pollen. Each bloom she kicked erupted in a dark cloud, and those eruptions led to more eruptions, setting off a chain reaction until a full quarter of the field was awash in toxic spores.

"Fuck," Cece said.

She couldn't go back. That much was obvious. But if she went forward, the mortifloria would knock her flat.

Amana chose for her. She was halfway across the field, running at an even clip, when she tripped. She kissed the earth with her fingers, stumbled forward three steps, and disappeared.

Damn.

Cece clenched her fists, took a deep breath, and just as she was about to run, she heard footsteps pounding up from behind. She twisted around and saw a dark form bounding out of the woods. It zipped past her and out into the field.

Sacha.

"Sacha, no!" Cece cried.

The dog hit a patch of pollen and skidded to a halt, sneezing and shaking her head. She retreated to the forest and trotted up and down the border, growling. Amana was on her feet now, reeling and unsteady. Sacha barked again, and Vic appeared behind her, a mask strapped to his face, a shotgun leaning on his shoulder.

"Quiet Sacha!"

Cece spun.

"Vic!" she cried. "Holy shit! Mueller and Warner, they're—"

"Shut up," Vic snapped.

He barked an order at Sacha in a foreign language. Was that Russian? When the dog didn't move, Vic repeated the command, and Sacha sat down with a grumble and a whine. Cece swayed on her feet.

"What the fuck is going on, Vic?"

He looked over her shoulder at Amana's retreating form.

"Who is that?"

"Vic. Lissen to me..."

Vic marched through the flowers, stopping a few feet away from where Cece stood.

"They're killing people."

"Killing people?"

"Jake. Aiko. Harlow..."

"That's a lot of people." Vic looked over her shoulder one more time. "One more shouldn't hurt."

And he struck her in the head with the butt of his shotgun.

THE DWARF, THE WITCH, & THE TROLL

A leg rotting on a bedspring.
Blood and fluids dripping into a pan.
Terrible flowers shooting toxic clouds into the air.
An exploding ball of fungus.
Skin sloughing off a face.

Amana sat up on her cot with a cry.
It's okay. It's okay. Just a dream. It was just a dream.
She rubbed her eyes, and her hands came away yellow. She looked down at her pillow. A thick layer of pollen coated it. Her arms, her shirt, her pants, all rimed with the stuff. She shook her head, and it pattered all around. The night rushed back in.

Cece. Ben.

She swung her legs over the side of the cot, and her foot landed on something solid. The filter mask. She picked it up. The strap fell loose from the plastic buckle. Pollen crusted the inside.

She tried to recall how she'd gotten back to the yurt but came up blank. The last thing she remembered was running through the field, Cece crying out for her to stop, those weird flowers erupting with every step. Then she tripped and fell and woke up in her cot.

A thought struck her, and she searched around with her hands.

"No, no, no."

She got up, more pollen shaking loose from her hair and shoulders and drifting to the floor. She upturned her cot. Nothing. Her father's cot. Nothing. Where was it?

With no other options, Amana knew she had to head out into Yurtville. If she was lucky, nobody would be up yet, and she could slip back out and try to retrace her steps. She put her hair up in a ponytail with one of her father's stray bandanas, dusted her clothes off, checked her image in the little mirror she'd hung from one of the tent poles. A streak of yellow from her temple to her neck. She licked her fingers and rubbed it off as best she could. Re-checked the mirror. Better than nothing.

Right before she left, she turned and grabbed the filter mask and shoved it in her back pocket, then pushed through the exit and into the morning light.

Yurtville wasn't necessarily dead, but it wasn't necessarily crawling with workers. A few exited their yurts or stood in line for the shower. A couple were walking over to the field kitchen. The smell of bacon and eggs and coffee made Amana's stomach grumble. No time for that. She marched across the commons and ducked into Cece's yurt.

It was empty.

Back out into Yurtville.

A boy she'd never seen before passed by on the way to breakfast, and Amana steeled herself. Counted to three.

"Excuse me?"

The boy stopped and turned, a dopey, peaceful expression on his face, his eyebrows slightly raised.

"Can I help you?"

"I'm sorry, but do you know the girl who's staying here?"

"Girl?"

"She's a little taller than me. Short, blond hair. Kind of a bitch—"

A troubled smiled passed over the boy's face.

"I'm hungry. Aren't you hungry?"

"What?"

"There's bacon at the kitchen."

"No, listen, I need to find—"

"Break your fast, avoid the lash!"

The boy sauntered away, leaving Amana alone and shaking her head. A door slammed behind her, coming from the direction of the main house. Warner and Mueller's raised voices floated out into the morning. She couldn't hear exactly what they were saying, but judging by the arms flung in the air and the jabbing fingers, they were not discussing what to have for breakfast.

"... told you to check her yurt!" Warner yelled.

Mueller folded his arms across his chest and leaned back on the tailgate while Warner continued his tirade.

Amana spun on her heel and turned her back to them. A small crowd of workers was heading over to the field kitchen, and she jogged over and blended in. When she was sure that she was out of the line of sight from the main house, she peeled off and aimed for the hoop-house.

If there is one thing most people can agree upon, it is the acceptable volume at which certain genres of music should be played. Rock and Rap were to be cranked at maximum decibels. Country music, depending on the tune, somewhat lower. R&B and jazz were acceptable only at levels somewhere below the sounds normal people make when fucking. Smooth jazz was an abomination, and those who listened to it at any volume should have their ears revoked.

Gypsy Jazz occupied a place somewhat below the first but well above the last. Choice of venue and age of audience matters, of course, for an AC/DC cover band playing at full tilt on Bourbon Street might not go over as well as, say, Stephane Wrembrel. When it came to greenhouses, other than Mozart or perhaps St. Saëns, no music, from Armstrong to Coltrane to The Clash, should reach decibels higher than 70. Even Gypsy Jazz.

That was why, when Amana stepped into the hoop-house, it was disconcerting to hear Django Reinhardt blasting from the back office at a level that would rattle even the stoutest incus. Amana was a fan of music. She even liked what she was listening to as she tip-toed through the aisle. It was old, certainly, but the instruments—the violins, the acoustic guitars, the double bass—sounded warm and pleasing. They reminded her of her grandfather, who liked to listen to Son Cubano while he gardened in the courtyard. But when Laszlo added his warbling disharmony to the mix? She did not like that. She did not like that at all. Once she heard the lyrics, though, she couldn't help but laugh.

After you've gone and left me cryin', he sang. *After you've gone, there's no denyin'/You'll feel blue, you'll feel sad/You'll miss the dearest pal you've ever had.*

The music hit a break, and Amana called out, "Hello? Laszlo?"

Laszlo sang on.

"There'll come a time, now don't forget it/There'll come a time when you'll regret it."

The solos came in, frenetic, hyper, wild. She made her way to the back, letting the violin take its turn. At another break, she tried again.

"HELLO?"

A crack, a bang, and a cartoonish ziiiiiip of a record needle. Laszlo opened the door and peeked out.

"Hello, yes?"

"What are you doing?"

"Listening to 'After You're Gone' by the great Django Rheinhardt and the Stéphane Grappelli."

"Why are you playing it so loud?"

"Loud? Oh, yes. Loud. It is an experiment."

Laszlo opened the door a little more.

"You see, flora and fauna respond to reverberations in the air. Those less cultured think it has to do with the sweetness of the song, the timber of the trill, but that is grievously inaccurate. Specific genres of music create more or less aggressive fluctuations in the atmosphere. Cannibal Corpse, for example—"

"Okay, well." Amana flapped her arms. "I'm here to work, so what are we doing today?"

"Work?"

"Yeah, you know. Work."

"Oh! Oh, yes. Work. Work, work, work."

Laszlo cast a look around.

"Ah ha! Here we are. Please to follow, please to follow."

He led her down a few rows and into Cece's old area, the toxic plant area.

"So how are you? Did you… hm, hm. Did you sleep? Well?"

"Fine, I guess."

Under his breath, Laszlo said, "Fine, she says. Fine." Then louder: "By chance have you had anything to eat? The morning meal is the most important of the day, you know. Avoid the lash, break your—"

"I'm not hungry. Hey, did I leave a black backpack in here yesterday?"

Laszlo thrust his hands in his lab coat pocket and turned up an aisle.

"No. No, you did not. Hm. Oh, well. Today I assign you to the mums."

"Mums?" Amana looked back at the protective gear hanging on the pegboard. "Shouldn't we wear gloves and stuff?"

"Nothing to fear, my dear, nothing to fear. These are not the mortifloria. These are much, much more different. Delightful little creatures, yes. Magnificent, even."

He stopped to the right of a listing pot.

"Such a naughty little girl. Such a naughty little beastie. They're always trying to escape, you see. It is a wonder that they haven't succeeded. One day, yes? One day!"

He laughed at his own joke, that hoarse hissing laugh that made Amana simultaneously amused and nauseous.

"Forgive me, miss. I am a jokester. My dear mother once said, 'whatever shall we do with you, Laszlo? Whatever shall we do?'."

"Why are you acting so weird?" Amana asked.

Laszlo grew serious.

"Yes. People have always called me that. Weird. All but Missus. She never did. Never once. Are you familiar with the Tale of the Dwarf, the Witch, and the Troll?"

"Like Harry Potter?"

"Who?"

"Never mind."

"Hold, please."

He righted another fallen flower.

"And we're walking. So, the Tale of the Dwarf, the Witch, and the Troll. The Dwarf, the Witch, and the Troll. Hmm. How does it go? Ah! Once, there was a dwarf. A naughty little dwarf. An evil dwarf. The naughtiest, evilest dwarf in all the land."

"Oh, my god."

"And this dwarf, he worked for a naughty witch. An evil witch. The naughtiest, evilest witch in all the land. It was such a delight! They took turns, you see, testing each other with their naughtiness. And their evilness. They concocted spells, naughty spells. And they created things."

"Evil things?"

"Yes! Yes! Potions! Elixirs! Tonics of the variety strange and unusual. One day, they created the world's most naughtiest, evilest tincture. A tincture so delicious that if they released it, the whole world would quake at their feet. Unfortunately, a troll, the evilest, vilest, toadiest toad of a troll stopped them, and… Oh, here we are."

Laszlo stopped in the middle of the aisle and put a single knuckle in his mouth, studying Amana's position.

"Could you…" he said, and he took a step to his right.

Amana stepped to her left.

"And one more," he added.

They continued their dance until they both had their backs to the tables on either side of the aisle.

"This is the mortifloria," Amana said. "You said we weren't—"

"Hold, please."

Laszlo turned around to futz with a flower. Amana scanned the expanse of the hoop-house, the flowers, the exit. A pair of scissors on the floor to one side. A red plunger on the table to Laszlo's left.

"I am most definitely sorry to have to do this, young miss," Laszlo said.

Amana pulled the mask out of her back pocket.

"Do what?"

"This."

Laszlo slammed the plunger. The pump whirred to life under the floorboards. Viscous, black fluid glurped out of plastic tubes. The mortifloria stiffened, retracted, and exploded with yellow dust.

Amana jammed her eyes shut.

A leg rotting on a bedspring.
Blood and fluids dripping into a pan.
Mortifloria shooting toxins into the air.
An exploding mungwort ball.
Skin sloughing off a face.

Cece sat up with a cry.
Or she tried to.

She made it about an inch off of whatever uncomfortable piece of garbage she was lying on, but when she tried to pull her arms along with her, she couldn't. They were restrained. Chained. Chained to a rusty bedspring. Her ankles, too. Exposed beams above. An IV stand next to an oxygen tank. Gleaming instruments on a medical tray. A body hanging from a meat hook on the wall. Was that Ben? She squinted, focused. No. Diego.

She yanked on the chains, banging and screaming and straining as hard as she could, but all that did was make the springs poke in her back and legs and buttocks.

"FUCK!" she screamed.

Someone chuckled from a dark corner of the basement.

"Easy, Butch. Don't strain your vag."

"Mueller, you sonofabitch!"

Mueller strolled out of the shadows, hand on the hilt of his knife, a typically snide leer on his face. His jaw was swollen and his left eye black and blue. Cece lunged and growled, but that only made him laugh.

"Them cuffs right there is 120 grade stainless steel." He held up his key chain and gave it a little jingle. "You ain't getting out of those unless you got one of these."

"I'm gonna rip your face off."

"No, you ain't."

He stepped over to the IV bag and inspected the clamp, flicked the catheter, checked the spike.

"I swear to god Mueller, try to put that shit in my arm, and I'll take a chunk out of your fucking neck."

Mueller sighed. He stretched his shoulders, his triceps.

"You know what?"

He slammed his fist into Cece's face with a heavy right hook. Cece's head rocked to the side, gashing her cheek on an errant spring. She snapped back with a grin. Spat blood.

"Fuck you."

Another punch, another gash. Her vision went black. This time, she left her head where it lay. Mueller smiled, rubbed his hand.

"That's right. That's what it feels like to fuck with a real man."

Cece's shaking chest resolved itself into a full-on belly laugh.

"Real man!"

Mueller worked her midsection this time, aiming for her ribs. The air whuffed out of her with each blow, fists thudding meat. He backed off after a moment, wheezing, his face red, sweat dripping from his chin. Cece took a long, hoarse in-suck of air that ended in a coughing fit. Then she started laughing again. Mueller leaned over and yelled in her face.

"WHAT THE FUCK ARE YOU LAUGHING AT?"

Cece spat blood right into his eyes. He jerked back.

"Fuck!"

He punched her one last time, a haymaker that caught her in the temple. Her head hit the spring again, and her eyes rolled back in her head.

"Still feeling funny?" Mueller snarled. He snatched the spike off the IV stand and shoved it in her face. "I'm gonna stick you with this."

He grabbed her arm, spiked the vein, and wrapped some tape around it.

"Don't make me nail that down."

He turned his back to her as she writhed, shaking his punching hand and taking a few turns to cool down.

After a minute, Cece, through cracked lips and bleeding teeth, muttered, "what's in that?"

"End of the line for you, Butch." Mueller pulled her cell phone out of his back pocket. "What's your password?"

"Go fuck yourself."

"I knew you'd say something like that."

He disappeared into the shadows again. A metal scrape. He returned, waving a little pair of bolt cutters.

"Love these tiny ones. Perfect for them fence links and fingers."

Cece clenched her fists.

"Mueller—"

"Laszlo says I'm not supposed to maim ya'll too much. Says it 'contaminates the tea'."

He stepped on Cece's wrist and unclenched her fist. Then he shifted his boot so only her thumb and index finger were showing.

"But Laszlo's a pussy."

He fixed the bolt cutters to the base of Cece's index finger and snapped it off. Blood spurted. Cece screamed. Mueller picked the digit off the floor and pressed the pad onto the home button of Cece's phone. The screen lit up, showing all of her apps.

"Damn. I thought for sure I was going to have to get the thumb, too."

He stowed her finger in his front pocket with a satisfied pat.

"Little souvenir from our time together. I'll post it on Yik Yak. 'The best summer of my life'. Now, let's see what kind of music you listen to."

He scrolled through the app.

"Crap. Crap. Crap. What's this? Led Zeppelin? Butch Rugmuncher! I. Am. ImPRESSED!"

Cece couldn't stop shaking. Her lips felt numb. Her toes, too. Blood spouted out of the stump where her finger used to be.

"Gonna bleed out."

"Warner don't like me to play my music down here. Says he can't think straight. But Warner's a sad old fuck."

"Mueller—"

"I played him some Nirvana once, and do you know what he said? 'What's this guy so depressed about?'. I mean, come on." He tapped the Settings icon. "Now, where is that speaker? Ah! Here we go!"

A blistering guitar solo filled the basement, and Mueller held up his hands in mock reverence.

"There it is! Fender Strats and Marshall stacks!"

Drums crashed in with a sonic wallop, and Mueller banged his head along in time. Cece gathered up her strength and screamed as loud as she could.

"No, no. Not yet," Mueller said. "Wait for the break."

The music stopped as Cece's scream petered out, then came crashing back in as the singer wailed the opening line.

"Bam!" Mueller cried. "Fuck yeah! Come on, Butch! This is your jam."

He noticed the blood pooling on the dirt floor under Cece's hand and grimaced.

"Well, shit. That's bad. Boss lady'd kill me if you died. Here."

He jammed the bolt cutters in his back pocket and took a tourniquet from the tray.

"You do anything stupid, I'll take the thumb, too."

"Fuck you."

"Uh-huh."

He tied off her wrist and patted her palm, then he paused, gazing down upon her.

"You know, I don't necessarily like doing this. The job has its benefits, but this part?" He waved at the machinery behind him: the barrels, the hoses, the pumps. "The maintenance is a bitch, and the clean-up afterward's worse. Plus, most of you guys are actually pretty okay to work with. I even liked one or two of them, like poor Sanchez up there. But he's grist for the mill now."

He leaned over and put his hands on his knees, looked her right in her one good eye.

"But you? Boy, howdy, I'm gonna enjoy watching you rot."

Cece whispered something.

"What's that?"

She whispered again, and he leaned closer.

"Speak up, Butch. I can't—"

Cece shot up and chomped into his cheek with her teeth. Mueller screamed and pulled back. Cece clamped down harder. Blood spurted. She thrashed her head back and forth like a dog and tore a chunk of his flesh off of his face. Mueller staggered backward, his hand flying up to cover the wound.

"You cunt!"

Cece spat the chunk out, laughing, her mouth and chin glassy with blood.

"I told you I was gonna do it!"

Mueller threw himself at her, grabbed her by the shirt, and punched her in the face. Her head rocked back. He did it again. She stopped laughing at the third blow. He pulled his arm back for one more punch when someone yelled, "hey!"

Mueller twisted around.

Amana was there, covered in blood, a shovel already swung up over her shoulder.

"Pendejo," she said, and she smashed him in the head.

Mueller flew to the side and crumpled to the ground. Amana stalked over and straddled his body. Raised the shovel over her head like a championship golfer. Mueller held his arms out.

"Wait!"

Amana brought the shovel down in a sweeping arc, striking him in the temple with a sick crack. Mueller went limp. She stood there, panting, waiting for him to move.

"Amana," Cece said. "Amana. Help."

Amana stepped away from Mueller's body and took in what he'd done to her. Her eyes fell on Cece's hand.

"You need something to cover that."

"No. Cut me loose first."

"How?"

"Keys. In his pocket."

Amana hesitated.

"Amana!"

"Okay, okay!"

Mueller still hadn't moved. A mark in the shape of the shovel, already turning purple, had formed on his face. They watched and waited. Ten seconds. Fifteen. His chest hitched, rose, and fell.

"Back pocket," Cece said.

Amana reached under him with a grimace, worked the keys out. It took a moment to find the right one, but she found it and unlocked the cuffs. Left wrist, left foot. Right foot, right wrist. She helped Cece sit up.

"Can you stay up on your own?"

"I don't know. I think I can."

Amana turned toward the body of her father hanging on the wall.

"I have to get him down."

"Amana, we have to get out of—"

"I'm not leaving him here, okay!"

Cece held out her good hand.

"Okay. Okay."

"Just wait here. I'll do it myself."

The rope Mueller used to haul her father up to the hook was still looped under his armpits. It ran up through a pulley in the ceiling, then back down to a winch bolted to the concrete floor.

Behind her, Cece limped over to Mueller's body and knelt, wincing. On his belt, her father's knife, still sheathed. She unbuckled the strap and took it out.

"Amana," she said, limping over. "Let me help."

They lowered him down faster than Cece thought they'd be able to. After she cut the zip ties binding Diego's hands and feet, she helped Amana turn him over, then limped away and leaned up against a beam. She closed her eyes and tried to focus on her breathing. The white noise of the basement was almost soothing. Amana's gentle weeping was not. She wanted to clean and dress the stump of her finger, but that wasn't an option. Her finger. That sonofabitch was still holding onto it. She half-turned, half-stumbled around, intending to retrieve it, and came face to face with Mueller himself. Blood coated one side of his face, and his swollen jaw was out of place.

"Bitches," he slurred.

He backhanded Cece, sending her tripping back toward Amana, who stood and caught her. Mueller shook his head, trying to clear it. A rill of blood ran down from his forehead and into his eye. He wiped it off on his shoulder.

"Would ya lookee here. Gonna get myself a hat trick."

Cece smiled, her teeth red with blood. She beckoned to him.

"Come on, asshole."

"You numb cunt. Never knock a man out and leave him with his favorite weapon."

He reached for his knife, and his face went slack. He looked at his belt, confused, and then, no longer confused, looked up. Cece was holding the blade out at him.

"Numb cunt?" she said.

MÉRIDA

Cece hated everything leading up to flying. Two hours to get through security. An hour to board. Thirty minutes to wait for take-off. It almost seemed like it would be more worth it to drive if the drive didn't take eight times as long. But now that she was up in the air, she could finally relax. The flight to Mérida, after a three-hour layover in Houston, was long enough for her to do some reading about the area, maybe go over the plan.

She raised the shade with her bandaged hand, wincing at the pain. No matter how many times she saw her missing digit, she couldn't believe it was gone. She inspected it, turning it over in the bright light coming in from the portal. Mueller's cut was clean but diagonal, and the surgeon had had to snip it down even farther. But that morning, the stub seemed to be pushing against the bandage, and when she removed the wrap, it looked different, like it had gained a centimeter. Clearly it hadn't, but maybe…

Ugh.

No use thinking about it. Might as well enjoy the view. They were too high to see anything but clouds. The blue skies were still beautiful, though. After a minute, she closed the shade and leaned her seat back as far as it would go, which didn't prove to be very far at all. Still, she was a little sleepy. Maybe she'd just close her eyes for a minute. A quick nap wouldn't hurt, not in the face of what she was about to do.

It only felt like Cece had closed her eyes for a second before she was back in Lilith's basement. Mueller lay at her feet, his body twisted, his eyes fixed and staring. Her arms were covered with blood, his blood, her blood. Someone was shaking her shoulder. A voice in her ear, muted and warped.

"Cece! CECE!"

It took all of her strength to shake herself present. It was Amana.

"Are you okay?" the girl asked.

When Cece spoke, her voice was slow and slurred.

"Yeah, I think so."

Amana went over to Mueller's body and kicked him in the head.

"Asshole."

She kicked him again. Spit on his face. Cece watched, impassive, trying to shake the fog out of her mind. They weren't in the clear yet. Warner was still out there. Lilith and Laszlo, too. That asshole, Vic. And this place. They couldn't just let it stand.

She shuffled around, looking for something, anything. There had to be some old gas cans down there. Maybe some kerosene. They could use the old nudie mags in those boxes under—her eyes fell on oxygen tanks next to the rusty bed spring. She dipped her hand, her good hand, into her pocket, and took out a lighter. Vic's lighter. Her face lit up.

Cece startled awake. The plane had hit some turbulence, a real rough patch at that, and the entire cabin had let up a collective gasp. The fasten seatbelt sign lit up with a bing, and the captain's voice came over the intercom.

"Attention all passengers, this is your captain speaking. We're heading into some mild weather. We're going to climb to 38,000 feet to get over it. At this time, the fasten seatbelt sign is up. Please remain seated."

Cece cleared her throat and sat up straighter. She looked out the window as the plane climbed higher. The sky had gone dark. The clouds turned black. A bolt of lightning flashed in the distance.

"First time flying?"

Cece turned to her right, eyebrows raised. The old woman in the middle seat was looking at her, an expectant smile on her face.

"Excuse me?" Cece asked.

"I said 'first time flying'?"

"Oh, no. I've flown a lot, thanks."

"My husband and I are going to Mérida."

"Aren't we all?"

"It's our fiftieth anniversary, isn't it, dear?"

The old woman patted the shoulder of the equally old man next to her. He was out cold, his mouth slightly open, head lolling on the rest. The woman tsked.

"Franklin could sleep through a hurricane."

"Mm."

"My name's Marjorie."

"Mm."

"And you are?"

"Poppy."

"Well, Poppy, if you get anxious, I have some mortifloria oil."

Cece snapped alert.

"Some what?"

"Floria oil."

The old woman dug around in her purse and withdrew a brown vial with a rubber stopper.

"Just one drop and all your worries disappear."

Cece took it.

"Where did you get this?"

"It just showed up on one of my feeds. I've been taking it for months."

Cece scoured the label.

Floria Oil! Brought to you by SingleCorp. A fresh, herbaceous aroma has a long-standing history of calming the mind and body. Floria is wonderful for relaxing all of your fears and concerns. Benefits & Uses Include: May reduce tension, system imbalance, migraines, respiratory illness.

Tired of all the nonsense on your feed? Stressed out about cancel culture? CRT? Floria is an excellent remedy for the progress of our modern times.

"I take at least two drops a day," the old woman said. "In fact…"

She retrieved the vial from Cece's hand, unstoppered the top, and squeezed two drops on her tongue.

"Gotta trust the plan."

"Plan? What plan?"

Another lightning bolt lit up the sky. Another patch of turbulence shook the plane. The old woman patted Cece's hand.

They waited until dark to execute their plan. A slow leak in the single oxygen tank. Vic's lighter sitting on the workbench, the flame up as high as it could go. The first explosion hit just as Cece squeezed through the break in the fence. Two more followed as she and Amana made their way up the drive, Amana in the lead, Cece lurching behind. The orange glow of the fire illuminated the dark sky over the tops of the trees.

"Amana wait," Cece called.

"Hurry up!"

Cece pressed a hand to her side. She knew her ribs were broken, how many, she wasn't sure, but every step was agony. Her hand throbbed and her vision swam. She was struggling so hard to keep up that she didn't hear the approaching engine until it was too late. A pair of headlights rounded the corner in front of them, and then Vic's truck was there, pinpointing Amana in the dark. Without a second thought, Amana bolted for the woods. Vic skidded to a stop and popped out of the cab, shotgun in hand. He planted himself firmly in front of the grill, aimed the gun over Amana's head, and triggered a blast. Amana skidded to a halt.

"Vic, don't!" Cece yelled.

She stumbled toward him, one hand out. Sacha barked and snarled in the cab, her teeth pressed against the passenger side glass.

He belted her in, Cece thought. *Here he is, about to kill us, and he belted his dog in.*

"Come on over here, little girl," Vic said. "Join your friend in the road."

Vic leveled his shotgun at Amana as she backed up, hands raised. He glanced up at the orange glow burning above the trees.

"You stupid bitches. What'd you do?"

"It's over, Vic," Cece said. "Just let us go."

He gazed at her, a hint of a smile on his face.

"No, I don't think I'm gonna do that."

He pumped a fresh round into the chamber, the used shell flying out to the side. Amana moaned.

"She's just a kid, Vic!"

"What's your point?"

He put the stock on his shoulder, squinted one eye closed. Sacha's bark turned into high-pitched squeals. Cece put out her hand. Amana squeezed her eyes closed. Vic's finger rested on the trigger. He let out a long breath.

Then the noise of another engine revving sounded in the night.

"What the fuck is that?" Vic said.

He lowered his shotgun as Warner's truck rounded the bend from the direction of the farm. Amana's eyes flashed open. She saw the lowered gun and bolted again.

"Fuck!" Vic cried.

He swung the barrel at her. With a growl, Cece leaped for him, knocking the gun up as he shot. The blast deafened her ears. Vic hit her in the back of the head with the stock, and she went down hard.

"You dumb fucking cunt!" Vic yelled.

Warner hit the gas, tires spitting gravel, aiming right for the pair. Vic shot it a look, frowning.

"What the fuck?" he said.

The truck slipped into third, picked up speed, and too late, Vic realized it was aiming for him. Cece rolled to the side. Vic swung his shotgun around, letting out a scream as the truck slammed into his body. He flew into the grill, his head smacked the hood, and he crumbled to the ground, his back twisted at an obscene angle.

Cece rolled onto her back on the verge. All she could hear was Sacha's hysterical barking and Warner's grumbling truck. He cut the engine. She heard him open the door.

"Cece?"

Holy shit.

She sat up with a groan.

"Ben?"

She saw Marjorie and Franklin one more time, standing in line at Customs. Marjorie gave her a wink and a little wave. Cece ignored her. Cece skirted through easily. She only had her backpack. She stopped at a snack bar called Snack Bar and ordered a snack at the bar.

Anything else? the bartender asked.

A beer, she said. *A big beer.*

The bartender popped the top off of a Dos Equis and set it down in front of her. She took a big mouthful and swished it around, relishing the taste. She had just finished the last swig when two men sidled up next to her. She looked up at one. Then the other.

"Boys."

The men all but frog-marched Cece out of the airport. When they ushered her out of the front doors, a black SUV rolled up to the curb. One got in the front. The other opened the back door. A handsome man wearing dark sunglasses was sitting on the far side of the middle bench, looking out the window.

Mr. Miguel? Cece's escort said. *She's here.*

Miguel took off his glasses and turned from the window, a smile on his face.

Please, Ms. Stone. Come in. Have a seat.

Cece shrugged her bag off her shoulder, but when her escort tried to take it, she pulled it away. He glanced at Miguel.

It's fine, Jose, Miguel said.

Jose released the bag and motioned for Cece to enter the car.

After you, he said.

They drove out of the airport and onto the highway, heading, as far as Cece could tell, southwest. She peeked at Miguel. He looked almost exactly like his brother. Their eyes were the same color, and their noses had the same flat end. But where Diego's face was round, Miguel's was oval. Where Diego had short, thick, almost curly hair, Miguel's was long and thin, and she could see the beginnings of a widow's peak forming. Miguel caught her looking, and she dropped her eyes. He smiled.

You certainly made an impression on my niece.

Amana's a very special kid.

That she is. Although I must say, Ms. Stone, you frightened my wife showing up like you did. How did you get past my security?

Cece smiled to herself.

Family secret.

Miguel pulled back, his brow furrowed. Then he burst out laughing.

You hear that, Jose? Family secret!

Yes, boss.

Miguel wiped his eyes under his sunglasses.

Still, you must know that people in my line of business don't like to have unannounced visitors.

I'm sure Amana explained why.

A solemn nod.

This woman. Lilith? She's the one who killed my brother?

Yes.

And you're sure she's down here, living in… he snapped at Jose. *What's the name of this place?*

Rancho de Dragones.

Dragones?

Yes, boss.

Who the fuck names their farm something like that?

I think it's her last name, Cece said. *Lilith Drake. It means "night monster."*

Miguel shot her a look.

I looked it up, she added. *And, yes. I'm sure she's here.*

Stunned by Ben's appearance, Cece let her mouth drop open.

"Don't look so happy to see me," he quipped.

"Ben, what the fuck are you doing here?"

"Saving your life."

"No, I mean, I thought you were dead."

Ben looked over her shoulder.

"Hey, Amana."

"You're alive?" Amana said.

"Barely."

"Ben," Cece said. "The last time I saw you, Mueller was stabbing you in the back."

"You fought him off, didn't you," Amana said. "That's why he had that black eye."

"Is that true?" Cece asked.

"Yeah, yeah," Ben said. "Actually, no."

He told them how after he tripped and fell, Mueller pounced on him and stabbed him in the leg.

"Then he stabbed me in the shoulder. I think he was aiming for my neck. He was about to stab me again when Warner cried, 'Mueller, goddammit! What the fuck is going on!'

"That distracted him, so I pushed up off the ground as hard as I could and sent him flying. Ran off into the woods and hid until I was sure they weren't going to look for me. I don't know why they didn't.

"This morning, I went for a swim in the pond. When I was all healed up, I snuck into the pantry in the big house and waited until it got dark. I thought maybe I'd try to hoof it into town, but then I remembered Warner always left his keys in his truck, and, well, here we are."

Another explosion from Lilith's house rocked the ground, and a fireball shot up over the trees.

"Good thing I left when I did," he added.

"Yeah, well, good thing that bitch is dead."

"Who, Lilith? No, she wasn't in there."

Both Amana and Cece said, "what?" at the same time.

"I heard her talking to Warner this morning. Said something about catching a flight south." He shrugged. "Guess she has another one of these in Alabama or something."

"No," Cece said. "Not Alabama."

Let me see it, Miguel said.

Cece unzipped her bag and was about to reach inside when Jose leaned over the seat and engulfed her wrist in his meaty paw.

"Dude, what the fuck?" Cece snapped.

It's okay, Jose, Miguel said.

You sure, boss?

Let her go.

Jose released Cece's wrist and sat back. One hand slipped into his jacket.

Cece reached into the bag and pulled out the torn scrap of cardboard she'd ripped off the box in Lilith's basement. The one with the Russian name and Mexican address on it. Miguel looked at it, then pinned his eyes to the bloody bandage covering the stump of her index finger.

You should see the other guy, Cece said.

Miguel smirked. Cece handed him the flap.

A name. An address, he said. *That's it?*

Contrary to the stereotype, Karen did not see very many cops hanging out in diners. At least not the ones she liked to frequent. When they did show up, it wasn't to shove donuts in their faces or eat fried food but to respond to a fight (she should have been more mystified by the number of drunk people who liked to eat pancakes and start fights in diners at three in the morning), or to grab a cup of mid-shift coffee. She nodded if she ever caught their eyes, but mostly she hunkered down in the corner whenever they showed up, kept her head down and her hat down lower.

One night toward the end of August, two of them took up residence at the counter where they ordered coffee and half-flirted with the waitress. Karen kept close tabs on them, careful to never meet their eyes when they looked over, which, over the course of thirty minutes, they did five times. They blew on their coffees but didn't drink. When one got up to go to the bathroom, which was behind Karen's booth, Karen found something interesting to read on her phone.

"You a trucker?"

Shit.

Karen looked up. The other officer had turned on his stool to face her. One hand was on the counter, but the other rested on his thigh.

"What?"

"I asked if you were a trucker."

A siren ramped up in the distance. Karen tilted her head to listen.

"Nah. I'm not a trucker."

"What do you do, then?"

"Do I have to answer that?"

"I'm just asking because I see you here a lot."

"You been watching me?"

The officer smiled, just a twitch in the corner of his mouth, but a smile nonetheless.

"Not like that."

Karen blew on her coffee. The siren was growing closer. A firetruck. Or an ambulance. Fuck. She was going to have to find a different web.

"I'm a headhunter," she said.

"Headhunter?"

"For a foreign multi-international technology conglomerate."

"Huh. Where from?"

"Moscow."

"That explains the night owl."

"Sure does."

The officer's radio squawked, and he turned it off.

"Do you mind if I show you a picture?"

"Look, officer, I'm just trying to enjoy my coffee in—"

He was already up, extending a flyer to her.

"It's a missing kid. We've been plastering these things all over the county. It'll just take a second."

Karen eyed the flyer. Then, with a sigh, she took it, looked at it, her heart beating faster than it should.

"Sorry, don't recognize her."

When the second fire truck sped by, the officer took notice.

"Your bat signal awaits," Karen said.

"Hey, Jim." It was the second officer, hurrying out of the bathroom. "We gotta go. Huge fire out at the old Drake property."

Officer Jim took the flyer back.

"Thanks for the help. Good luck with the hunting."

Karen stared at her coffee as they paid the tab and gathered up their hats. The cowbell on the door rattled, and then they were gone. She didn't breathe easily until their cruiser squealed out of the parking lot, siren blaring. The waitress came over, one hand on a cocked hip and a steaming coffeepot in the other.

"You want a refill, hon?"

"Sure."

The cowbell rattled again as the waitress poured.

"Be with you in a jiff!"

Jeez, Karen thought. *This place is a regular train station tonight.*

The waitress finished pouring and spun away.

Standing behind her were Cece and Amana.

Both were covered in blood, both gripping bone-handle knives. Karen nodded as if she'd been expecting them. She picked up her mug, steam rising off of the surface.

"Alright then," she said. "Let's get this over with."

Ben was leaning on Karen's truck, the legendary F250, when the diner door flew open. Amana came out first, then Karen, then Cece, limping behind. It was so late that even the traffic on 95 had died down considerably. The only cars in the lot belonged to the waitress and the cook, both of which were parked under the lone functioning light pole. A motorcycle revved to life somewhere nearby. Ben bumped himself off the truck.

"Holy shit, I remember her."

"You mind keeping your fat ass off my truck?" Karen said. "I just had that waxed."

Cece pushed her shoulder.

"Shut up, Karen."

"You're Cece, right? The one with the karate boyfriend."

"I said shut up."

"Guess I underestimated you, huh?"

"Passenger side," Cece said as they came upon the truck. "Ben?"

Ben pulled a machete from the farm out of the truck bed.

"Ready."

Cece pressed her knife into the small of Karen's back.

"Give me your keys."

"Alright, alright."

Karen reached into her front pocket. Cece pressed her knife in harder. Karen hissed.

"Take it easy, Cece."

"Slowly."

Karen did as she was told. The fob hung from a ring on her finger.

"Give them to the girl," Cece said.

"What is she, twelve?"

"Thirteen," Amana said.

"Well, excuse me."

Ben put his blade up under her chin. Karen dropped her keys into Amana's open palm, and Amana trotted around to the driver's side, pressing the button on the fob. The car beeped, the doors unlocked.

"Just like we discussed, Amana," Cece said.

"Got it."

Cece stepped around to face Karen. She pulled out her phone, swiped at the screen, and started recording.

"What's your name?"

"Is this really necessary?

Ben pressed the blade into her throat.

"What's your name?" Cece repeated.

"Karen Boemer."

"Who do you work for?"

Karen cleared her throat.

"Lilith Drake."

"And who does she work for?"

Confusion crossed Karen's face.

"Lilith doesn't work for anybody."

Cece pulled the torn flap out of her back pocket, the one with the Russian name and Mexico address.

"Is this where she is?"

Karen's eyes betrayed her.

"Thought so. Amana?"

"I found the mask but not the other stuff," Amana replied.

"Keep looking. It should be behind the dash."

A cracking sound came from inside the cab.

"If she trashes my truck, I swear to god—"

Ben slashed Karen's face with the tip of the machete.

"Gah! Fuck!"

Karen slapped her hand over the wound.

"*Der'mo*! You guys are fucking dead! Do you know who I work for?"

"You said you worked for Lilith."

Karen laughed. She wiped off the blood running down her face.

"That was a lie, you dumb cunt."

"I know."

Cece circled around and kicked her in the side of her knee. Karen crumbled to the ground. Ben put the machete on the back of her neck.

"No way are you really going to do that out in the open," Karen said. "They'll lock you up and make you ride the lightning."

"We're dead anyway, right?"

"Found it!" Amana called.

"Bring it over here."

Amana came around the truck wearing Karen's filter mask and holding a bag of yellow powder. Cece focused her camera on Karen.

"Now tell me where this is, or we're going to douse you with your fairy dust."

"Fuck you."

Cece considered kicking her again, but the one she already delivered had strained her ribs, so she nodded at Amana.

"Alright. Go ahead, Amana."

Cece opened up her camera app, found the video, and hit play with her middle finger. Karen's face, encrusted with yellow pollen and streaked with blood, filled the screen. The lens zoomed out. She was kneeling on the blacktop. When she spoke, her voice was slow and slurred, and her eyes were barely open.

"Jeez. Did'ja use the whole bag?"

Cece spoke off-camera.

"State your name."

"My name's… KAREN BOEMER!"

But she didn't pronounce it like an American: CARE-IN BOW-MER, but rather KAH-RIN BOO-MUYER. She broke down into peals of laughter.

"Stop laughing, Karen."

Karen stopped abruptly.

"Where are you from?"

"Moskva."

"And what are you doing here?"

"I'm a headhunter for a multi-international technology conglomerate."

Off-camera, Ben said, "what the fuck, man?"

"What's the name of the company?" Cece asked.

"SingleCorp."

"Is this who Lilith works for?"

Karen swayed on her knees and shook her head hard, like a dog trying to rid itself of a pest.

"I… can't…"

"Does Lilith work for SingleCorp?"

Karen put her hands up to her head. A drop of blood fell out of her nose and she moaned.

"Karen, stop."

"It's like bees!"

"STOP."

"Don't ask me that anymore!"

"Okay, I won't."

Karen, hunched over on her knuckles, stopped moaning. A final drop of blood on the blacktop. A siren in the distance. Ben spoke again.

"Cece."

"I know."

"We've got to get out of here."

"I said I know. Karen, sit up straight."

Karen rose sharply off the pavement. A rustling sound, then the flap of cardboard replaced Karen on the screen. The lens adjusted, and then the Russian name and Mexican address came into focus. Cece flipped it so Karen could see.

"Is this where Lilith is?"

Karen was swaying again, muttering to herself, her eyes closed.

"Hey!"

Karen's eyes snapped open.

"Is this where Lilith is?"

"Yeesssss."

"What is this place?"

"That place?"

"Yes."

Karen chuckled again, and the chuckle turned into laughter.

"Answer the question, Karen."

"That place? That place is the end of the world!"

She leaned back and shouted it to the sky.

"THE END OF THE WORLD! THE END OF THE WORLD! THE END OF THE WORLD!"

The camera shook and dropped, and right before she stopped recording, Cece said, "knock her out, Amana."

Miguel glanced at Cece as she put her phone away.

What the fuck was that?

You tell me.

She's crazy.

I'd say the same thing if I was you.

What did you give her?

It's called mortifloria pollen.

Floria? Like in the ads?

Cece blinked.

You're the second person to tell me that. What ads?

Miguel motioned at Jose, who said, *On it, boss,* and started tapping away at his phone. He reached over the headrest to show them. A picture of a man doing a cartwheel on the beach popped up on the screen. FEEL BETTER THE NATURAL WAY WITH FLORIA! Improved MOOD, Incredible ENERGY, Decreased ANXIETY. Tired of doctors prescribing pills that don't work? Ineffective Therapies emptying your wallet and your patience? Try ESSENCE OF FLORIA! Because the world is a scary place, and you just want to take it easy.

Holy shit, Cece said.

Jose pulled his phone back.

You say the lady who's responsible for this is growing it in the peninsula?

Proof's on the video. If you don't believe me—

I believed you before, Ms. Stone. Amana said I can trust you, so I trust you.

Good. I've got your money, too. I gave it to Amana to hold on to.

Miguel scoffed.

I don't want your money. I only want one thing. When you're done with that crazy bitch, hand her over to me.

That wasn't the deal.

Miguel sucked his teeth and looked out the window.

It is now.

Lilith lay back in her tub and rested her head on the waterproof pillow on the edge. It had been a hard week. The flight to the peninsula was delayed, she missed her connection, and she had to spend the night in Peoria of all places. Then when she finally made it to the ranch, the staff hadn't been informed of her late arrival and had all been sent home. And now she received news of the catastrophe in Virginia. A direct call from Warner himself. The poor man sounded like he was going to soil himself. The first thing he said was, "it's gone."

"I'm sorry, who is this?"

"You know goddamn well who this is."

"I can only assume this is Mr. Warner, yes?"

"Will you stop playing games and listen to me? The farm is gone."

"What are you talking about?"

"Burned down. The house, the farm, the land all around it. The whole place went up like a roman candle."

Lilith sat down hard. Her mind traveled to a hundred places all at once. Warner kept jabbering away, talking about the police showing up, the bodies they found in the aftermath.

"I think it was ET. No, I'm sure it must have been him. Him and that spic ya'll done in. Thanks for telling me about that, by the way.

It's okay, though. They found the oxygen tanks. I told them you had emphysema. They ruled it an—"

"And the hoop-house?"

"What?"

"The nursery? My babies? Are they okay?"

"That actually made it. Most of it. All that glass and steel, I think."

Lilith let out a breath.

"Good. Let Laszlo know I've been made aware of the situation, and—"

"Yeah, about him."

Lilith closed her eyes. Paused.

"Go on."

"Do I have to spell it out?"

Warner's voice dimmed as Lilith's world closed in around her. Laszlo? Dead? That couldn't be. He was the lynchpin of all of this. She caught a snippet of something Warner said, something about having found Laszlo's body in the nursery, and snapped to attention.

"You mean he didn't die in the fire?"

"No. I told you. I found him in the hoop-house."

"Did his creatures get to him?"

"No, I don't think so."

"How do you know?"

"Unless them things can wield scissors and stab him in the temple, I think it was someone else."

Lilith let that sink in.

"It was her, wasn't it?"

A statement, not a question.

"Maybe. She's nowhere to be found. Her fag hag friend, too."

Lilith stared out into space, trying to take it all in. A car horn honked on Warner's end.

"Mr. Warner? Are you on a public phone?"

"You think I'm fuckin' stupid? I bought a burner."

"But you're out in public, yes?"

"I'm sittin' on a bench in Hurkamp. What the fuck difference does it—"

Lilith pressed the End Call button.

Now she was lying in a clawfoot tub in the middle of her massive private bathroom. Handmade tiles (imported from Peru!) decorated the floors and walls. The shower featured twenty heads designed to keep her body constantly massaged by hot water. Up a short step in the corner sat a golden toilet. A golden toilet with a gold-plated bidet.

Tchaikovsky's Symphony No. 6 played on her stereo Hi-Fi. A glass of white wine rested on the stand next to the tub. Candles flickered and glowed. Water dripped and plashed as she reached for the wine. She took a sip and exhaled, letting the alcohol and the music work their magic. The symphony moved into its ninth minute, the sweet woodwinds lulling her deeper and deeper, fading into an impossible quiet. She was on the verge of sleep, that blissful moment when the body was completely relaxed, the mind empty of all worries and cares, when someone spoke up.

"Pathétique?"

The horns blasted in with a ferocious shot. Lilith sat up with a gasp. Cece was standing next to the wi-fi, reading the back of the record sleeve. She tossed it aside with a bandaged hand.

"Sounds about right," she said. "Given the company."

Lilith regained her composure. She leaned back in the tub, her arms draped along the edges.

"Cece Stone. What a wonderful surprise."

"Mm."

"I'd ask you how you found me, but it seems like a moot point. Whatever it is you're planning on doing, you should know that my bodyguard is right outside in the hall."

"Yeah, about that." Cece addressed the locked door. "Jose?"

The door burst open, and Jose heaved Lilith's dead bodyguard inside. His eyes were wide open, and blood washed down his slashed throat. Lilith stared at the body in horror.

"Everything okay?" Jose asked.

"Yeah," Cece said.

"I'll leave you to it."

He closed the door with a gentle click, leaving them in silence. Cece plonked a wooden dressing stool next to the tub and sat down. She withdrew her knife from the sheath on her belt. Lilith pulled her knees up to her chest, shrinking as far back as possible.

"Gold toilet, huh?" Cece asked.

"Cece, please."

Cece lashed out and slapped Lilith across the face. The old woman's head rocked to the side, and she started to weep. Cece pulled a plastic bag filled with yellow powder out of her pocket and held it up next to her knife.

"Pick your poison."

TURN THE PAGE FOR AN EXCERPT FROM
THE HIVE

BEST DOG I EVER HAD

When most people think of an alien invasion, they think of the dumb movies Hollywood pumps out every summer. Robots and spacesuits. Lasers and spaceships. What they don't think of is the thing that dropped onto our neighbor Mr. Gomez's farm and smashed his barn to smithereens, along with his horses, his pigs, his goats, and probably about a zillion rats. We didn't see it happen, Daddy and me, but we felt it. It was seven o'clock on a Wednesday morning, and I was laid up with a broken leg on the couch, dozing in and out while I watched sitcom reruns on the TV. *Hogan's Heroes. Gilligan's Island. The Love Boat.*

The broken leg came courtesy of Ruth Grace Hogg, starting fullback for the Caroline Cavaliers' Varsity Girl's Field Hockey team. I played forward for the Spotsylvania Knights, and for good reason, too. I lived in Spotsy, for one, and I was fleet and fast and good with my stick. Unfortunately, I didn't weigh much more than a hundred pounds. Ruth Grace Hogg tipped the scales at about a buck ninety. I had legs like a colt. She had arms like a gorilla.

When she saw little old me cutting up her team, she knew what she was about. She ran up to me, cocked them big hairy arms of hers, and whacked my leg like it was a piñata. Two hours later, I was laid up at home on the couch, two pins in my femur and forty mgs of Vicodin in my head.

"Ain't you going to do something about it, Daddy?"

Daddy was in the kitchen, sipping a cup of coffee.

"Like what?"

"I don't know. Complain to the school board. Call the president."

"I'll get on my personal line to him directly."

"It's rude to tease an invalid. Can't you talk to her parents?"

Daddy looked like someone had just asked him to solve a calculus problem with a fish.

"Why'd I want to do something like that?"

"Because I'm your daughter. And she broke my leg. On purpose."

Daddy chuckled and shook his head.

"'Manda, you know I love you, right?"

"I'm starting to question the depths of that love."

"Well I do. But let me ask you something. You do know how much Ruth Grace Hogg weighs, right?"

"Who don't? The whole county shakes when she gets out of bed in the morning."

"And you know how much you weigh, right?"

I waited a long time before I answered.

"Yeah."

"I couldn't be more proud of you. You had you a job, and you didn't let nothing back you down. But you did try to run down someone nearly twice your size, and you lost. So let that be a lesson to you."

"I thought you said you were proud of me?"

"I am."

"So why're you telling me to back off the next time?"

"I didn't say that."

I ever tell you Daddy could be infuriating? I sighed, took a deep breath, and said, "You mind telling me what you are telling me, then?"

"Next time," he said. "Run faster."

So anyway, the invasion.

It was late summer, and school hadn't even started yet. The August heat and humidity weighed down on everything like a wet blanket. Our house was built in 1921, as Daddy was fond of telling just about everybody who cared to listen. To him, that was an accomplishment. To me, it meant that nearly everything was broken or breaking down. The pipes froze every winter, the windows were like sieves, and in the summer we didn't have air conditioning. Oh, Daddy did his best. He planted a couple of recycled, wheezing window units in the windows, kept them alive with a healthy application of duct tape and freon, but all they did was make a racket while blowing not-really-cold air a few feet into the house.

Daddy'd just come in from loading Sparkles up into his truck, Sparkles being an old dog of his he'd gotten stuffed. It was a sad day for the old girl. The years had been unkind, and she stank. Daddy brought her to his regular taxidermist to fix the issue, but she gave him some sorry news: old Sparkles was rotting.

"Well, no shit, she's rotting," Daddy said. "She's been dead fifteen years."

Apparently pointing out the obvious didn't improve Sparkles' condition. It was finally time to lay her to rest, and Daddy was going to do it Spotsy style. He got himself ahold of a remote-controlled detonator and some explosives—cherry bombs and fertilizer and the like—and stuffed her full to the brim. The plan was simple. He and his friends were going to drive Sparkles out to the country, set her up in a field, get drunk, and blow her up.

Daddy showed me the detonator as if seeing it would make me want to go.

"You sure you don't want to come?"

"No thanks."

"Alright then."

He put it in his back pocket and went over to fill his thermos up with coffee. That's when I felt this horrible pressure build in the air. It pushed down on me, like the atmosphere itself had gone feral and decided to attack. I held my hands to my ears, but the pressure kept building and building. I opened my mouth to scream but couldn't hear anything at all. Then it released and I could hear again. A sonic boom thundered in the distance, and the house shook and rattled and nearly jumped off the foundation. I thought it was an earthquake. Or maybe Ruth Grace Hogg having a fit. I almost fell off the couch. Plates and cups clattered in the cabinets, and Daddy's ham radio fell over and cracked on the floor. Then it fell quiet and still. I pulled myself into sitting position.

"What the hell was that?"

Daddy was kind of squatting down, hands out, looking like he was waiting for another blast. His overalls were covered in coffee.

"I dunno. And don't say hell."

"You say it all the time."

The phone rang and I gasped. I could tell he wanted to chew me out, but something big had just happened, and when the phone rang after something big had just happened, you answer it.

"Aw hell," he said and snatched it off its cradle. "Yeah? Yeah, Gomez, I felt it."

He covered the mouthpiece and mouthed "It's Gomez" to me like I couldn't hear. Gomer Gomez. Our next-door neighbor. (Out here a next-door neighbor could live ten miles away.) I turned my attention back to the TV. We didn't have a remote. Not that I minded. We was lucky to even get a signal at all. I struggled off the couch and hopped over to change the channels. I was looking to see if any of the local news stations were making a special broadcast. Channel 4, nothing.

Channel 7, nothing. Channel 9, nothing. Daddy kept jawing away in the kitchen.

"Calm down, Gomez. I can't understand a word you're . . . Uh-huh. Your whole barn? Uh-huh. You get a look at . . . no, I wouldn't go out there. It'd be best if you didn't. I can't, I got 'Manda here, and she's got a—" Gomez screamed something and Daddy pulled the phone away from his ear with a grimace. "Gomez? You there? Damn." And he hung up the phone.

"What's wrong with Mr. Gomez?"

"Says a spaceship landed on his barn."

Daddy went over to his gun safe and started dialing in the combination.

"Spaceship?"

"Uh-huh."

"Out here?"

"Uh-huh."

"Damn."

"Dammit, 'Manda."

"He say what it looks like?"

"Uh-huh."

"You mind telling me?"

"Said it looked like a big wasp's nest."

The gun safe unlocked with a click, and he pulled it open and started grabbing boxes of ammo. Then he took out his favorite Remington .30 .06 and slung it over his shoulder and put a couple of .357's in a bag.

"You gonna kill it?"

"Gonna try."

"Can I come?"

"You're gonna stay right here, young lady."

"Why?"

"Because you're all busted up. And if there really is a spaceship out there that looks like a wasp's nest, there ain't much you'll be able to do."

"I can shoot one of them .357s."

"I know."

"Aren't you the one who always said its better to have a man on your six?"

"Yeah, I did say that."

Daddy was already putting on his jacket and hat. He was halfway out the door.

THE HIVE

"You really think Mr. Gomez's gonna have yours?"

That made him stop. Daddy wasn't that much of a thinker. I don't mean he was dumb because he wasn't. I mean that when a decision needed to be made, he liked to make it fast. Just like that, he said, "If you can get out to the car before I leave, you can come with me."

Mr. Gomez's farm was down Brock Road a stretch, just past Todd's Tavern. Take a few turns back toward Locust Grove, a few back roads, and there it was. Fifty acres smack dab in the middle of Spotsylvania County Virginia, the northernmost southern county in the whole damn state.

Daddy turned up the long gravel drive that led to the house, sending rocks clattering in the wheel wells and dust clouding in our wake. I bounced around in the front seat like a baby in a bucket, hoping the rifle on the rack didn't accidentally go off. Or the .357's in the bag, for that matter.

"Slow down, Daddy! You wanna break my other leg?"

He didn't reply. He had a way about him when he got set on something. He called it 'Enthusiastic Designation.' I called it 'Acting Like A Jerk'. I knew better than to bring it up. He just got cranky if I did.

He ganked the wheel and skidded to the right, steering around the side of Gomez's worn out farmhouse. Gomez was the type who liked to keep all sorts of things in his yard. Old tires. Rusted out tractors. Landscape drags and farming tillers. Daddy slalomed through it all like he was an expert, tearing up the grass, finally slowing down when he made it to the pond a few hundred yards behind the house.

Mr. Gomez's barn was just off to the side. Or it used to be. Now it was scattered all over the field like it'd been blown to bits from the inside out. In its place was something that I don't even know how to begin to describe, but I'll say this: Either Mr. Gomez'd never seen a wasp's nest in his life, or he was the stupidest man on God's green earth. The thing that landed on his barn was round and greenish-brown with spikes sticking out all over the surface. Looked more like a sweet-gum ball than a wasp's nest.

Steam or smoke or something poured off the top, and there was a crack at the bottom—an opening or a door or something—with a warm, orange light pulsing from deep inside and green stuff oozing out. And boy did it stink. Hit us full-on even with the windows rolled up. I couldn't think of anything worse I'd ever smelled.

Daddy, in his usual way, summed it up nicely.

"Smells like roasted goat shit."

Mr. Gomez's neighbors were already standing in the field between the barn and the house. Mr. Sokolov and his boy, Vlad, and old Mrs. Freeman, who looked as spry as ever in her work jeans and red flannel. Mr. Gomez's sons, Gomez and Gomer, Jr, were in the middle of trying to restrain their mother who kept pulling away from them. Daddy pulled up to Mr. Sokolov's truck and put it in park.

"You stay here and watch Sparkles."

"Seriously?"

He got out without another word, leaving his door open and the keys in the ignition. I ain't one for whining, and I'm sure he was just trying to protect me, but the day I'm compared to a stuffed dog and come out equal will be the day I can fly and shoot bullets out of my nose. I wrenched the passenger side door open, hopped out, and grabbed my crutches. It was hard going, but Daddy didn't raise no bleater, and I caught him just as he tipped his hat at Mr. Sokolov.

"Hey, Skip." (Mr. Sokolov's name was Viktor). "What's going on?"

"That thing lands on Gomez barn. Gomez, he's sucked inside."

"Sucked inside?"

"Sucked inside."

Mrs. Gomez, or should I say the Widow Mrs. Gomez, seen us, pulled herself free of her sons, and came galloping over.

"Bill! Bill, please! You've got to do something! That thing has my Gomez!"

She collapsed into Daddy's arms sobbing and carrying on, and I never saw Daddy so uncomfortable. He was not a man to show his emotions. I think they embarrassed him. And if he wasn't already embarrassed enough by his own emotions, he was damn well mortified by other people's. He patted Mrs. Gomez on the back a few times and then peeled her off and held her at arm's length.

"Okay, Mrs. Gomez. I need to you calm down and tell me what happened."

She nodded and tried to get herself together, and after a few deep breaths, she was finally able to talk.

"Gomez went about bonkers when that thing fell on our barn. After he made a couple of phone calls, he jumped in his truck and went speeding on down here, tearing up the lawn and my peonies."

Her eyes wandered back to the house.

"I told him not to go, that this was an issue for the president, but he wouldn't listen. You know how crazy he gets about the government."

"Yes, ma'am, I do."

"He wouldn't let me go with him, neither. Me or the boys. So we watched from the kitchen window. He drove his truck right up to that thing, got out with his hunting rifle, and started shooting."

"Don't look like he did much damage."

"None at all. And then as God as my witness, as he reloaded, that crack opened up, and a tentacle slithered out, wrapped him up, and dragged him in. I don't remember what happened after that. I was too busy screaming."

Daddy looked around at everyone, seeing if he could muster them up to do something, but they toed the ground and refused to meet his gaze. Mrs. Gomez worried the front of her dress, her face reddening when she realized that nobody was going to do anything.

"If you all ain't man enough to anything, I am!"

And she marched off across the field, her sons right behind her, calling out "Momma! Momma, wait!" I tell you what, Mrs. Gomez'd worked herself up into a state. She was screaming and yelling (what exactly she was saying, I couldn't tell) tearing at her hair, jamming her finger into the air. None of us moved a muscle. She was going to do what she was going to do, whether it was good for her or not.

Daddy said, "Y'all think we should call the president?"

Mrs. Freeman spat on the ground.

"I ain't too sure what Slick Willie'll be able to do about this."

The Gomez boys did their best to stop her. Gomer, Jr. jumped on his momma's back and Gomez. latched onto her legs, and they all got to screaming and yelling and clapperclawing. It might've gone on like that forever, but I guess that spiky ball'd had enough because three tentacles shot out of it, wrapped around each of the surviving members of the Family Gomez, and started reeling them in. That seemed to be enough for Daddy.

"Aw hell," he said and marched right back to the truck. He grabbed the .30 .06 off the rack and the .357's out of his bag and started loading them. "Y'all bring yours?"

He needn't have asked. Mrs. Freeman already had her shotgun out, Mr. Sokolov had a .30 .30, and Vlad'd gotten himself a machete for some reason.

Daddy, Mr. Sokolov, and Mrs. Freeman positioned themselves in a line facing the thing and started shooting. Bam! Bam! Bam! Bam! Round after round. Bullets whumped into the thing's meat, but other than a little more smoke and what looked like green syrup pouring out of its side, they did about as much harm as a squirrel chewing on an elephant.

When they were done, the air smelled like goat shit and gunpowder, but it didn't do a thing to stop the tentacles. All we could do was watch as Mrs. Gomez and her boys were sucked inside with a syrupy slurp. Daddy waited a tic before he made his final assessment of their work.

"Well, crap."

And that's when the tentacles shot out again. Four this time.

The first one grabbed Mr. Sokolov and heaved him off his feet. Another one grabbed Mrs. Freeman. The third whipped out and snatched Daddy around the waist. The last one tried to get Vlad, but he sliced it off at the tip with his machete. The tentacle went wild, spraying purple gunk all over him that burned and sizzled. Vlad fell to the ground, screaming. Daddy fixed his eyes on mine.

"'Manda," he said. "Sparkles."

Oh yeah.

Sparkles the stuffed dog. Stuffed with explosives.

I don't know if any of you ever tried to run on crutches, but it ain't like pulling a string out of a cat's ass. Hurts your armpits, too. So I dropped one and hopped back to the truck, jumped in, and turned the key. The old thing cranked to life and I slammed it into gear and stepped on the gas, aiming straight for the hive.

That old hive must've known something was up because it shot three more tentacles at me as I sped toward it. One crashed through the windshield. Another hit the grill. The third missed entirely, but swung back around and grabbed the truck by the rear bumper. It yanked sideways, and I realized I didn't even need to drive no more. The only thing I had to concentrate on was getting out before it pulled me into them slimy green and yellow guts.

I forced the driver's side door open, but one of the tentacles slammed it closed again. Another swung at me through the busted windshield and I threw myself onto the bench seat. It smashed the driver's side window and wrapped around the frame, breaking off hunks of metal. Purple ooze splattered onto the dashboard and sizzled, eating its way through it. I scrambled across the seat for the passenger side door and managed to get it open, and right when I was going to dive out, praying I didn't break my neck when I landed, my broken leg exploded with pain.

It was another one of them tentacles. Damn thing'd wrapped itself around my cast and got to squeezing.

If breaking my leg was the most excruciating thing I'd ever felt, squeezing it when it was already broke ran a close second. The vision in the corners of my eyes went black and I felt like I was going to vomit. The thing yanked again, and I felt something give in my knee. I was in so much agony that I couldn't even think straight. Another squeeze, another yank. I slapped around for something, anything I could use as a weapon, and happened upon a nice, long, hunk of the metal frame.

My body was halfway out the door, and I could see the opening of the hive, pulsing and squelching as we drew near. With a scream, I sat up and stabbed that tentacle with that hunk of metal. It pulled back, ripping my cast off and sending me tumbling ass over elbows out of the truck. I flipped once and landed strange, and then I was laying on my back in Gomez's field. Next thing I heard was an explosion, and a ball of fire filled the air.

One week later, both me and Daddy were sitting on the couch eating ice cream and watching *M*A*S*H* reruns. His arm was wrapped tight to his chest and he was wearing a neck brace. He didn't like it very much, and I didn't blame him. August in Virginia was hot enough in shorts and a t-shirt without adding a neck brace. I kept catching him in the middle of taking it off, saying it "cramped his style."

"Daddy, you try to take that thing off again, I'm going to sprain your other neck."

"I don't know what that means, but message received."

My new cast was even bigger and thicker than the one before, and the itching drove me nuts, and since I wasn't allowed to take a shower, and since Daddy told me that under no circumstances was he going to give me a sponge bath, I was starting to get a little ripe. He would, though, spring for ice cream.

"I personally like me some praline myself," he said, scooping a spoonful into his mouth.

"Yuck."

I took a bite of mine, trusty, dusty Neapolitan, and watched the TV. Hawkeye and Trapper John was in the middle of fixing a prank on that old stick-in-the-mud Frank Burns again.

"Well, one thing's for certain," I said. "I'm glad that old stuffed dog's finally out of the house."

Daddy gave me a playful slap.

"Don't you talk about Sparkles like that. Sparkles saved the world. Best dog I ever had."

TURN THE PAGE FOR AN EXCERPT FROM
THE RABBIT, THE JAGUAR, & THE SNAKE

THE WIDOW

The Widow Mrs. Feldman leaned her elbows on the sill, her ample belly pressing against the radiator, testing the limits of her coarse, black skirt. She sniffed the early evening air, the wart on her nose quivering with each whiff. The neighborhood stank as usual: a bouquet of garbage perfumed with mildew and gutter rot, and riding beneath that, the musk of the homeless men who laid up in the alleys during the day. It had always smelled that way, for years and years. Sometimes worse, sometimes better. But the new century had brought with it new odors. Car exhaust and gasoline, bleach from the factories, chemical and stringent, with a soupçon of cancer. Not that The Widow Mrs. Feldman cared. She was there long before the white men constructed their towers and poisoned the land, and she would be there long after they were gone. She was an element of the earth, as timeless and indestructible as dirt, susceptible to nothing but the nuclear tides of the sun.

She looked up and down the block, scanning for any signs of trouble, then zoomed in on the old abandoned townhouse right across the street. It was in as poor condition as ever—the bricks were stained, the windows streaked with grime, and moss hung out of the leaf-choked gutters. She paused, peering hard at the door, searching, waiting for the slight shimmer in the air, the rippling that signaled that something had come over from the other side. Nothing.

Unsatisfied, she hawked up a lunger and spat it out onto the sidewalk below.

"Demon!" she snapped. "Demon! Come here you little... demon."

A thump sounded from some far off room above. Demon liked to hunt in the attic. The insects were juicy there, the rats juicier, and, if the crone had some leftovers from her own nocturnal adventures, he had his pick of the best vital organ meat in the city. Lungs untouched by smoke, livers unsullied by alcohol. The Widow Mrs.

Feldman pulled the stump of a cigar out from the folds of her sweater and plunked it into her mouth, lighting it with a snap of her fingers. Smoke carpeted her lips, and she watched the shadows loom over the street. The best time to use the door was right before the sun set, in the gloaming, the transition from safety to terror, and the gloaming was coming soon. That's when the beasts crossed over.

A city kid ran down the street in front of her, shouting "yeah you and what army?" over his shoulder. His voice reminded her of BG, King of the Goons. She thought about her last conversation with him and snorted.

"'Oh but they ain't coming over here,' he says. Oh, yeah? Tell that to my Demon. He's gained five pounds in the last month, the little pig."

She took another pull on her cigar and blew out a heavy gray cloud.

"Tells me to do my job. You do your job, I say! Pah. Stupid goon. The faces change, but they're always the same. Demon! Come here you brute!"

But Demon was a long time coming, and she drifted off into her memories, back, back, back, all the way to her beginnings. She didn't remember a father or a mother. She had no siblings. She just was. In those early times, she wandered the landscape, cold and alone. She spoke no language, had no tongue of her own. She sang to the plants and the water, and they provided for her. She drank from the streams, and they were cool and clean. She ate what she could catch, first the little creatures, the mice and the rats, the frogs and the fish, but it was never enough to fill her belly. In time she learned the songs of larger game, and she sent sweet sweels of melody out into the air, and they came to her, and she feasted on their flesh.

But with the bigger beasts came prodigious danger, horn and hoof, teeth and claw, and she didn't always win. Even worse were the things that walked upright. They made tools and knew fire. They were cagey and knew how to fight. She had only tasted a few before the rest came for her, chased her through the forest with bone clubs and spears. They cornered her in the foothills, and she cowered against an outcropping. She could still see the flicker of their bared teeth in the angry red flames of the torches, the thrusting spears. She reached up around her back to rub the old wound. The skin was shiny and smooth beneath her hairy hand.

"Demon!" she yelled again. "Oh!"

Something tickled the back of her legs just above her dirty brown hosiery. Demon. Or his tail, rather. He was a gray Bengal cat with black stripes and striking blue eyes, prone to mischief, yes, but sagacious and loyal. And powerful. He rarely used it, for the transformation drained him, but if tested, if threatened, he let it loose. And woe to the creature stupid enough to be on the receiving end. He wound his way in and out of her skirt, rubbing his face against the scratchy stockings and purring. The Widow Mrs. Feldman chuckled.

"There you are, you nasty little creature. Where you been, huh? Up in the attic? Get yourself a bellyful?"

He meowed, blinking up at her.

"That's what I thought. You're a good little demon, huh? A good little devil." She scratched his ears, then patted the sill. "Come on up here now. C'mon. Time for you to earn your keep."

Demon followed the sound, tail swishing, and jumped up, sinking his claws into her finger before she could pull it away.

"Ach, you demon, Demon!" she cried, and popped the digit into her mouth.

Then she took a few bits of smoked meat out of a fold in her sweater and sprinkled them on the sill. He sniffed them, wary. She'd tricked him before. When he was satisfied that there wasn't anything wrong with the meat, he chomped in. The old crone waited for him to finish, then sang him his song. He watched her, mesmerized and blinking, before turning toward the street and sitting down, his tail swishing back and forth like a pendulum, irregular at first, then falling into a steady rhythm—swish-swish, swish-swish.

The Widow Mrs. Feldman leaned over and peered between his ears. She watched the air, waiting for the right moment. The shadows of the brownstones lengthened on the street. The air began to cool and... there! A shimmer in the door of the old abandoned townhouse. She took a pull from her cigar and blew a plume of smoke between Demon's ears. He didn't even flinch as it expanded in front of him, a dark gray cloud. The crone bored into it, concentrating, willing it to stay, to hover, to reveal what it was meant to reveal.

And it did.

The front door of the old abandoned townhouse flickered in and out, in and out, and then the passage opened and a monster leaped through, shrouded in shadows. Demon yowled and the smoke dissipated, and by the time it had all cleared, the creature had galloped halfway up the street.

The Widow Mrs. Feldman winced as she stood up, her spine popping. She put her hands on her back and stretched. Plonked the cigar in her mouth. Took a few puffs.

"Well, Demon." The cat looked at her. It blinked. "What do you think?"

She waited a moment for a reply, and when none came, she stubbed the cigar out on a black spot on the sill and hid it in the folds of her skirt. Then she grabbed a walking stick from its place next to the window and limped over to her front door, the heels of her boots clonking on the hardwood.

"C'mon you mangy beast," she said. "Time to sing for your supper."

THE RABBIT

Hey, how's it going?

Lemme tell you the story about the time I saved the world.

Looking around right now at the burned out buildings and the churned up streets and the bodies in the gutters, I know what you're thinking: "This is how you save the world?" So I guess my answer is that I don't really know. And I don't really care. I kind of look at it as something that happened to me, like jury duty or a colonoscopy. But hey, that's jumping ahead now, ain't it? Let's start from the start. And there ain't no better place to start with than my Ma and Pop.

Pop came to America from the old world before the Model T, if you can believe it. Met my dear old Ma on the boat on the way over, and even though I knew it wasn't the truth, I like to think that the whole thing was a whirlwind romance. Love on the high seas. A jealous suitor. Fist fight in first class, a triumphant right hook followed by a wedding on the main deck, with the ship's captain and the clear blue skies and the icebergs floating by. In reality, pop was a penniless Jew from Minsk, and ma, she wasn't no better off. Their getting together was probably more like a scrum and a moan behind a crate in steerage, a pauper's union at the neighborhood temple, and nine months later, me.

I grew up in the slums of the Bottom with about five million other street rats. Living in a place called the Bottom was exactly like what you'd think it'd be like living in a place called "the Bottom." The one room tenements, the baking hot summers, the midnight bumrolls, the cholera, the TB, the dysentery. Ah, the golden years. Ma toiled long hours as a seamstress in a heat box deathtrap, and Pop worked a whole bunch of miserable jobs. He was a fish monger, a ditch digger, a stone-cutter. He buried gas lines. Dug subway tunnels. I don't know how he did it, but eventually the old codger saved enough money to buy his own business. A newsstand. Established himself as a true entrepreneur.

Me, however, I was free as a bird. Lived like a king. I hung out the usual gang of gutter punks. Skinny Pete. Squinty. Slappy. The Mangler and the Jew. We got up to all kinds of hi-jinx, me and them. Alley smokes. Heel hacks. Knife fights. But then Ma died in a factory fire, and Pop didn't know how to put up with me. Granted, I was a bit out of control, and short of drowning me in the river, there wasn't nothing he could do to keep me in check. Plus, he'd just got that newsstand off the ground, and he couldn't have a liability running around, that liability being me, so his only option was that free school them papists run.

And by that I mean Catholic School.

And Catholic School was Catholic School.

I know what you're thinking. You're thinking, "ain't you a Jew? Them papists don't let no Jews in Catholic School."

Well, you're right, you're right. But pop, he wasn't no dummy. About three months before he signed me up, we started attending mass. Every Sunday morning, every Sunday night. Pop got himself in thick with the priests, told them that he wasn't no religious type, that it was too late for him but that he didn't want his only son to go to Hell. Next thing I knew, they're swinging that censer all over the place and tracing the sign of the cross on my forehead with water. And just like that, I was a mackerel snapper, with all the privileges and blessings and hope of heaven.

He packed me off to Our Lady of the Bleeding Hands and Slit Throat that very fall, and then my education began in earnest. And boy oh boy did it suck. Sure I got me a nifty uniform and three squares a day, and oh yeah, they taught me how to read, rite, and rhythmatic, but I also got myself a hefty backhand whenever I done anything to offend anybody, which, given my natural constitution, equated to a considerable amount of backhanding. I'd always thought I was pretty clever, a real yuk yuk guy, you know? I even got The Mangler to laugh on occasion. In my opinion, my mouth was the best part about me, but them priests didn't seem to share my sentiments. (Well, they did and they didn't, but more on that in a sec.) They hit me so much their knuckles'd swell up just looking at me. Unfortunately, the kind of behavior in which I specialized also drew a different kind of attention, the kind ain't nobody want, and from there my story went from pitch black to pitch blacker.

Satan black.

THE RABBIT, THE JAGUAR, & THE SNAKE

Ninth bolgia of Hell stuff.

I don't feel like going into all the details cause there ain't no point in grossing nobody out. The only thing you need to know is this: all the things that happened to poor kids with no resources in Catholic School happened to me. Pretty unconceivable a century later; run of the mill back then.

I got my revenge, though, right? Not after they fucked me up permanent, and not until I was much older, old enough for everybody who hurt me to forget about who I was and what they done, but revenge was got. I won't go into the particulars. That story's been told already anyhow. Some jerk wrote it up in some dumb book he published. *A Stick in the Eye* or... what's that? Oh yeah. *A Knife in the* Back. Anyway, it's a good read. A real potboiler. Seven short stories and a novel. You should check it out. Especially the one about me.

Go ahead.

I'll wait.

Okay, maybe we ain't got the time for that kind of thing right now. For those of you who don't want to, or who ain't got the time or the patience, or who can't read, think of it this way: That priest's head looked good up there on my wall, didn't it? Not as good as them two goombahs, dumbass Basilio and fat little Arko, but good enough for government work.

So look, enough with the exposition. Here's where the story really begins.

About a year after that, I was killing time at Pop's newsstand, selling the typical newsstand type stuff, like newspapers, and magazines, and chocolates, when The Widow Mrs. Feldman stuck her head out her window.

"Howzit," she said.

It was a slow day. The war'd been over for three years, and the twenties was roaring like a lion. After the morning rush, ain't nobody was interested in the good news, so I sat back and put my feet up on a stack of City Sentinels to read the science section.

"Fuck you, you old witch."

"Hey, language, language. Is that any way to talk to your elders?"

"No. But it's the way I talk to you."

She laughed that chuffy laugh of hers. Half phlegm, half soot: "Huh huh huh. Huh huh huh."

"Jesus," I said. "You inhale a smoke stack or something? You gonna be alright?"

"You're a funny one," she said. "Real wiseass. You get that from your pop or your ma?"

Ma'd been dead for centuries, but Pop, he kicked it only a few months before. Lasted pretty long, him. Ninety-five years. Not bad for a time when most people died at half that age. It's fantastic, actually, unless you consider how he died, because he died kind of shitty, if you ask me, with the cancer eating away at his lungs until there wasn't no lungs left. I was already irritated before she reminded me of all that, but now I was irritated considerable more. I took my feet off the papers and plonked them on the sidewalk.

"You need your attitude adjusted?"

She waved me off.

"You don't scare me. Mr. Feldman was the last one who tried and look at what happened to him. Plus," she nudged her chin at the old abandoned townhouse. "I know what you done over there. And I like it."

I gave the old place a glance. It was all blackened at the base from when them two idiots tried to burn it down, and the windows was still cracked and grinning at me, but it was still standing, proud and unbeaten. I returned my attention to the article I was reading.

"Oh, yeah?"

"Yeah. You got style, kid. And I know you been thinking about expanding your services."

Now that one shocked me a little. How the fuck she did know about that? She wasn't wrong, but, well, after I finished "The Unholy Triumvirate," I ain't had no inclinations to carry on. I felt I'd done my duty, purged my demons. Lived along with the knowledge them fucks who did what they done to me and mine would never be able to do it to somebody else and theirs. Until recently.

I'd heard things about what was still going on at that school. Good old Ronnie Resnick told me about it, and let me tell you something, I was none too pleased. In fact, I was so unhappy that I was actually thinking about giving them a little taste of my scalpel and bonesaw, add a few more trophies to my wall. But that was as far as I got, just the thinking about it, and as far as I knew, thinking about a crime wasn't a crime. That wasn't the problem, though. The problem was that The Widow Mrs. Feldman knew about the crime I was only thinking about.

"You know fuck all about it," I said.

"About what?"

I stared at her over the top of my paper. She wouldn't look me in the eye. Looked everywhere but, mumbling and muttering to herself. Dead giveaway. Finally, I said, "You know fuck all about fuck all."

"You're a laugh riot. A gaggle of giggles. I don't know fuck all? You just told me everything I needed to know."

"Ah you're a crazy bitch," I said.

But she wouldn't let it go. Kept laughing that hoarse laugh. I won't lie to you. It pissed me off.

"The fuck you laughing at?" I snapped. She laughed harder. A little ball of energy swirled up in my chest. I tried to keep reading, but it wasn't no use, so I folded the paper and slapped it down on the stand. "Can I help you with something?"

"No, but I can help you with something."

"Not interested."

"No, really. Listen. You look in the mirror lately? You look good for a guy your age."

"Watch it, you old hag. I might be horny, but I ain't desperate."

"What are you? Thirty-three? Thirty-four? You don't look a day over twenty."

"Sorry, you're not my type."

"I heard that about you."

Sometimes a body just got to absorb the insult. That was one of them times.

She said, "I know you know what I'm talking about. I know you seen it, too. You're in your prime. You'll never look better. I'm just trying to help you out a little. Give you a boost." I pretended to read again. "Look. I'm on your side here. You wanna stop them fucks from doing what they do?"

Fine. Fuck it. She knew. How she knew what she knew, I don't know. But she knew. I put the paper down.

"Yeah," I said. "I do. I'm gonna kill every last one."

The Widow Mrs. Feldman nodded.

"That's what I thought. C'mere a second."

"Fuck that. I ain't going nowhere. You come here."

"Got a bad hip." Her cat jumped up on the sill next to her and arched its back against her shoulder. She pet it. "Hey there, Demon. You come out to say hello?" Demon meowed. The Widow Mrs. Feldman reached behind her and put a glass of something on her sill. "Demon made you something to drink."

I looked at it. It was tall and skinny and filled up with something green and goopy looking.

"I ain't drinking that."

"It's cool and fresh, and it's a hot day, no?"

"Yeah, but I ain't drinking that."

She seemed to take that in, studying me, reading me, but she finally shut up so I was able to get back to the news. Whoo boy, the world was in a ton of shit. The Great War really fucked things up good. Unemployment rising in Germany. Some asshole in Italy and his black shirts. The old lady started to hum a tune. I didn't notice it at first cause she sung it under her breath, but then it seeped into my head, into my bones. I'd heard me a lot of music in at that point in time. "I Ain't Got Nobody." "Ain't We Got Fun?" "I Ain't Nobody's Darling." Streets was positively filled with that new jungle bunny shit. But this was something different, eerie and earthy, like the trees and the rocks and the wind all got together to start a band. It was the most beautiful thing I ever heard, and I felt transported by it back to a time when there wasn't no bricks or buildings, no assholes or asphalt, just the sky and the ground and the oceans and the rivers, and the next thing I knew, I felt something rub my calf, and when I looked down I seen Demon winding his way around my ankles. I got dizzy. And out of the haze came The Widow Mrs. Feldman's voice.

"You sure you don't want that drink?" she said.

And you know what? I did get a thirsty right then. Parched, even.

Years passed, and it was around that time that I started noticing something different about me. My old friends, Slappy and the like, they got older. Fatter. Sicker. Slappy caught a case of the Nationalism, enlisted in the Army, and ended up a corpsesicle when he tried to fight the Bolsheviks in Siberia during the Russian Civil War. The Mangler was too smart to sign up for any government sham but dumb enough to get himself killed in a drunken pub brawl. I heard Squinty went blind, which anybody with half a brain could of predicted, and then I never seen him again. The Jew was the only one who made it out somewhat prosperous. Owned himself a pawn shop near the Industrial District. I seen him every now and then, always alone, muttering to himself, stooped over and worn, like the trials of life weighed on his shoulders so heavy that he couldn't take it no more.

But me?

I stayed the same. Like my body got to the ripe old age of twenty-two and said, "Fuck it. I'm done." And that's when I knew. I knew what I was going to do. I was going to follow through on all them thoughts I'd been thinking.

Look, I got a lot of regrets in my life. Who don't? I regret not running away from them fucks at the Our Lady of the Bleeding Hands and Slit Throat before they got to me. I regret not taking on extra work somewhere so Ma didn't have to work in that heat box deathtrap. But one thing I don't regret is drinking the potion old Mrs. Feldman made me that afternoon. Changed my life, it did. Or at least I think it did. Who knows? All I know is that once I realized what was what, all them ideas that'd been swirling around in my head solidified, and the guy I was after wasn't the guy I was before, and everything I'd ever known, the fear, the pain, the helplessness, vanished, replaced forever with an anger that nearly consumed me.

So I expanded my services. And by that I mean killing any fucks what fucked with the well-being of a helpless kid. This took some creativity. You know, before you start in on the judging, you should remember who I was going after. I wasn't duping no co-eds into helping me carry my groceries up a flight of steps. I wasn't leaping out at grandma from alley corners. I went after the kiddie diddlers, the pedo-pokers. Remember what I told that priest?

"I wish I had someone like me around when I was a kid."

Well, I took that serious, and for a while, it worked out pretty well. I find you been diddling kiddies, I hunted you down and slit your throat. Worked out well for about five or six years, but unfortunately, no matter how skilled or careful or sneaky or creepy, there comes a time in every great killer's career when he ends up caught. Well, not every one, because has anybody ever heard of Jack the Ripper?

So, yeah, this was some time around '51? '52? I got wind of a local cop whose tastes ran unconscionable. First some kids started spreading rumors. Scumbag took Jerry Blumczech for a ride in his cruiser. Gave Arnold Gold an option in an alley. Then this new cop showed up, lo and behold, fresh out of nowhere, young guy, slicked-back hair, square jaw, and a bit swarthy in the palms if you know what I mean. I seen him talking with the kids on my street, and then he's walking them to school, buying them ice creams. Classic profile. I also noticed that little Robby Resnick—Ronnie Resnick's grandson—wouldn't go near the guy, avoided him at all costs, ran across the street when he offered him a chocolate, took the long way to school. Once I seen that . . . there ain't no words for it. I felt an anger I ain't never felt before, and not for me, but for that poor kid. I didn't save Ronnie Resnick's ass from a priest way back when just to have his grandson get his plowed by no cop.

If only I'd known.

Them kids was paid to spread them rumors.

Robby was paid to act like he was afraid of the jerk.

Blumczech never took no cop car pleasure cruise.

Gold remained just as pure as his name.

And I fell into it like the sucker I was.

One night, returning home drunk from a date with one of The Widow Mrs. Feldman's bottles, an opportunity presented itself. I seen that sonofabitch pedophile cop walking across the street a block in front of me, and the dark twirlies descended. I didn't normally snatch nobody on the spur of the moment, and I definitely didn't do it when I'd been drinking, but up until that point I'd enjoyed a string of successes and I let it go to my head. Isn't that always the case with people like me? They call it a cycle or something; we plan and we stalk and we kill and we drink to forget it, even if we're not supposed to be bothered by it, and then we plan and we stalk and we kill again, a little sloppier this time, and a lot sloppier the next time, and worse and worse and then you're spiraling out of control like an idiot. So yeah. Pedocop spotted. Dark twirlies descended. I don't remember what happened after that. One second I was walking behind the guy, the next I'm surrounded by a bunch of dicks screaming at me to hold up my hands, goddammit or they'll shoot.

"Alright, alright," I said, and did what I was told.

Unfortunately for me, my hands was covered with gore. So was my face. And my chest. And them cops is shining the lights in my eyes and I can't tell if it's real or fake, can't see nothing, really, except them lights, and suddenly I realized I was straddling somebody, and when I looked down I seen a busted open chest cavity between my legs.

"Oh shit," I said.

"Oh shit's right," someone said, and slugged me solid right in the temple.

What'd they do? What do you think they done? They dragged my ass to the station and worked me over with a rubber hose. Ripped out my adenoids. Showered me with the old lead sprinkler. They could have saved their breath. I had no intention of lying. I wanted them fuckers to know what I done. Maybe they'd see the light. Maybe they'd understand that I was actually trying to help them out. So that's why when the beatings stopped and my face had time to unswell, and they hauled me into a little room with a bright light overhead and a two-way mirror (you seen TV), and the one cop was breathing down my neck and the other acting all official and polite, and they asked me "Did you fucking do this shit?" I said, "Yeah, I fucking did that shit" and that was that.

I don't think the cops expected me to do that, kill their boy so soon. I think they thought they were going to do some serious investigating, whip up the media, maybe fabricate an event, something they could use during an election year. They certainly didn't think any of theirs was going to die, and if they did, they didn't think it'd be as unpleasant as the way I made it. The guilt must have been phenomenal. The one I killed was fresh out of the academy. Top of his class. Asshole tighter than a corncob. True blue, him, and his dumbass superiors set him up to be gutted like an animal.

I seen the realization dawn on them right then and there in the interrogation room. Their eyes went dead, and they broke out another round of rubber hoses and wooden clubs and brass knuckles and beat the ever-loving shit out of me, punched my half-swole eyes until they was fully swole, pummeled my bread-basket until it was mush. When it was all done and I wasn't nothing more than a bloody pulp, they drug me down to the deepest, darkest, dankest part of the jailhouse, threw me in the moldiest cell, slammed the door, cut out the lights, and marched off, slapping each other on the back and giving each other hand jobs. Okay, maybe they wasn't giving each other hand jobs, but they was jerking each other off. I'd like to say I took it all professional, but I was scared out of my mind. I soiled myself silly. Them fuckers threw away the key. I was gonna die down there. I curled up on the thin mattress in the corner and cried myself to sleep.

The main think I had was "what happened?" Why didn't they parade me around in shackles? Publish my picture in the newspapers? Slap me in the chair and let me do the electric jiggle on live television? I'll tell you why. Because things didn't turn out the way they planned. Because I didn't do it the way they wanted me to. Because I didn't follow the rules, didn't fit into a box, and that makes normals itch, and no matter what anybody tells you, no matter how many times they say "live your dreams and be an original," they don't mean it true. Sure, live your dreams. Sure, be an original. But don't do nothing too dreamy or original or you'll freak us the fuck out and we'll throw you in the dungeon.

And that's all it was, them sticking me in that cell. Fear. Pure fear. I educated them on the limits of all that freedom they said they loved so much, and all the sudden they thought maybe too much of it wasn't such a good idea, that were was people like me who took them serious, took them at their word, who didn't give a fuck. That scared the crap out of them more than anything else, because where there was one dumb enough or sloppy enough to get caught doing the kinds of things I done, there were probably a hundred more waiting in the wings, just itching to cut and slash and slaughter, and once they seen what the people in charge had in store for them, who do you think they'd be coming for?

Well that wouldn't do.

That wouldn't do at all.

Fortunately, there was another group of people that'd took notice of my talents. Powerful people. People like me. Violent, ageless. Better than that, they were from the Neighborhood. Not the neighborhood, the Neighborhood. There's a difference. What's the differ . . . ? Just give me a minute. You'll see.

One morning after breakfast (a rotten orange and moldy bread) I got a knock on my cell all polite like, like I had a choice not to answer.

"Yeah?" I croaked.

The voice on the other side sounded like the streets. Asphalt and brick. Dumpsters in alleys.

"That you?"

I worked my jaw and it clicked.

"Yeah it's me."

"Lemme in."

"What do you mean, 'lemme in'? I'm in here. You're out there."

"No. You're in there, and I'm out here."

"Six to one, and go fuck yourself." A pause. "Please."

Another pause. Then the guy said, "You gonna let me in or what?"

Seeing as I'd just spent the last few weeks getting my adenoids ripped out, I really didn't feel like screwing around, you know? "Remember what I said before about 'go fuck yourself'?"

He laughed. Can you believe that shit? Laughed.

"That's a good one," he said. "Good to maintain a sense of humor. But you know what? You ain't got no manners."

"I got plenty manners. For example, I said, 'Go fuck yourself,' then I added 'please'."

The silence on the other side of the door hung thick in the air. A mausoleum at midnight.

He said, "Maybe I'll come back another time."

His footsteps clopped away down the hall.

"Hey, I can be good!" I cried. "You come in here and I'll give you a shot of my bologna, how about that!" I couldn't stop laughing. "Oh sure, I got some cheese to go with it, too. And a little grease for extra flavor!"

After that, nobody came to visit no more. They stopped everything, the beatings, the food, everything. The former was a relief, the latter, a problem. I got creative. You ever eat a spider? It's not as traumatic as people think. I mean, sure, you gotta, you know, actually eat a spider, but then the stomach acid burns it to bits and you're ready for more. I became quite the arachnid connoisseur. Never reached Renfield status, but after ten days, twelve days, thirty days—who the fuck knew—I decided that, yeah, there really wasn't going to be a trial, and, sure, there really wasn't going to be no electric chair, neither, but the cell? The cell was my sentence. Twelve feet by twelve feet of eternal punishment. Four water-stained walls, a gray, concrete slab, a metal bed bolted into the wall, and that slate iron door.

So I ate spiders.

And flies. And silverfish. And cockroaches. And ants. And anything else that showed up. Catching a rat was like Christmas dinner.

Years passed, I guess. I stopped keeping track. Toward the end there, though, I couldn't really tell what was what no more. I can't remember when I started seeing things, but I started seeing things. Entire cities demolished by a ball of fire. Houses swallowed by earthquakes. Children snatched from porches. At first, I knew it wasn't real, then I thought it might be real, then I wasn't sure no more, and at a certain point, it didn't matter. There it was, and I was seeing it, so it was real.

And then one day the guy came back.

I was standing on my bed trying to coax a roach into my cupped hand when the knock came at the door again. I eyeballed it. Thought for a second. Almost had the fucker. Just. One. More. Second.

Another knock came and I said, "Just a minute."

The third knock came harder, and my hand shifted and the roach scurried up and away into a crack in the mortar and I pounded the cinderblock with my fist, crying "Motherfucker!" I turned my anger at the door. "You sonofabitch! You just cost me my lunch!"

"Tsk tsk," the guy said. "I see we haven't learned our manners yet, have we?"

I stared at that friggin door a long, long time. Sometimes when things started talking to me, if I stared at them long enough without saying nothing, they went away. So I stood there kind of hunched, my hands held up like I was about to pounce, my stringy hair covering my eyes. What was left of my prison uniform hung in tatters off my shoulders, and I didn't have no hips left, so I had to make a belt out of a strip of one of the pant legs to keep them from falling off. Not that it mattered. When the guy didn't speak again, I relaxed.

Phew, I thought. *He wasn't rea—*

"Hello?" he called. "You still there?"

"Oh," I said. "It's you."

He snickered.

"Yeah. It's me. You want to let me in now?"

"We gonna have this conversation again?" I sat down on my metal bed.

"I guess we are. So what's it gonna be?"

"Let's see. How's it go again? You want me to let you in, but you're out there and I'm in here."

"Noooo . . ."

"Yeah, yeah, I know. I'm in here and you're out there. Still don't change nothing."

"I don't begrudge you your bitterness."

"Bitterness? Bitterness? You got any idea how long I been down here? Because I don't. You should get a look at me. I'm a ghost. A fucking wraith. And all for what? Getting rid of the scum who did what they done to them poor kids? I was helping them out! And they locked me away!"

There was a long pause after that, and ice formed in my belly. Did I scare him off? Right when I was about to plead with whoever it was not to go, he said, "You mind I can ask you a question?"

Oh thank fuck.

"Go ahead."

"You ever wonder if there was other people out there like you?"

I thought for a minute.

"Like scraggly macs who's been thrown in a hole until the sun explodes?"

"I think you know what I mean."

I took a deep breath.

"Yeah," I said. "The thought did cross my mind from time to time."

"That's good. That's real good. So you wanna let me in or what?"

"I can't," I whispered.

"What's that?"

"I said I can't!"

"Oh, yes you can. Yes you can. All you go to do is stand up and open the door."

"But it's locked! They locked me up! They threw me down here and melted the key!"

"So you won't do it?"

"The door. Is. LOCKED!"

"Is it? You ever try opening it?"

The fuck was he talking about? Of course I'd tried opening it. I hung on the handle until my fingers broke, kicked it until my toes bled. Or maybe not. Who knew. One second oozed into the next down there. I could cup my hands against the wall for hours, waiting for a beetle to crawl into it, or lick at the water trail until my jaw ached, and I wouldn't know if it was the next day or the next week.

"I dunno," I said. "Maybe I haven't."

"Well, why don't you give it a shot? If it opens, great. If it don't, well, it ain't like you'd be any more disappointed than you already is."

That was some hot logic right there. Couldn't even start to think of an argument against it, so I said, "Okay."

I stood up shaky and shuffled toward it, and the whole time I'm thinking, "It's a joke. The fucking fuck is fucking with me." I knew that when I grabbed it, I'd feel the metal in my fingers, the same icy handle that I'd been yanking on for years (or hadn't been), and once again I'd push on it, and once again it'd creak and whine, and once again it wouldn't open. And then that son of a bitch on the other side would laugh and laugh, and I'd scream until my voice gave out.

Well. No time like the present, right?

I put my hand on the handle.

I pushed down.

You can imagine my surprise when, with a rusty squeal, the frigging door swung in at me.

THANK YOU FOR READING THE EXCERPTS FROM *THE HIVE* AND *THE RABBIT, THE JAGUAR, & THE SNAKE*!

If you enjoyed these excerpts, you can pick up the full novels wherever you buy books. Or you can buy it directly from me at **silverhammer.studio.**

A NOTE FROM JAMES

Hi there! Thank you for reading my latest novel. I truly appreciate all of my readers, especially those who like my books enough to make it to the end. :)

If you are so inclined, it would really help me out if you left an honest review of *Mungwort*. Just hop on wherever you buy your books and dial up your two cents. Thanks!

ABOUT THE AUTHOR

James Noll is a freelance writer, an educator, a musician, and a novelist from Fredericksburg, VA. *Mungwort* is his sixth novel. When he's not writing, he takes long naps. When he's not napping, he's probably thinking about it.
Check out his work at **silverhammer.studio**

Made in the USA
Middletown, DE
03 March 2023